D0500200

Independence Public Library

CITY *of* ORPHANS

INDEPENDENCE PUBLIC LIBRARY
175 Monmouth Street
Independence, OR 97351
3814-7853

Nineteenth-Century Novels by Avi

The Barn

Beyond the Western Sea
Book I: The Escape From Home
Book II: Lord Kirkle's Money

*Emily Upham's Revenge: Or, How Deadwood Dick Saved
the Banker's Niece: A Massachusetts Adventure*

*History of Helpless Harry: To Which Is Added a Variety of
Amusing and Entertaining Adventures*

The Man Who Was Poe

Punch with Judy

The True Confessions of Charlotte Doyle

Iron Thunder

Hard Gold

The Traitors' Gate

CITY
OF
ORPHANS

AVI

WITH ILLUSTRATIONS BY GREG RUTH

A Richard Jackson Book

Atheneum Books for Young Readers
New York London Toronto Sydney

ATHENEUM BOOKS FOR YOUNG READERS

An imprint of Simon & Schuster Children's Publishing Division

1230 Avenue of the Americas, New York, New York 10020

This book is a work of fiction. Any references to historical events, real people, or real locales are used fictitiously. Other names, characters, places, and incidents are products of the author's imagination, and any resemblance to actual events or locales or persons, living or dead, is entirely coincidental.

Text copyright © 2011 by Avi Wortis, Inc.

Illustrations copyright © 2011 by Simon & Schuster, Inc.

All rights reserved, including the right of reproduction
in whole or in part in any form.

ATHENEUM BOOKS FOR YOUNG READERS
is a registered trademark of Simon & Schuster, Inc.

For information about special discounts for bulk purchases, please contact Simon & Schuster Special Sales at 1-866-506-1949 or business@simonandschuster.com.

The Simon & Schuster Speakers Bureau can bring authors to your live event. For more information or to book an event, contact the Simon & Schuster Speakers Bureau at 1-866-248-3049 or visit our website at www.simonspeakers.com.

The text for this book is set in Scotch Roman.

The illustrations for this book are rendered in sumi ink and brush.

Manufactured in the United States of America

0711 FFG

First Edition

2 4 6 8 10 9 7 5 3 1

Library of Congress Cataloging-in-Publication Data

Avi, 1937–

City of orphans / Avi ; illustrated by Greg Ruth. — 1st ed.

p. cm.

"A Richard Jackson Book."

Summary: In 1893 New York, thirteen-year-old Maks, a newsboy, teams up with Willa, a homeless girl, to clear his older sister Emma from charges that she stole from the brand new Waldorf Hotel, where she works. Includes historical notes.

Includes bibliographical references.

ISBN 978-1-4169-7102-3 (hardcover)

ISBN 978-1-4169-8260-9 (eBook)

[1. Mystery and detective stories. 2. Family life—New York (State)—New York—Fiction. 3. Homeless persons—Fiction. 4. Gangs—Fiction. 5. Immigrants—Fiction. 6. Waldorf-Astoria Hotel (New York, N.Y.)—Fiction. 7. New York (N.Y.)—History—1865–1898—Fiction.]

I. Ruth, Greg, ill. II. Title.

PZ7.A953Cit 2011 [Fic]—dc22 2010049229

For Dan Darigan

New York City, 1893

Amazing things happen.

Look at someone on the street and you might never see that person again—*ever*. Then you bump into a stranger and your whole life changes—*forever*. See what I'm saying? It's all 'bout them words: "luck," "chance," "coincidence," "accident," "quirk," "miracle," plus a lot of words I'm guessing I don't even know.

But the thing is, I got a story that could use *all* them words. 'Bout a kid by the name of Maks Geless. That's Maks, with a *k*. M-a-k-s.

Now, this Maks, he's regular height for a thirteen-year-old, ruddy-faced, shaggy brown hair, always wearing a cloth cap, canvas jacket, and trousers, plus decent boots. He's a newsboy—what they call a "newsie." So he's holding up a copy of the New York City newspaper *The World*, and he's shouting, "Extra! Extra! Read all 'bout it! 'Murder at the Waldorf. Terrible Struggle with a Crazy Man! Two Men

Killed!' Read it in *The World*! The world's greatest newspaper. Just two cents!"

Now, not everything gets into the papers, right? But see, the only one who knows what really happened up at the Waldorf is . . . Maks.

You're thinking, how could this kid—this newsie—know?

I'll tell you.

This story starts on Monday, October 9, 1893. That's five days *before* the day of that headline you just heard. It's early evening, the night getting nippy. Electric streetlamps just starting to glow. In other words, the long workday is winking.

Not for Maks. He's still on his regular corner, Hester Street and the Bowery. Been peddling *The World* for *five* hours and has sold thirty-nine papers. Sell one more and he'll have bailed his whole bundle. Do that and he'll have eighty cents in his pocket.

Now listen hard, 'cause this is important.

In 1893 newsies buy their papers and *then* sell 'em. So next day's bundle is gonna cost Maks seventy-two cents. *Then* he sells 'em for two cents each. Means, for his five hours' work, he'll earn a whole eight cents. Not much, you say? Hey, these days, six cents buys you a can of pork and beans, enough eats for a day, which is more than some people gets.

You're probably thinking, eight pennies—that ain't hardly worth working all them hours. But this is 1893. These are hard times. Factories closing. Workers laid off. Not many jobs. Housing not easy to find. Fact, people are calling these days the "Great Panic of 1893." And the thing is, Maks's family's rent is due *this* week. Fifteen bucks! For them, that's huge.

All I'm saying is, Maks's family needs him to earn his share, which is—you guessed it—eight cents a day.

Now, most days when Maks finishes selling his papers, he likes staying in the neighborhood to see how his newsie pals have done. Don't forget, this is New York City. The Lower East Side. Something always happening.

This night all Maks wants to do is to get home and eat. No surprise; he's hungry twenty-five hours a day, eight days a week. And last time he ate was breakfast—a roll and a bowl of coffee-milk.

So Maks holds up his last newspaper and gives it his best bark: "Extra! Extra! Read all 'bout it! 'Joe Gorker, Political Boss, Accused of Stealing Millions from City! Trial Date Set! Others Arrested!' Read it in *The World*! World's greatest newspaper. Just two cents! Only two cents!"

Sure, sometimes crying headlines, Maks gets to head doodling that someday *he'll* be in the paper for doing something great, like maybe making a flying machine. So *The World* would pop *his* picture on its first page, like this here mug Joe Gorker. Then Maks reminds himself that his job is selling the news, not being it. Besides, *The World* is always laying down lines 'bout Joe Gorker, screaming that the guy is a grifter-grafter so crooked that he could pass for a pretzel.

Anyway, Maks's shout works 'cause next moment, a fancy gent—top hat, handlebar mustache, starched white collar, what some people call a "swell stiff"—wags a finger at him.

Maks runs over.

The guy shows a nickel. "Got change, kid?"

"Sorry, sir. No, sir."

I know: Maks may be my hero, but he ain't no saint. Like I told you, for him, pennies are big. Needs all he can get.

"Fine," says the swell. "Keep the change."

"Thank you, sir!" Maks says as he slings his last sheet to this guy.

The guy walks off, reading the headlines.

Maks, telling himself his day is done, pops the nickel

---

into his pocket. Except no sooner does he do that than who does he see?

He sees Bruno.

This Bruno is one serious nasty fella. Taller than Maks by a head, his face is sprinkled with peach fuzz, greasy red hair flopping over his eyes, one of which is squinty, and on his head he's got a tipped-back brown derby, which makes his ears stick out like cute cauliflowers.

But the thing is, Bruno may be only seventeen years old, but he's head of the Plug Ugly Gang. Lately, Bruno and his gang have been slamming *World* newsies, beating 'em up, stealing their money, burning their papers.

So Maks knows if Bruno is giving him the eye, things gonna be bad. And it's not just 'bout being robbed. If Maks loses his money, he ain't gonna be able to buy papers for next day. No papers, no *more* money *and* the family rent don't get paid. In other words, no choice. Maks has to get home with his money.

Trouble is, his home is a three-room tenement flat over to Birmingham Street, near the East River. That's fifteen big blocks away, which, right now, feels as far as the North Pole.

In other words, if Maks wants to keep his money, he's gonna have to either outrun that Plug Ugly or fight him.

Don't know 'bout you, but Maks would rather run.

Maks looks over his shoulder. There's another Plug Ugly down the street. Next moment, he sees a *third*. Then *three* more. Six Plug Uglies in all, including Bruno.

Maks looks for help. He ain't exactly alone. People like to say the Lower East Side is the busiest place in the whole world. Crowds of people buying, bargaining, begging, strolling. Kids, grown-ups, dogs scrambling for dropped food. Oh, sure, some stealing. These days, folks are really hungry.

Sidewalks packed with hundreds of curb-stalls, two-wheel handcarts, plus backpack peddlers selling anything and everything, whatever jim-jam a person should want, might want, could want, can want. Food, clothing, or fur-niture. On the Lower East Side you can buy bent spoons, used books, four-fingered gloves, one-eyed eyeglasses, or a shoe for your best left foot. Hey, one old beard is selling cracked eggs.

Sellers crying out their goods in English, German, Italian, Yiddish, Chinese, Spanish, Hebrew, Romanian, plus so many other languages, it's like the cheapest boardinghouse in Babel.

Even the air is crowded. Crisscrossing telephone lines make the smoky sky look like ruled paper. Hundreds of signs posted here, there, everywhere. It's like someone plucked a newspaper clean of words, then stuck 'em all on walls, windows, doors, and sandwich boards, telling people to *buy, buy, and buy some more.*

Overhead, the clattering elevated steam train—called the "El"—rains down smoke, sparks, hot ash. Every time a train rackety-racks by, Maks wishes he could ride one. Trouble is, costs a nickel to ride the El. That's five cents Maks's family can't spare. If Maks wants to go somewhere, he walks.

And the neighborhood stinks too. Stinks of rotten food, sweat, smoke, plus horse dung piles. Don't forget, this is before motor cars.

So streets are clogged wheel to wheel with wagons, trolleys (bells ting-a-linging), cabs, and carts. All hauled by horses. During rush hour, if you don't look out, you're gonna be mashed or rolled out dead by metal-rimmed wheels or iron horseshoes. Maks knows kids who've been hurt, killed even. Hey, cabbies and teamsters don't care.

Neither do Bruno and his Plug Uglies.

You're asking: How come Maks don't cry for a cop? 'Cause coppers don't like newsies. Call 'em "street rats," "guttersnipes." Besides, these times, city police are hardly better than crooks. Fact, lots of those cops *are* crooks, ready to be bribed if you have the clink. Don't forget: This is before Commissioner Teddy Roosevelt started bending things straight.

Anyway, Maks ain't supposed to call for help. Kids' doings—good or bad—are just for kids. Keep that in mind.

Not that it matters. 'Cause right now, when Maks looks around, ain't a cop in sight.

In other words, Maks is gonna have to get home on his own.

Maks takes another look at Bruno, shoves a hand into his pocket, makes a fist over his pennies, checks to see where the other gang guys are.

MAKS

Closer.

Maks yanks his cap down tight and shoots the only way open to him, right down the middle of Hester Street. But the crowds are so thick, he can't keep from knocking folks.

"Excuse me, ma'am. Sorry, sir."

At Chrystie Street, Maks halts and looks back.

Plug Uglies are coming hard.

Maks keeps shooting south. Gets to Canal Street and races 'cross in front of two horse trolleys. One horse shies, causing the driver to scream curses.

Still pounding down Chrystie Street, Maks searches for a hiding place along the walls of brick tenement buildings. Can't find one. Now his side is starting to ache. Getting hard to breathe. Worse luck: An ice-block wagon and four fat drays pull in front of him. He tries to get round, only to squeeze up 'gainst a stall where an old Chinese lady is selling baskets. Wiggles free, but the Plug Uglies are gaining on him.

That's when Maks remembers that up ahead is an alleyway, a shortcut to Forsyth Street. If he can get through without the gang seeing, he might be safe.

Galloping like a runaway horse, Maks reaches the alley. Gives it a quick check. It's four feet wide, dismal, gloomy, with grimy brick walls on either side, garbage on the ground.

Maks dives in.

Trouble is, halfway through the alley, a high wooden fence blocks his way. The fence is smack against the bricks, making it impossible to get round. He tries jumping but can't reach eight feet, not with one hand in his pocket clutching pennies.

As Maks tries to think what to do, he sees, right there on the ground, along the base of the wall, a body. The body's so tangled in rags, he can't tell if it's a he, a she, someone sleeping, drunk, maybe even dead.

Next second, he swings round just in time to see the Plug Uglies—Bruno in the lead—coming down the alley. In other words, Maks has to fight.

Maks wedges himself into the corner where the wood fence butts 'gainst the brick wall. Figures that way, the gang won't be able to get behind him.

Then he taps up his cap (so he can see), licks his

knuckles (wet knuckles sting your enemy), and sets his fists the way he's seen that heavyweight champ Bobby Fitzsimmons do on the sports pages of *The World*.

Bruno comes to a halt right in front of Maks. Stands so close, Maks feels his heat and smells his beery breath.

The mug plants his feet wide, hooks his thumbs into pockets, rocks back on his heels like some hotshot ward heeler. His nasty grin—some teeth missing—reminds Maks what people say 'bout Bruno: The guy is crazy, crazy mean.

The rest of the Plug Uglies squeeze in right behind Bruno, leering, laughing.

"Good run, kid," says Bruno, holding out a dirty hand, palm up. "Let's see your brass."

Maks is pressing against the wooden fence, hoping it gives way. Same time, his heart is going *bump-bump, bump-bump*, like a fire wagon bucking to a blaze. "I . . . need . . . it," he says, the words squeezing out between gasps. "To buy . . . papers . . . tomorrow. And our rent is due this week. And . . . and times are hard," he adds, something his papa is always saying.

"Right," Bruno sneers. "Hard times for everyone. And that includes me. So just tell all your dumb newsie pals at *The World*, greetin's from their new boss. I'm gonna take care of yous fine.

"So give!" he shouts into Maks's face. His other hand is balled into a fist.

Though Maks's legs are shaking, his eyes blinking, he keeps his dukes up.

"Don't be a wind-sucker!" yells Bruno. "Hand over your money or your nose gets clocked." To prove it, Bruno slaps Maks so hard, the kid's cap falls to the ground.

Maks manages to throw a putty punch. Misses.

Bruno gives a phony laugh. "Warned yous!" he says, and conks Maks's nose. It not only hurts god-awful, he starts bleeding enough blood that he's tasting it.

That gets the other Plug Uglies howling. "Lop him, Bruno! Lay him out! Collar him!"

Bruno slugs Maks on the side of his head so hard, it makes the kid dizzy. The only thing keeping Maks up is being wedged into that corner. And though he knows he's gonna be turned into dog meat, he manages another jab.

"Stupid mug!" Bruno yells, and cocks his arm, ready to sling his slammer.

That's the moment Maks does what he never done before in his whole life: He cries, "Help!"

And that's when the body on the ground jumps up. Rises so fast and unexpected, all Maks can see is that whoever it is has this big stick and is swinging it like a whirligig

gone wild, smacking Bruno on his shoulder, arm, face—
thwhack-thwhack-thwhack!

Bruno—taken by surprise—yelps and stumbles back, colliding into the Plug Uglies behind him. Those guys tumble, causing two more to crash. The others, shouting and yowling, try to duck out of the way.

But the alley, being narrow, and the stick-swinger swinging a storm, first one Plug Ugly then another gets whacked: arms, heads, and backs. *Crack! Crack! Crack!*

The gang breaks and runs, chased all the way out of the alley by the stick. In moments the Plug Uglies are gone.

Maks, hardly believing what's happened but having no idea who saved him, leans back into his corner, awful glad he's still got his money.

All the same, his legs are shaky, his chest hurts, his eyes are foggy with tears, plus his nose hasn't stopped dripping blood.

Meanwhile, up at the alley entryway, the stick-whacker is looking out onto the street.

Maks bends over to scoop his hat. As he wipes blood and tears from his face, he looks up. That's when he sees that the one who saved him has turned round and is coming back, stick in hand—as if the work ain't done.

Which is when Maks sees who it is.

Only thing, he don't believe what he's seeing.

The one who saved him is a girl.

She's taller than Maks. Skinnier, too. So he's looking up at her, she down, with a face smeared with grime. Her hair is dirty, long, snarled, and twisted into greasy knots. She's wearing a faded green shirt, which must have been some lady's 'cause bits of lace, like a tattered spider's web, are curled round the collar.

As for the girl's skirt, it's brown, long, filthy, ripped at the hem. Don't even reach her ankles, so Maks can see her bare, bruised feet with their nasty, scabby toes. And in that narrow space she smells like sauerkraut gone south.

Truth is, the girl makes Maks think of an alley cat, one of them howlers nobody wants. Except most cats *try* to clean themselves, but Maks is thinking, *Nothing clean 'bout this girl.*

And that stick of hers, it's still in her hands. Maks can see it's some tree branch, looking hard and nubbly.

Course, Maks got no idea who she is or why she was sleeping in the alley. His best guess is, she probably just arrived in America, one of them immigrants pouring off that new Ellis Island—what Maks and his pals call "greenhorns." Fact, Maks wonders if he'll even be able to understand whatever crack-jaw language she speaks.

As for the girl, she's just standing there, stick twitching in her hands, staring at him, saying nothing, but blocking his way.

Now, the thing is, Maks don't have no more fight left, not against this girl, not with *that* stick, not after seeing what she done with it. But deciding he better say *something*, he says, "Hey, thanks."

"What for?" the girl says, a hard voice, with a scowl that seems to be stuck on her as much as the dirt on her face.

"For . . . for getting rid of them guys," says Maks, glad she can at least talk American. "They was gonna bust me bad."

"I guess you called 'help' loud enough," she says.

To Maks, that sounds as if she's making fun. "Yeah," he says, "but you got 'em pretty good." Soon as he says that, the thought pops into his head: *This girl don't hear "pretty" too often.*

The girl lowers her stick, hitches her skirt, and fiddles with her shirt. Wipes her nose with the back of her hand, using the same hand to push hair from her face. That's when Maks sees her eyes, which look as if she's expecting something sneaky coming every next moment from ten different ways. Same time, she's still leaning 'gainst the alley wall studying Maks, the way a cat might mark a mouse.

"That your nose bleeding?" she says. "It doesn't look too good."

Maks feels like saying she don't look so good neither. But since she ain't beating on him—not yet, anyway—he wipes some nosebleed away. "I'm okay," he says.

"What did you do to them?" she asks.

"Nothing. They like slamming newsies."

"Don't look like you have anything worth robbing."

"Just sold my papers," says Maks, patting his pocket. "Still got my money."

Course, soon as he says that, Maks realizes he just gave the girl a reason to rob him.

All the girl says, though, is, "Lucky you."

Wanting to stall so he can get strength enough to run by her, he says, "What's your name?"

"Willa."

"What kind of name is that?"

"In German it's Waddah. You know how people change names here."

"Yeah. My name is Maks. With a 'k.' Danish. Didn't get changed."

"Where's Danish?"

"'Cross the ocean. We live over to Birmingham Street now. Where you live?"

"Here."

"This alley?"

"Other side of the fence."

Maks glances at it. "How come?"

"In case you didn't know, it costs twenty-five cents a night in a flophouse for cot, locker, and screen. Fifteen cents for just cot and locker. Even a cot costs ten cents. A nickel only buys a piece of floor. That's all too rich for me. It's free here."

As she talks, Maks notices that this girl, unlike most street kids, has an uptown way of talking.

He says, "If you live round the other side of the fence, how come you was sleeping here?"

"Too tired to climb."

Maks eyes the high wooden fence.

Willa hefts her stick. "You doubting I can climb it?"

"Maybe," he says, hoping that if she starts to climb, he'll have a chance to get away.

The girl, looking annoyed, goes to the fence, feels round its surface. Finding some chinks, she hoists herself up, keeping her stick with her.

Maks gets so interested in her climbing, he forgets to escape. Then, once on top, Willa straddles the fence, one filthy bare leg dangling, stick across her knees. "See," she says, looking down. "Easy."

Maks feels challenged. "I can do it," he says.

"Try."

Maks searches the wooden fence for grips, finds some, climbs—though a lot slower than Willa. Loses his cap too.

Maks peers over to the other side. There's another fence four feet on. Between the two is a three-foot gap. Though mostly dark below, Maks can make out an old blanket and a wooden crate with some things—he can't see what—in it.

"You really live down there?" he says.

"Isn't that bad," she says. "Has a sewer grate that lets up some warm air. I suppose that's why they built the fences. It's so narrow, not much weather comes down either. Don't mind the smell. And when people come along, they can only do it single file—like just happened. Long as I have my stick, I can handle them."

"Where's your family?"

She scowls. "What about them?"

"They live here too?"

"None of your business."

Her words make Maks study Willa. In the dim light he don't see much of anything. No sadness. No gladness. No nothing.

Maks drops to the ground. Plucks up his cap, dusts it off, sets it on his head. "Hey," he calls up to Willa, "thanks for helping."

"Sure."

Relieved that Willa ain't gonna hold him, Maks heads down the alley trying to act easy. But then he starts thinking: *What if them Plug Uglies are waiting to ambush me when I step onto the street?*

Maks turns round and sees Willa's up on her fence, watching him. He can't help asking himself if she—and that stick—might be willing to defend him a second time.

He starts to say something, but it ain't easy asking a girl for help. Just did, and though it worked, he's not sure he likes it. Sure, he knows this girl can be fierce, but he ain't sure what he feels 'bout her, who and what she is, living in rubbish. Truth is, Maks thinks her something strange.

Next moment, he reminds himself he knows plenty of okay mugs who live on the streets. Besides, this girl saved him. According to kids' rules, he owes. Shout "Help!" and get it, you gotta give back.

Not sure what to do, he pokes his head out of the alley, onto Chrystie Street. It's dark. The dark might give some protection. Then again, it could make things worse. 'Cause the thing is, Maks is pretty certain Bruno's gonna want revenge. 'Specially since a girl beat him out. And unless Bruno does something, news like that got more legs than a centipede.

Still, Maks ain't sure how he should ask Willa for help again. Thinking how skinny she is, he turns and shouts: "Hey, if you walk home with me, my mama will give you something to eat."

Willa don't reply.

"Mean it!" says Maks. The more he asks, the more he feels he needs her.

"You asking for my help?" she calls.

Maks, admitting nothing, says, "You coming or not?"

After a minute Willa says, "You mean it?"

"Said it, didn't I?"

"I guess I can always eat," Willa says, and climbs down.

"Hey," Maks says, "just bring your stick. In case."

When Willa gets close, Maks peers up and down Chrystie Street again. "Guess they're gone," he says. "Let's go." He starts off.

Though Willa is barefoot, she follows close, saying, "They really make you nervous, don't they?"

"Hey," he says, "them guys are mean. People say that Bruno—he's the redhead, the gang's leader—is crazy six ways. How'd you like to be attacked like that?"

"People leave me alone."

Maks can guess why, but he don't say.

"Who are they?" she asks.

"Call themselves the Plug Ugly Gang. Been busting *World* newsies. Trying to take us over."

"Why?"

"Don't know. 'Cept everybody says Bruno's getting protection from somewhere."

"What kind of protection?"

"Someone greasing someone to let him do what he does."

"Who?"

"No idea. But if you sees any of 'em Plug Uglies, keep away. They'll be wanting to get you now. And lemme tell you, they're poison in a pistol."

Willa holds up her stick as if to say, *Long as I have this, they won't bother me.*

Walking fast, they go for a while without talking, Maks keeping his eyes skunked for the gang 'cause, like always, the neighborhood is crawling with crowds.

See, these days, people live on streets and sidewalks as much as in their small rooms. Men gather in groups, standing under streetlights, talking, laughing, spreading the day's news. Women doing the same, laughing, talking, shopping. Food pushcarts doing good business. Lot of small saloons, too—what people call "drums," which are open and crowded. Midst it all, plenty of beggars.

If it's music you want, there's an Italian music grinder, with these little kids dancing round and laughing. But then there's always more kids on the streets than anyone. Thick as summer flies, playing, fooling, watching, waiting on the world. Take away kids, you ain't hardly got city in the city.

Maks, starting to relax, keeps taking half looks at Willa, trying to sort her out.

But it's she who says, "You make a lot of money selling papers?"

"Don't go home 'less I make my eight cents."

"I'm lucky," she says, "if I make a dime a week."

"Where you work?"

"Pick rags at the East River dumps."

"Get enough?"

Willa shrugs. "Ten cents a week. And there's a midnight breadline at St. Peter's Church on Fulton."

"Where your parents?" Maks asks again.

She don't answer. Then, realizing Maks is waiting on her, she says, "Gone."

"Where?"

Shakes her head.

"No idea?"

This time she gives him nothing.

"Hey," says Maks, "this city, people disappear all the time. Fathers. Kids. Mothers. Yours gone long?"

"While."

"You look for 'em?"

"Can't go everywhere."

"Got this newsie friend," Maks says. "Irish kid. We calls him Chimmie. Told me 'bout a mug who's got a business hunting missing people. A private detective."

"What's private about him?"

"Beats me. You got any sisters or brothers?"

Willa stops. "You know what you sound like?" she says. "The Children's Mission Society. I don't like all the questions."

"Sorry."

Maks, not speaking, pokes up the pace, going back to keeping watch for Bruno.

After a while, as if sorry for sounding so pout-mouthed, Willa says, "Your father around?"

"Oh, sure," Maks says, glad she's willing to talk again. "Papa works in a shoe factory over on Stanton Street. Back where we came from, he used to make small boats. Got one on the East River. Loves fishing. Sometimes I go with him. You been on your own since your family left?"

She nods.

"That okay?"

"I do what I want."

Maks says, "I got a big family."

"How big?"

"Papa. Mama. Three younger brothers. Two older sisters."

"You like them?"

"Sure. 'Specially my big sister Emma. She's a lot of fun. Works at that fancy uptown hotel that just opened. You know, the Waldorf? Up at Thirty-third Street."

"I don't go past Fourteenth," Willa says. "Cops run me off."

"Papa says Emma got the job 'cause she's pretty," Maks goes on. "Mama says it's 'cause she's so clean. She gets a uniform—all blue—and two dollars every other week. Plus tips. More than Papa makes, sometimes. Most nights she sleeps in the hotel dormitory. They feed her too. Comes home every other Monday afternoon and gives Mama her pay. You'll see her when we get home. Oh, yeah. Mama does laundry—a few shirts—for Bothwell's store.

"Agnes, my other sister," Maks continues, "she's our smart one. Goes to night classes. Does sums in her head. Reads books. Works daytime in the factory with Papa." Maks grins. "Only thing, when the labor inspector comes, she's got to hide in the bathroom 'cause she's just fourteen."

Willa says, "You like to talk, don't you?"

"In my family you got to. Anyway, Agnes says it's being

American. Have three younger brothers. Goofs. Tighter than sardines in a can. When'd you come to America?"

"Born here."

"If you was a boy, you could be president. I got here when I was two. So I'm not gonna be president neither. How old are you?"

She stops. "I told you, I don't like questions."

"Just asking," says Maks, but he switches his mouth to shut.

They keep walking awhile without talking. But after a few minutes Willa says, "I'm not sure how old I am. You?"

"Twelve. No, wait, turned thirteen two weeks ago. You go to school?"

She shakes her head.

"Used to," says Maks. "Too old. You know. Get to be thirteen, fourteen, got to work. Only work's hard to find nowadays. But when I went to school, learned to read. That's something."

Willa says nothing.

They come to a crowd, and Maks wants to see what's happening. Turns out people are just looking at a dead horse on the street, so Maks and Willa start up again. Hey, these days, you can see dead horses on the streets most anytime. People work 'em that hard.

As they go on, Maks glances back and stops short. *It's Bruno!* Or is it? 'Cause when he stares at the spot, no one's there.

Willa, sensing something happened, says, "What's the matter?"

"Nothing," says Maks, deciding being nervous is making him see things. Even so, he walks faster.

Few minutes later they pass two boys who know Maks. "Hey, Maks mug," one of 'em cries. "Find yer girlfriend in the dump?"

Embarrassed, Maks shouts back, "Buzzers!" Still, he steals a look at Willa. She don't give no reaction, but Maks ain't too happy being seen with this dirty girl. Trying to be less jumpy, he starts talking again.

"This building where we live," he says, "got twenty apartments. Agnes—my smart sister—she once added up all the people who live there. Hundred and eighty-one. Families come and go faster than the El. The landlord's never put in water. No gas, electricity, neither. My younger brothers born there. All eight of us been living there eight years. Papa says it's decent and cheap. Sometimes I think I'd rather live on my own. Plenty of mugs do."

Willa says, "Try it."

Maks steals another look at her, telling himself, *Something's bothering this girl.*

As the kids keep going, Maks don't see no sign of Bruno. But thinking 'bout what those mugs said 'bout Willa, he starts worrying what his parents are gonna do when *they* see her.

Point is, Maks knows Mama is always trying to keep their flat—and her kids—clean. Sure, Maks has invited plenty of kids home, but nothing like this girl, who's so filthy. Besides, his parents are always asking questions of the mugs he brings home, wanting to know who and what. Willa already told him she don't like neither.

So Maks reminds himself that he's the one who called for help, and since she gave it, he promised her food. Which means he's gotta keep going, first over Division Street, then down Pike, until they reach his street, Birmingham.

Now, you need to know about this Birmingham Street, where Maks lives. It's like a lot of old downtown city streets.

Short, narrow, with cobblestone on the street, both street sides lined with soot-dark brick tenements, each of 'em twenty-five feet wide, five or six stories high. Couple of the buildings have them newfangled iron fire escapes, already draped with drying clothes that look like old drippy wax. Each floor has four windows across, so at night you can see burning candles or oil lamps behind sooty windows.

Hate to say it, but piles of garbage everywhere. Sure, cleaners come, maybe once a month.

At the far end of the street, Eliscue's horse stables. If the wind blows north, you smell 'em. At the other street end, Zunser's tiny Hebrew printing shop, which smells of ink. Actually, Maks likes that smell.

Mid-block—right across from Maks's building— there's an electric streetlamp. Though it's a cold night, a bunch of kids—Maks knows 'em all by name—are playing hopscotch in its puddle of light.

"Here's my place," Maks announces, stopping before a five-step stoop.

Glad to be home, Maks looks up and down the street to see if they've been followed.

No Bruno.

"We're not supposed to go down there," Maks says, nodding toward one side of the stoop where, just below street level, there's a small saloon. "Calls itself The Vineyard," says Maks. "Run by Mr. Cicolone."

A concertina is playing and someone's singing a sad Italian song.

"Does good business afternoons and nights," Maks says. "Guess what? Agnes once told me—she heard it at her school—fifteen thousand saloons in the city. She's always telling us stuff like that.

"Over there," says Maks, pointing toward the other side of the stoop, "that's Tyrone's fish store. Opens early, but stinks all the time."

Maks nods down the street. "In daylight," he says, "you can see Brooklyn Bridge. Papa says we'll walk it one of these days. Come on."

Maks climbs the stoop steps to his house only to realize that Willa is staying on the sidewalk.

"Hey, ain't you coming?"

Even as Willa stands there, her stomach gurgles so loud, Maks hears it. He grins. "Guess you do want some food."

Willa, pressing her lips together, just keeps staring up at him.

"Hey, you nervous 'bout coming?"

She don't answer.

"When's the last time you ate?"

Willa gives a small shoulder shrug.

"Let's go," says Maks.

Willa, one foot on the first step, her stick in her hands, says, "You sure your mother won't mind?"

"Naw," says Maks, though he's sorry now he had promised this girl anything 'cause he's pretty sure his mother *will* mind.

Figuring he owes her one more try, he says, "Hey, Mama makes bread. Be a lot better than your breadline bread."

Willa comes up the stoop.

Maks, wishing he hadn't said that, starts to push open the front door, only to stop. "Any blood on my face? My jacket? Mama don't like brawling."

Willa looks him over. "You're okay. That what you call her—Mama?"

"Yeah."

"All right to take my stick?"

Maks, remembering Bruno, and that Willa will be going out again after eating, says, "Better keep it."

"You sure my coming is okay?"

"Hey, everybody's gonna love you," Maks lies, wanting nothing more than to get this girl in and out—fast.

***

It may be dark on the street, but it's even darker inside the building's narrow entrance hall. Cracked linoleum on the floor. Ceiling covered with pressed tin, bulging in a few places. Walls painted ugly brown. Everything smelling of dirt, old fish, sour beer. And, sorry to say, sometimes mugs from the saloon use the hall as a privy.

The kids come inside, Maks getting more nervous. "Just so you understand," he says, "my folks are glad to be in America. Just once in a while they want it more like where they came from. You know, old-fashioned."

Willa turns back to the door. "I'll visit another time."

"No, honest, it'll be fine," Maks says, grabbing her arm and realizing how thin it is. "I promise, you're gonna get something good to eat. Just hold on to my jacket. We're top floor and ain't no light. But there's one good thing with being top."

"What?"

"Steps that go to the roof. In the summer, easy to get

up there for sleeping. A lot cooler. Mr. Floy—third floor, back—he's nuts 'bout birds. Keeps pigeons up there. Chickens in the backyard. Once he gave me an egg. Mama cooked it. Not bad. Come on."

Willa says, "You ever stop talking?"

Maks grins. "Only if you tells me."

They start climbing.

Now, in tenements like these, each floor has four flats, two on each side, front and back. A flat has three rooms: front room, kitchen, plus small back room. Walls so thin, you hear what people are saying on the other side.

You can smell the foods people are eating too. Bacon on the second floor. Bread on the third. Potatoes on the fourth. Get it? The higher the floor, the cheaper the eats. Same for rents.

On the second floor the Palbeck kids—from the back flat—are playing jacks in the dim hallway. They can't be bothered to look at Maks and Willa as they go by.

On the third, the door is partly open. Someone is shouting.

"Mrs. Tinglist," Maks says. "Hates America. Drinks a lot. Always shouting at her husband and kids."

On the fourth floor the door is wide open. A family— all seven of them—seated at a table, working.

"The Vershinskis," Maks tells Willa. "Speak Polish. All they do is make brooms. One of their kids told me they get ten cents a broom. Takes 'em an hour for each. Trying to get enough money to buy a ticket for their mother to come here from that Poland.

"My parents speak Danish. So does Emma. I can't. Not really. Anyway, my sister Agnes makes us speak American. Warn you, she can be bossy."

Just as they near the last flight of steps, farther up, a door slams. Next moment, a big guy holding a lit lantern comes thumping down the steps. Maks sees his high-domed helmet, the double row of gleaming brass buttons on his coat, his silver badge.

A cop.

To let him pass, Willa and Maks have to flatten themselves 'gainst the wall.

"Why's a policeman here?" Willa whispers when he's gone.

"Don't know," says Maks. Suddenly uneasy, he bolts up the rest of the way. On the top floor he rushes to the front of the building and shoves the door open.

There's enough light from the oil lamp on the kitchen table to show Maks's mama—Mrs. Geless—standing in the middle of the room. She's a small woman with her arms wrapped round her chest, as if to keep herself in one piece.

Though strands of hair are covering part of her face, Maks can see her eyes, and they're full of fright. Maks's three young brothers are clinging to her, crying.

"What is it?" Maks cries. "What's happened?"

Mama opens her mouth. No words come. She keeps swallowing, gasping for air. Tears slide down her face.

"Tell me!"

"It's . . . Emma. She's been arrested."

"*Arrested?* What do you mean?"

Mama struggles to speak. "They put her in that jail. The one over by City Hall."

"The Tombs?" cries Maks.

Mama bobs her head and smears tears from her face with the heels of her small, red hands.

"But . . . why?" Maks says, slamming the front door to keep the news inside.

Mama says, "A policeman was just here. He said that"— she takes a breath—"Emma stole a watch."

Maks, mouth wide open, can't believe what he's hearing.

"At her hotel," Mama explains, with a frantic gesture. "They arrested her."

"Emma would *never* steal," says Maks. "She wouldn't!"

"The policeman says she did." Mama's voice is miserable, her face pinched. "They don't lie."

"Yes they do!" Maks is so upset, he's almost choking. Shoving aside his younger brothers—Eric, Jacob, and Ryker—he takes Mama's arm and leads her to one of the three chairs by the kitchen table. "You better sit."

Mama sits and uses her white apron to wipe away tears. "It's terrible," she says as much to herself as to anyone in the room. *"Frygtelig,"* she adds in Danish.

Maks, not sure what to do, stands over her. His brothers—frightened—stay huddled in a corner, staring at him and Mama.

"Does Papa know?" Maks says. "Does Agnes?"

"Not home from work."

"Tell me what happened."

"The *politistyrke* said—" She shakes her head. "The policeman—"

"Don't care what the policeman said!" Maks shouts. He heads for the door. "Gonna get her."

Mama, her face blotchy, looks up. "You can't. Not till morning."

Maks, hand on the doorknob, says, "Why?"

"The policeman said the prison's locked. Won't open until morning."

"But—"

"Said she'll stay there 'less she has a lawyer."

"What's a lawyer gonna do?"

"I don't know!" Mama shouts, bursting into full tears.

"Then I'm getting a lawyer," Maks says, pulling the door open while trying to remember where he's seen lawyer signs round the neighborhood.

"Maks! Please! Wait for Papa."

Frightened, Maks stands there.

Only then does Mama notice Willa. Maks had forgotten her too. The girl's standing 'gainst the wall, tense, fingering her stick.

"Who is this . . . girl?" says Mama. "Why is she here?"

Maks's brothers also stare at Willa.

Maks don't know what to say. With his mother there, he's seeing how bad Willa really looks. The ragged clothes, the bare feet. Her smell. All he can manage is, "She's a friend."

"Friend?" says Mama, wrinkling her nose. "What . . . what kind of friend? Why does she have that stick?"

Willa's jaw tightens. She wants to get out of there, but Maks is blocking the door.

"Why is she here?" Mama repeats.

"Saved me from getting a beating," Maks says. "I wanted to thank her. Give her some food."

Mama looks at Willa as if *she'd* done the beating. She turns to Maks, "Is that blood on your face?"

"From that Plug Ugly Gang," says Maks. He's almost crying. "I told you 'bout 'em! They're hounding newsies. They was coming after me and"—he gestures toward Willa—"she beat 'em off."

"But she's so . . . dirty."

"Come on, Mama," cries Maks. "Dirt ain't people. I was the one who asked for help. She hadn't given it, I wouldn't have my money. And her name is Willa."

"Willa?"

"German name."

"German," his mother echoes.

Maks, suddenly remembering his mother don't like Germans, quickly adds, "Born in America. That's more than me."

Wanting to turn Mama's talk from Willa, Maks scoops his pennies from his pocket and dumps them on the table.

"See," he says. "Sold all my papers. Made my share."

Mama barely looks at the coins.

"You should thank her," Maks says as he divides the coins into two piles—what he needs for the next day's paper buy, and his own eleven-cent profit. Grabbing a cigar box from the shelf over the stove, he shovels in most of the pennies.

Mama turns back toward Willa and gives a nod. "I'm sorry if I sounded so—" She stops, interrupted by the sound of footsteps.

"It's Agnes and Papa," says Mama. "Dear God. The news will kill him." She puts out a hand toward Maks, whispers, "Help me stand."

Maks helps Mama pull herself up. Once standing, she faces the doorway, trying to dry her eyes and shove back hair that keeps falling over her face while smoothing her faded blue dress—all at the same time. Then, as the steps draw closer, she squeezes her hands together as if praying.

Maks's brothers stay in the corner.

Willa presses herself against the far shadowy wall, trying to make herself small.

As for Maks, he just stares at the door, hoping his father will tell 'em what to do.

11

The first one to come in the door is Agnes—thin, pale, large eyes rimmed with pink. Got a shawl round her head.

Papa comes right behind. He's slightly stooped, bald, with a shaggy, tobacco-stained mustache, all of which make him look older than he is. In his hand he's got a tin lunch pail.

Everyone in the room stares at him. Takes him only a second to know something's wrong.

"What is it?" he says. "What's happened?"

Mama twists her hands. "Emma."

"*Emma!*"

"She . . ."

"She what?" Papa cries.

Mama tries to speak but can't. 'Stead, she drops back into the chair, lifts her apron, covers her face. Shoulders shaking, she cries.

Agnes looks to Maks. "Maks!" she says. "What is it?"

Papa also turns to him.

Maks says, "Emma's . . . Emma's been . . . arrested."

It's as if Papa has been struck in the chest. Goes all cream-faced. Takes a step back. Drops his lunch pail with a clatter.

Agnes stares. She can't speak.

In the corner the boys start crying again.

"Arrested?" Papa gasps. "But why?"

Though it's hard to say it, Maks gets out what Mama said.

Papa turns to Mama. "Is that true?"

Mama, crying, nods.

"Tell me!" Papa shouts.

Mama starts speaking in Danish.

"No Danish, Mama," Agnes pleads. "American!"

Mama gulps, swallows, tries again. "A policeman came here and—"

"Here?" cries Papa. "A policeman?"

"Said Emma stole."

"Great God!" cries Papa. "Why would Emma do such a thing?"

"Emma didn't steal!" Maks shouts.

Papa looks to Mama. "Did she or didn't she?"

Mama nods.

All Papa can do is stand there and pull at his mustache.

Agnes, coughing, shuts the door. Yanks off her shawl, so her blond braids tumble. Clearing her throat, she sits on one of the kitchen chairs, takes up Mama's hands, squeezes them.

Papa hasn't moved. He can't.

Maks says, "Papa?"

"What?"

"We gotta find a lawyer."

"What will a lawyer do?"

"Get Emma out of jail."

"Is . . . is she in *jail*?"

"The Tombs."

Papa looks at Mama. "That *gigantic* prison?"

Mama nods.

"Papa," Maks pleads, "we gotta do *something*."

Papa suddenly lifts a fist over his head.

Frightened, Maks steps back. Mama calls out something in Danish. Papa's body sags. His hand opens. Drops by his side. His body seems to shrink. In a ragged voice he cries, "Dear God! I don't know how things work here. How we going to help her?" He looks round at his family's faces. "Maybe Emma just picked up something by mistake.

Or maybe something fell into her pocket. Without her knowing. These things happen. Terrible mistakes get made."

"Papa!" Maks shouts again. "Emma didn't steal!"

"No, of course not," says Papa. "I didn't mean—not for a moment. But . . ." He stands still, his breathing ragged, words sputtering. "Dear God. These are . . . hard times. Just today . . . we were told the factory will be closing for a time."

"How come?" says Maks.

Agnes says, "They say we're making too many shoes. Can only sell them for two dollars."

"What's wrong with cheap?"

"They can't make a profit," Agnes says. "When we closed last fall, we were off for two weeks. It could be worse this time. In school we learned that capitalism needs profits to—"

"Stop that talk!" Papa shouts. "Nothing to do with anything! Lots of factories are closing. It's what I said. Hard times." He makes a vague gesture. "The panic . . ."

The room is full of silence.

Papa takes a deep breath. Says, "I got to pay the landlord the key money this week. Merciful God, we have money. For now. But with Emma . . . Agnes and me, we can't miss any work. We'll need every penny." He looks to Mama. "Mama, you'll go to the prison and—"

"No!" Mama cries. "I can't. I know nothing of prisons. I'll be afraid. I . . . I forget English when I'm upset." She looks round. "What if I do something wrong? They might . . . they might keep me there."

"Mama," says Agnes, "they wouldn't dare."

No one speaks.

That's when Maks says, "I'll go to The Tombs."

"Good, Maks," says Papa, and Maks hears relief in his voice. "Yes. You'll go."

"Will they let him?" says Mama. "Won't he be too young?"

"Don't care," Maks says. "I'm going. In the morning. Soon as the jail opens."

"There," says Papa. "Emma will like that. You and her, you're good friends. And tomorrow I'll speak to that friend of mine, you know, Mr. Strande. He's a lawyer."

"Papa," says Agnes, "Mr. Strande was a lawyer in Copenhagen. Here he's just in an insurance office."

"Fine," says Papa. "Then you and me will ask people at the factory if they know a lawyer. Someone will. Though I suppose lawyers are expensive.

"Never mind," he hurries on. "Mama, you'll find food for Maks to bring to Emma. Maks, when you go, you must ask her what happened."

The three boys, crying less, look on.

"There," says Papa, looking round the room, his eyes full of tears. "Yes," says Papa, letting a breath out. "My poor, beautiful child. But see, we're all working together."

"And perhaps," Mama says to Papa, "you'll be allowed to go before a magistrate. You could . . . you could tell him we could send Emma home to Denmark."

"Send her back?" cries Maks.

"Better than prison."

"But she's a good girl!" cries Papa. "An honest girl." Then he adds, "But yes, we'll make sure they know that. One way or another, we'll get Emma out of that place. Absolutely. No question."

Too upset to look at his father, Maks turns to Willa. The girl is standing 'gainst the wall, staring at Papa. Maks wonders what she's thinking.

Papa follows his look, finally notices Willa. "Forgive me," he says. "But . . . who are you?"

Maks quickly tells him what happened.

Papa sighs. "Maks, I've told you. Too many fights. It leads to no good."

"Papa—"

"What?"

"I sold all my papers. Made my eight cents, and more." Maks goes to the table, scoops up his pennies, and puts them into Papa's large, dye-stained hand. "Wasn't for Willa, wouldn't have 'em."

Papa gazes at the pennies. "Every bit helps, doesn't it?" he says. Closing his fingers round the coins, he turns to Willa. "We thank you," he says to her. "You see, this family works together. More than ever." Nodding, he looks round for agreement.

Mama sighs, wipes a tear away, and struggles to her feet. "I'll make supper," she says. "Just need water."

"I'll get it," Maks says, wanting to be out of the room.

Snatching up a candle stub from the stove shelf, he lights it from the lamp. Grabs two pails from under the kitchen table, goes to the door, stops and looks at Willa.

"Water's out back," he says, hoping she'll come along.

Willa, darting a shy look at the rest of the family, leaves the apartment too.

Once in the hallway, Maks shuts the door behind them, takes a deep breath. "Hey," he says, "why'd you bring your stick? Just going to the yard."

Which is when Willa says, "I'm not staying."

"How come?" says Maks. "Don't you want no food?"

"Your family is too upset. They don't want me here."

Soon as Willa says it, Maks knows it's true. Makes him feel bad for what he thought 'bout the girl. And the thing is, now he *wants* Willa to stay. 'Cause with the whole family miserable, he's sure the night is gonna be awful. But if Willa is there—a stranger—they won't talk so much 'bout how bad things are. Besides, Willa knows Bruno. So he *can* talk 'bout that.

Except he don't know how to say any of it.

"Don't you want that food I promised?" he coaxes. "Probably fish soup. Mama makes it good."

Willa shakes her head.

Maks, not knowing what to say, stares at the girl, but she won't look up. "Okay," he says, too exhausted to argue.

Using candlelight to show the way, they go down the five dim flights without talking. As they go, Maks keeps glancing at Willa. Keeps seeing that sadness on her face. Makes him feel worse.

They get to the front door. Stand there, still not saying nothing.

Willa looks up. "Hope your sister is okay."

"Yeah."

"You know where I live. You don't have to be chased to come and tell me what happens to her."

"Sure," says Maks.

He pulls the door open. And what's he see? Right across the street—standing under the streetlamp—it's Bruno.

Maks slams the door shut.

"What's the matter?" says Willa.

"Bruno. That redheaded guy from the gang. 'Cross the street. He must have followed us."

Willa reaches for the door.

"Don't!" Maks says, blocking her way. "That guy'll kill you soon as look at you. Better he don't know we seen him."

Willa just stands there.

"Might even be more of 'em," Maks presses, afraid to look out again. "Won't matter you're a girl. Honest, they're terrorsome."

Willa don't move.

"Don't worry. You can sleep here," Maks pleads, really scared for her, upset that he's the one who got her into this.

Willa eyes the door. "I'll be in the way."

"Naw. Honest. We always got room. And in the morning, be lot safer. People on the street. Anyway, be a favor to me if you stayed."

She looks round. "Why?"

Maks, nodding toward the top of the house, says, "Up there, with everyone upset, it's gonna be bad. Be good to talk to someone who ain't family." He touches her arm. "Come on. You don't wanna get hurt. And you'll get some food. Mean it: Mama's a good cook. Just have to get some water."

When Willa still don't move, Maks says, "What's the matter?"

Willa, eyes down, says, "Your mother said I was dirty. Can . . . that place where you get water, can I wash my face?"

Maks snorts. "That all? Come on."

He leads Willa out the back way, down the rickety wooden steps, into a small, muddy yard.

On all four sides of the yard, tenement buildings rise up. Light enough from windows—plus Maks's candle— to see.

Middle of the yard, surrounded by puddles of dirty water, is an iron water pump. Couple of chickens strut 'bout. Back of the yard is what looks like a row of closets.

Maks shoos the chickens away, points to the closets. "Privies," he says, handing Willa the candle.

Willa hurries to use one of them. When she comes back, Maks is finishing filling his buckets. She hands him the candle, then holds out her hands.

Maks pumps up water, which she throws over her face and rubs. Dirt flows off. "Any better?" Willa asks, peering at him.

It's almost as if Maks is seeing her for the first time. She's got a small, thin face, with a slightly turned-up nose. Her mouth is small, tight.

Maks mutters, "You look fine."

"You sure?"

"Honest." He hands her the candle and hoists the buckets. She picks up her stick.

As they climb the dim steps, Willa says, "Why do you think that Bruno is out there?"

"Told you. Wants revenge. Beat us up."

Willa halts and looks down at Maks on the step below. "*Us?*" she says.

"Sure. Betcha anything he thinks we're together."

With tiredness filling her face, Willa says, "He doesn't know anything about me."

Maks shrugs. "Don't matter to him."

She sighs.

Maks looks up at the girl. The candlelight lets him see her eyes. And what he's seeing now is that she's scared.

Willa seems 'bout to speak. Instead, she swings round and heads up the steps again.

Maks follows, thinking, *Hey, I'm scared too.*

Maks and Willa step into the kitchen.

Now, this room, this kitchen—maybe ten feet by ten—

what it's got is a square table covered with yellow oilcloth and a lamp. Plus three chairs and a deep tin sink, which is really a tub. Also, an iron cookstove, a coal scuttle, a storage closet for food, and a cabinet for dishes and pots. There's a small icebox, but the family only gets ice during hot summers. During winter, they use window ledges to keep things from going worse.

There's also a big tin bucket—with a scrubbing board—for Mama's laundry work and for giving baths. On a shelf over the stove are three heavy pressing irons, which Mama also uses for her work.

Not much, but it's crowded.

The ceiling is tin. The floor is wood. As for walls, they're all faded green with a few cracks and not much peeling. Two paper pictures stuck to them. One is of Queen Louise of Denmark—Emma found it somewhere. The other is a chromo of President Lincoln, which Maks got from some ward heeler for Election Day. There's also a wooden clock on the wall.

When Willa and Maks get there, the room is hot 'cause Mama has the stove going. Agnes is sitting at the table near the oil lamp reading a book. The book's pages are loose, its cover bent, but she don't seem to care. As she reads, she coughs.

Maks stands in the doorway, Willa right behind him. He says, "Willa's sleeping here tonight."

Mama, at the stove, says nothing, just stirs the pot. Agnes keeps her eyes on her book.

Maks, guessing they're not happy 'bout Willa staying, don't want to explain that Bruno's outside. There's enough trouble. All he says is, "Where's Papa?"

Agnes, not lifting her eyes from her reading, says, "In the back room. Very upset."

"Where the boys?"

"Front room. Not happy either."

Maks brings the buckets to Mama. To Willa, he says, "Come in."

He sits at the table, glances at Mama. He can only see her back, but from the way her shoulders keep twitching, he can tell she's weeping—silently.

Trying to push down the pain he feels, Maks looks over to Willa. The girl's still standing by the door, not sure where to go. Maks pats the chair next to him.

Not wanting to draw attention, Willa shuts the door softly and sits on the chair's edge. With downcast eyes, her stick is resting 'cross her knees, as if she's gonna rush off any moment.

Maks leans toward her and says, "Soon as we get

enough money, Papa's gonna get more chairs."

Willa barely nods.

Usually at this time, everybody in the family would be in the kitchen talking 'bout what they did that day, with Papa reading a newspaper and announcing what's happening. This being Monday, Emma should have been home, which means lots of laughter. But this night, other than the clock ticking, the only sounds in the room come from Mama scraping a spoon 'gainst her black iron pot and, every once in a while, her sighs.

"I'm hungry," Maks blurts out.

"Think how Emma must feel," says Agnes, not looking up.

Maks slumps down and thinks, *Maybe I should go to Denmark.*

Sitting there, Maks notices that though Agnes is acting as if she's reading, she ain't turning no pages.

Agnes looks up. "Do you mind my asking," she says to Willa, "where are your mother and father?"

Willa, her voice small, says, "I don't know."

Agnes's cheeks redden. "Forgive me," she whispers, coughs, bends over her book.

Maks fidgets, leans over the table, pokes his sister, and says, "What you reading?"

Agnes holds up her book. On the cover it says *Every Girl Her Own Clerk: How to Get a Job in a Fine Business.*

"Reads better than any of us," Maks tells Willa. "Never pays more than three cents a book. Always reading. Goes to those free night classes at that Educational Alliance over on East Broadway. Trying to get out of the factory." He glances at his mother. "Mama thinks that's too high-and-mighty. Says she should stay at the factory." He pokes his sister again. "Tell Willa what you're studying."

Agnes don't even look up. "Accounting. Typing."

Willa gives Maks a puzzled look.

"Accounting. Business adding," says Maks. "Typing is machine writing."

"Oh."

Frustrated, Maks jumps up. "Come on," he says to Willa. She grabs her stick and follows him into the front part of the apartment.

This front room is the flat's largest, maybe twelve feet all ways, with two windows on the street side. Got five narrow beds—one against each wall, one in the middle.

"The boys' room," Maks explains.

His three brothers are sitting side by side on one of the beds. Not talking, looking miserable.

To Willa, Maks says, "When Emma's home, she shares a bed with Agnes in my parents' room. Me and my brothers sleep here. This here middle bed's for our boarder, Monsieur Zulot. He's a Frenchy. Be home soon."

Maks goes to one of the windows and peers down. When he sees Bruno leaning against the streetlight, he feels sick.

16

Maks turns back into the room. Willa, having guessed what he's doing, looks him a question. Maks just nods.

Not wanting to talk 'bout it, he sits on the middle bed, opposite the boys. "Whatcha doing?" he says, same time offering Willa a place next to him, which she takes.

Jacob, almost eight, the oldest of the three boys, glances toward the kitchen, leans forward. Small-voiced, he says, "Maks, did Emma steal?"

"Didn't you hear?" says Maks. "No. And don't no one go telling nobody she did. Understand? Nothing to nobody."

Eric says, "We know. But what's gonna happen to her?"

"In the morning," says Maks, "first thing, I'll get her out of jail."

"How?" Ryker asks. He's six.

"She shouldn't have been arrested. It was a mistake. Don't worry. I'll get her out. This here's Willa. She's my new friend. Staying here tonight."

"How come?"

"I invited her."

Eric grins, wrinkles his nose. "Is Mama gonna give her a bath?" he asks.

"Shut up!" says Jacob.

Maks introduces his brothers to Willa. "Jacob. Oldest. Sometimes he sells my papers when I can't. This one is Eric. Thinks he's funny when he ain't."

Eric giggles.

"And Ryker. Youngest. Just started school."

"Maks," says Ryker, "she gonna live here?"

"Have my own place," Willa says.

"Where?"

"By Chrystie Street."

"How come you don't have shoes?" Ryker says.

"Don't want them."

"Papa and Agnes make shoes," Ryker tells her.

Jacob says, "You really chase that gang away from Maks?"

Maks says, "With that stick."

"How?" Ryker says.

"Whacked 'em," says Maks.

The boys' eyes grow big. "Can I hold it?" says Eric.

Willa hands him the stick. The boys give it a study, running fingers over its bumps.

"Maks," Jacob asks, "what's a lawyer?"

"Does stuff with the law."

"That Mr. Strande," says Eric, "Papa's friend. He's a lawyer, right? All he does is tell stupid jokes in Danish."

Wanting to get off the subject of Emma, Maks says, "What happened in school today?"

"Guess what?" says Jacob. "Ryker got a new name."

"Why?" Maks says.

"Teacher said I needed an American one."

"What she give you?"

It's Eric who says, "Ronald." He grins.

Maks makes a face. "You like it?" he asks Ryker.

"Naw."

Shyly, Willa says, "My name used to be Waddah."

Eric giggles. "Willa's better."

"You get it in school?" Ryker asks her.

"My mother gave it to me."

"Our mama," says Jacob, "says we should always keep being Danish."

"But Agnes," Ryker puts in, "is always saying we need to be American."

"Maks," says Eric, "guess what? Papa says he'll take us fishing on Sunday."

"Good." Maks stands up and looks out the window again. Sees Bruno and wonders if he'll stay till morning.

Dinner is fish head soup with barley and potatoes. There's also bread, which Mama bakes 'cause she can make it cheaper than the bakery five-cent loaf.

As always, Papa and Agnes eat first. Mama serves. No one talks. Halfway through his bowl, Papa throws down his spoon. "Can't eat!" he says, and goes into the back room. Slams the door behind him.

No one says anything.

Agnes, eyes cast down, now and again coughing, resumes eating.

Maks, not able to get Emma or Bruno out of his head, can't keep still. He's up, down, in and out of the front room, stealing looks out the window.

Bruno hasn't moved.

Coming back into the kitchen, Maks looks round, says, "Where'd Mama go?"

Agnes whispers, "With Papa. They're really frightened," and she puts a finger to her lips.

She calls the boys to dinner and ladles soup into their bowls. Maks cuts a thick slice of bread for each of them, then steps back and watches.

The boys, silent at first, keep looking from Agnes to Maks.

Willa's stomach rumbles. Eric tries to keep from giggling.

Jacob, giving his brother a punch on the leg, says to Willa, "Hope you like fish soup. What we eat most of the time."

"Get cheap fish from Mr. Tyrone," Eric tells her. "When it's old."

"But not rotten," Jacob adds with a look to Agnes.

"But sometimes Papa gets a fish from the river," says Ryker.

"On birthdays Mama makes *smakage*."

Willa glances at Maks, who's pacing restlessly up and down. "Danish for 'cookies,'" he explains.

"When's your birthday?" Ryker asks Willa.

She looks down. "I forget."

"How can you forget a birthday?" Eric hoots.

Willa shrugs.

"Maks," says Agnes, "your pacing is making me jumpy."

"Sorry." Maks sits on the floor, back against the wall. Keeps shifting his legs.

"Willa," says Agnes, "where do you live?"

"Near Chrystie Street," Ryker answers for her.

"Guess what?" Jacob says to Agnes. "Her name used to be Waddah. Willa is her American name."

"Her mother gave it to her," says Ryker.

Agnes says, "I thought you lived alone."

"I do," Willa says softly.

"You live alone?" says Jacob, soupspoon stopping halfway to his mouth.

"Lots of people do," Maks calls from across the room. "Half the newsies I know ain't got parents."

Agnes says, "It's 'do not have,' not 'ain't got.'"

"Where they live?" Jacob asks Maks.

"Different places," says Maks. "On the street. Newsboy lodging houses cost a nickel a night."

"Everything costs a nickel," says Ryker.

"Hokey-Pokey ice cream is a penny," Jacob reminds him.

"Maks," says Ryker, "how come they call it that?"

"Don't know," says Maks, and he jumps up and goes to the front room and looks down again. Bruno's still there. Maks comes back to the kitchen. Willa looks at him. He turns away, not wanting to share his growing panic.

18

The door to the apartment opens, and the boarder, Monsieur Zulot, comes in.

See, these days, with cheap rooms hard to find and immigrants filling up the city, lots of people take in boarders. Helps with the rent.

Zulot's a stocky young man with a thin, pale mustache, who's been in America 'bout a year. He's always wearing a long coat over an old black suit. Shoes scuffed and the fingers of his right hand smudged with ink 'cause all day he's copying letters for some business near Wall Street.

When he comes in, he's carrying a rolled-up magazine.

"Bon soir," he says, bowing to the boys first, then to Agnes. "Mademoiselle Agnes," he says softly. When she turns away, Zulot's face becomes red. That makes the boys grin.

Zulot holds up his magazine. "A new story," he announces to the boys.

"Can we hear it?" cries Ryker.

"With permission. Mademoiselle Agnes?" Zulot asks, making another bow toward her.

She don't answer.

Zulot stands straight and goes into the front room. Trying so hard not to look at Agnes, he don't even notice Willa.

As soon as he's gone, Maks says to Willa in a low voice, "Our boarder. Monsieur Zulot."

"Frenchy," says Ryker.

"Pays us a dollar a week to board," Eric adds.

"We like him," says Ryker, "'cause he reads stories to us."

Giggling, Eric says to Willa, "And guess what? He's dead stuck on Agnes. Wants to marry her."

Agnes blushes.

"But Papa says no," Jacob says, grinning.

"'Cause she's too young," says Eric.

"Uh-uh," says Ryker. "Mama says it's because he's Catholic."

"Stop!" Agnes cries.

Jacob punches Ryker's leg.

Urgently, Agnes whispers, "Don't any of you tell him what's happened to Emma."

"We won't," Jacob says.

"Scoot," Agnes says to the boys. "Tell Monsieur Zulot his dinner is ready." The boys horse it into the front room.

"Your turn," Agnes says to Maks and Willa as Monsieur Zulot returns. No longer wearing his coat, the Frenchman dips his hands into one of the water buckets, washes off ink. He puts a dollar coin on the table. "My rent," he says, and sits down at the table.

Agnes picks up the coin. Puts it in her dress pocket. "Thank you."

Maks says to Zulot, "This is my friend, Willa."

The Frenchman jumps up and makes another bow.

"My great pleasure to meet you." He sits, tucks a napkin under his chin.

Agnes ladles the remaining soup into bowls while Maks cuts three more bread slices.

Agnes sets down the three bowls, the last one for Monsieur Zulot.

Willa don't even wait, but gobbles her bread fast. When a crumb drops, she pops it into her mouth.

Agnes, acting as if she's not noticing, says, "Maks, you know the rule: No hats when eating at the table."

Maks snatches his cap off.

Zulot bows his head, makes the sign of the cross over his heart, presses his hands together, whispers a prayer in French. All the while, he's stealing looks at Agnes. She's acting as if she's ignoring him, but Maks sees her glance round once in a while.

No one talks.

Willa spoons up her soup so fast, Agnes gives Maks a look. Maks, ignoring her, pulls his own bread apart, slides one half to Willa.

His dinner finished, Monsieur Zulot stands up. "Mademoiselle Agnes, I thank you. Mademoiselle Willa." Another bow. "Mademoiselle Agnes, may I read to the boys?"

"Of course."

He leaves the room. Soon as he does, Agnes steps close to Maks. "Maks," she whispers, speaking low before turning aside to clear her throat, "when you see Emma tomorrow, what are you going to tell her?"

"That we're gonna help her."

"'Going to,' not 'gonna.' How?"

"Not sure."

"You need to find out everything that happened."

Maks says, "You don't think she stole, do you?"

"Of course not."

"Why'd they put her in jail, then?"

Agnes says, "That's what you have to learn. I'll help Papa get a lawyer."

"Not that stupid Mr. Strande."

"I know."

"Ain't a real lawyer gonna cost a lot?" says Maks.

"'Isn't,' not 'ain't,'" Agnes says. "I'm not supposed to know, but Mama saves money for some uptown doctor for me. So there's some. But we're going to have a lot less."

"How come?"

"Didn't you hear Papa? The factory is closing. For a while, anyway." Agnes glances toward the back room,

WILLA

hoping Mama and Papa can't hear her. "It's going to be you and me who'll have to think of what to do."

"What 'bout Emma?"

"We should be all right, if we can get her out of jail and she can keep her job."

"They ain't really gonna send her back to Denmark, will they?"

"Don't know."

"Agnes?"

"What?"

"We gonna be all right?"

Agnes, clearing her throat again, don't answer, just turns away.

Maks glances at Willa. She's staring into her empty bowl. Maks looks to Agnes. "Any more soup?"

Agnes, not able to talk, shakes her head.

Maks, upset, washes the soup bowls in a bucket, then takes the dirty water down to the yard, where he throws it at a clucking chicken. When he gets back, Willa is sitting in the dark kitchen alone.

"Your sister says good night," she says. Then she adds, "You have a nice family."

"Yeah. But everybody's tumbled. Want another piece of bread?"

Willa hesitates, then says, "Can I?"

Maks cuts her a piece and gives it to her. "Where's the lamp?" he asks.

"Your boarder took it." Then Willa says, "Agnes has a bad cough. And her eyelids are pink."

"Mama told Papa it's something called 'wasting disease.'"

Willa stops eating. "You sure?"

"Yeah. Why? What's the matter?"

"I know . . . someone who had that."

"What happened?"

"She died."

Maks, afraid to say anything, only murmurs, "Get you a blanket. We got some thick Danish ones." Nods to the back room, where his parents are. "They brought 'em over."

He goes into the front room, where he finds everyone sitting on the beds, the lit lamp on the floor. Monsieur Zulot has the magazine open on his lap.

"Maks," says Zulot, "do you desire to hear the story?"

"It's really good," says Eric. "'Bout detectives."

Jacob, squirming with pleasure, says, "It's called *The Bradys and the Missing Diamonds.*"

"*Or*," Ryker adds, "*The Boy Detective.*"

"Tell Maks who wrote it," cries Eric.

Monsieur Zulot reads: "'By a New York Detective.'"

Maks says, "Lemme get Willa."

Before he gets her, he steals a quick look down at the street. Bruno's still there.

Not saying anything to Willa 'bout Bruno, the two of them sit on Ryker's bed.

"I'll start again," says Monsieur Zulot, flipping to the first page. "*Bien.* Here we go. 'Chapter One: The Detectives Get the Case.'"

The story is 'bout two detectives—one an old mug, and the other his kid. They're trying to figure out who stole this lady's diamonds. Maks likes the way the story describes the boy detective: "He looked like a mere boy, with a handsome face, a pair of keen eyes, and a dashing, aggressive air that showed he was of a bold, intrepid character." Maks wishes he were bold, but he don't know what "intrepid" means.

Then there's that lady, the one who lost the diamonds.

The story says she's "tall and splendid, with raven black hair, soft red lips, and gentle brown eyes, all of which gave her an air of great refinement."

"Aw," pleads Eric when Monsieur Zulot stops reading. "Can't you read more?"

"Tomorrow." He brings the lamp back into the kitchen.

Maks fetches blankets from the front room. As he does, he looks out the window to the street below. Bruno hasn't budged.

Back in the kitchen Maks says to Willa, "Bruno's still there."

"Do you think he'll be there in the morning?"

"Hope not," Maks says as he lays out a blanket for Willa.

"He won't come up, will he?"

Maks hasn't thought of that. "I'll sleep out here."

He sets his blanket in front of the door.

Willa lies down on the floor and covers herself. Keeps her stick by her side.

Maks sits on the floor, back against the door, legs stretched out. He says, "You like that story?"

"Okay."

"I'd like to be that boy detective. Wanna be that tall and splendid lady?"

"Not sure."

For a moment there's silence, until Maks says, "Hey, Willa, when was the last time you ate?"

"Three days ago."

"Want another piece of bread?"

"I'm okay."

Neither speaks till Willa says, "Maks?"

"What?"

"I can't read."

"Lot of kids can't," says Maks. "Mama can't. Not American. But you know what? That story Monsieur read gave me an idea. 'Member I told you what my friend Chimmie told me? 'Bout that detective he knows? Maybe we could get him to help Emma. Might be cheaper than a lawyer."

"What's a detective going to do?"

"Like in that story. Find the real crook. My sister didn't steal nothing. I know she didn't. And if a detective could prove it, the police would have to let her go, right? I'd die if she went to prison. Or Denmark."

Willa don't say nothing.

Maks blows out the lamp, then lies down with his hands back of his head. "Yeah. I'm gonna ask Chimmie." Maks stares up at the dark. "Willa?"

"What?"

"Ever been to The Tombs?"

"No."

"They put crooks in there. Have trials. Then people go to jail—Blackwell's Island, Sing Sing—for *years*." He pulls himself up on one elbow. "Whenever someone in a uniform or a boss tells my parents to do something, they just do it. As if they never left Denmark. Papa's always telling us how bad it was there. But you know what Mama says? 'People are freer in America. But there are more tears.'"

Willa is quiet. "Maks?" she says after a while.

"What?"

"If you want, I'll go to The Tombs with you."

"Okay." Maks shuts his eyes only to suddenly realize the clock ain't ticking. He jumps up, stands on a chair, and adjusts the chains. The clock starts ticking.

"That clock," he tells Willa when he lies down again, "was a present someone gave my parents when they got married. Papa winds it every night. Guess he's so upset, he forgot. Mama loves it. But she thinks that if it stops, someone in the family will die."

"You believe that?"

"Don't know. Hard not believing what your parents believe."

After a moment Willa says, "I don't know what my parents believed."

"Don't you have no idea where they went? Or why?"

When Willa don't answer, Maks says, "Thanks again for saving me in the alley. Glad you stayed. If you like, we can be friends."

After a moment Willa says, "I don't have friends."

"Can have one now."

Willa don't reply, and it's not long 'fore Maks hears her sleep breathing.

Everything is still.

Maks closes his eyes. Can't sleep. Too many worries. Emma, mostly. Bruno, too. That his father and Agnes gonna lose work. Then there's Agnes and her coughing. He wishes they had more money. What if they have to use Agnes's doctor money for a lawyer?

He starts thinking 'bout Willa, all her silences. Like she ain't all there.

Maks starts wondering what he'd do if *his* parents died. Or Agnes did. Or Emma.

He gets up and slips into the front room. His brothers and Monsieur Zulot seem to be asleep.

Standing before one of the windows, Maks looks down. To his relief, Bruno is no longer there.

"Maks? What you looking at?"

Startled, Maks turns. It's Ryker. He's sitting up in his bed.

Maks says, "Nothing."

"Did Emma get home?"

"Tomorrow. Go to sleep."

"Maks, you know what? I'm scared for her."

"Told you, everything's gonna be fine."

"You sure?"

"Yeah. Go to sleep."

"Okay."

Maks goes back to the kitchen, lies down on the floor, and pulls the blanket up. Lying there, he can hear Mama and Papa talking in their back room. Mostly in Danish, so he can't understand it, though he keeps hearing Emma's name. It all sounds tense, full of fear. Then, to his horror, he hears Papa crying, Mama trying to calm him. But she's crying too.

Maks sits up. It's something he's never heard. It scares him like nothing before. His heart pounds.

Emma. He thinks about her. She's a pretty girl, sixteen, taller than Mama, not skinny like Agnes. Light hair, dark brown eyes, happy most of the time. Always laughing, mostly over silly stuff, which makes Maks laugh. He loves being with her. Makes him happy.

She and he like to take walks together. Nowhere in particular. Just to talk. Emma tells Maks her secrets. Not that she's got many. Recently, she spent a nickel to ride the elevated train to come home. That was her first time. She did it—secretly—so as not to be home late. She told Maks the ride was exciting. Promised to take him.

Then there was the time she went to a dance hall with some girls from her work. Wanted to learn that new two-step. That was big. Mama wouldn't have liked that. A week later she bought a penny ribbon to look nice. She never wore it at home.

Maks didn't tell no one 'bout these things.

So hard to think of her in jail. Maks ponders if it will make her different. If she goes to Blackwell's on the river, it'll be like she died.

Maks wonders how scared Emma is. Then he thinks, *Willa's scared. I'm scared. The whole world's scared.*

———

What if we can't get Emma out? Maks thinks that question ten million times. How many answers does he get?

Not one.

Maks, trying to guess where Bruno went, finally closes his eyes.

21

Even dreaming, Maks couldn't imagine the scene at the Roof Garden Dance Hall: part dance hall, part restaurant. It's atop the American Theatre on Forty-second Street, which is farther uptown than Maks has ever gone.

The place is crowded. From the stage, a banjo twangs "Oh, Dem Golden Slippers"—a new, hot tune. A few couples dance the two-step on the polished floor, gliding past the iron arches holding up a high ceiling. The arches are decked out with electric lights.

Lots of whiskered men in dark suits sporting derbies or fedoras on their heads. Women in long dresses with high collars and feathered, flowery, wide-brimmed hats.

The air is blue-gray with cigar smoke. Not many

women are smoking—not considered decent. Most of the people are just sitting at the hundred small tables on the dance floor, eating, talking, looking round.

Ignoring the clatter, the music, and the people, there's a man sitting alone in a far corner finishing his dinner of steak and potatoes. He's wearing a new black suit, he's smooth-shaven, and his hair is slicked back. Not interested in the crowd or, for that matter, his dinner. From time to time, he picks up a cigar from an ashtray, takes a puff, blows smoke up.

Nothing on his face shows what he's thinking, though now and again he pats his left jacket pocket, feeling for what's there: a Colt pistol.

From his right-hand pocket, he plucks up a gold watch—a Breguet—the hours marked by Roman numerals. He checks. Shakes his head, annoyed to be kept waiting.

He puts the watch away and in its place takes out a photograph. Glued to a card, it's a photograph of a face. Bruno's face.

A barefoot newsie approaches the table. "Paper, mister?"

The man makes a dismissive gesture. The boy backs off only to bump into someone. He looks up, sees who it is, scrambles away.

The man looks up. "Ah, Bruno," he says. "You're late."

"Had some business." Bruno is staring at the photograph in the man's hand.

"Sit down," says the man, nodding to an empty chair.

Angry, Bruno yanks out the chair and sits. Rubs his squinty eye, adjusts his derby. "Whatcha doing with that picture?" he demands.

"I like to make sure I have it." The man returns the photo to his pocket. "Because I may need to use it, if necessary."

Bruno sits there, fuming. "Yous forced me to have my picture taken," he blurts out. "Stole my face."

"Now, Bruno," says the man, "it was you who tried to hold me up and steal my money. It was my revolver"—the man pats his pocket—"that kept you from stealing it. Correct?"

Bruno just glowers.

The man goes on: "Just know that the police are looking for a criminal responsible for a whole series of holdups. All I need to do is give them this photo and they'll use it to identify you. And when they do, you'll be arrested. And—"

"Don't need to go telling me all that stuff again," grumbles Bruno. "It's blackmail, that's all."

"Perhaps. Do as I tell you and you'll avoid working the stone quarry at Sing Sing prison for ten years."

"I can leave town."

The man smiles. "Bruno, there are police everywhere. And they cooperate. I can make copies of the photo. Send them anywhere you might go."

Bruno says nothing, but the muscles on the side of his face tighten.

The man leans forward. "That a welt on your cheek? Looks like you walked into a wall."

Bruno mutters, "Something like."

"Anyone I know?" says the man.

"Only if yous knows a lot of walls."

"My dear Bruno, do what I ask and you won't have to see the walls that should worry you the most. Prison walls. If not . . ."

"Just don't go thinking you're better than me," says Bruno.

"But I am better," the man throws back. "Smarter, too. And I have powerful friends."

"Who's your boss? Tammany Democrat? Republicans?"

"You don't need to know."

"A swell mobsman, that's all yous are," Bruno says with a sneer. "Where do yous come from?"

"I was born here."

"Yeah. But all yous got is a pistol. And connections."

The man nods. "And a photo of you."

Bruno, feeling hatred, clenches his fists.

"I don't care if you like me or not," the man says. "Just keep doing what I've told you to do. And if you don't . . ." He spreads his jacket, revealing the pistol.

"Aw, never mind," says Bruno, wishing, not for the first time, he had that pistol and the photo in his own hands.

"Good," says the man. "Now, how did things go today?"

"Fine," Bruno says. Reaches down, sets a small sack on the table. Coins clink. "From four newsies."

"Four is a sad number, Bruno. You need to work harder," says the man. "Faster."

"Don't know why yous bother," says Bruno. "Shagging pennies from mugs."

"I don't care about pennies. The point is, newspapers in this city are powerful. They have a lot of influence. Don't they?"

"I don't know. I just like the Sunday funny pages."

"But to get their influence, they must sell the papers to people, correct?"

"Suppose."

"How do they sell them?"

"Newsies."

"Hundreds of them."

"So what?"

"Bruno, for once, *think*," says the man. "If someone could control those newsboys, keep them from buying and selling papers, that person would control that newspaper."

"What you're always saying."

"Because you don't seem to grasp it. That boss of mine, the man *I* work for, wants to control *The World* and what it says about him. It's as simple as that. So, Bruno, we start by controlling those boys. I've made sure the police won't interfere. So just harass those boys. Hound them. Make them fear you. Don't let them slip from your grasp."

"They never does," says Bruno, grinning.

"Except when you run into walls," says the man. "Never mind. Keep the pennies. I don't need them." He stands up. "It's late. I must go home."

Bruno squints at the man. "How come yous never tells me where yous live?"

"Because you and I live in different worlds," says the man. "We have no trouble meeting, do we? Fine. I'll see you tomorrow. Here. Make sure you're on time. Ten o'clock."

"Hey," says Bruno, "if yous don't like me, how come yous wants me to do your work?"

The man leans over Bruno and grasps his shoulder hard. "Because you're dumb. Just make sure not one newsie escapes you," he says. "Not one. Remember: You answer to this." He pats the pocket where he keeps his pistol.

Releasing Bruno's shoulder, the man snaps the welt mark on the young man's face.

Bruno, wincing with pain, turns away.

The man plucks up the still-burning cigar from the table and offers it to Bruno. "I'm done with it," he says. "You can have it."

Bruno, fighting tears, takes it.

Grinning, the man walks off. Once outside on the sidewalk, he hails the first hansom cab in the waiting row.

"Where to, mister?"

"Waldorf Hotel."

"Sure."

The man climbs into the cab. The driver shakes the reins. The horse moves forward at a brisk trot.

Bruno, on the curb, watches from a distance. *Someday,* he thinks, *I'm gonna fix that mug for good. I swears I will.*

Okay, now it's the next day—Tuesday. Six o'clock in the morning. In the flat on Birmingham Street it's mostly dark.

Mama, her breath misty in the cold air, is up first. She lights the kitchen lamp, starts the coal stove by shaking down old ashes. Using matches, twists of paper, and wood scraps, she gets the coal burning. Finding wood bits on the streets—that's one of Eric's and Ryker's jobs.

Since Willa and Maks are sleeping in the kitchen, they get up too.

Right off, Maks sneaks into the front room to see if Bruno is on the street. He's not, which makes Maks feel a whole lot better.

He comes back, grabs the pot of cold, gray ashes and the two water buckets from under the sink. As he does, he looks at Mama.

Her long hair, yellow and gray, hangs down her back.

Her eyes are dark, deep, and sad. Maks guesses she didn't sleep too much with so much worry.

Like him.

Lit candle in hand, he goes down the stairs, meeting and passing neighbors going to work, to the water pumps, or to the privies. In the day's early shadow, people seem just half there. A few mumbled greetings, not much more.

On the second floor one of the Palbeck kids is sleeping in the hallway. He's sucking his thumb.

Once outside, Maks dumps the ashes atop the high pile of street curb garbage, then goes back through his building to the yard. He has to wait on line. First it's to use a privy—twelve people before him. Then it's to get to the pump. As the chickens cluck round him, he blows out the candle and puts the stub in his pocket.

Shivering, Maks gazes at the patch of graying sky above and notices it's the same color as ashes. Least it don't look or feel like rain.

Standing there, knowing he's gonna visit Emma in The Tombs, makes him tense. He's hoping that when he gets there, they'll have decided arresting her was a mistake. Be a lark meeting Emma on the street coming home.

With a heavy pail in each hand, plus the empty ash pot, Maks trudges back upstairs, trying not to spill any water.

The Palbeck kid is still sleeping in the hall.

On the third floor Mrs. Tinglist is quiet.

On the fourth floor the Vershinski family is already making brooms, trying to get their mother from Poland.

Maks leaves the buckets in the kitchen, takes up the tin milk can, and rushes out round the corner, to the tiny, crowded grocery store that belongs to Mrs. Vograd. Maks can never figure out how so many things can fit in such a small space.

As Maks dips his pan into the milk barrel, Mrs. Vograd makes a mark in her ledger and calls, "A good morning to your mother! Be so good—thank you—as to tell the lovely lady that family accounts are due Friday. Cash only!"

Maks hurries home with the milk.

When he gets back to his stoop, Mr. Tyrone's fish store has opened. A barrel of herring is on the sidewalk. At the end of the block Mr. Eliscue is leading out one of his horses hauling his ice-block wagon. The white-bearded printer, Mr. Zunser, stooped and slow-moving, puts a hand-lettered OPEN sign on the door of his shop and waits for business.

As Maks walks through the door of his flat, he announces, "Mrs. Vograd says accounts are due Friday."

He don't know if Mama even hears him.

While he's been gone, Mama gave Willa a shirtwaist

dress. One of Emma's old ones, it's short for Willa. Makes her seem taller. But it's a lot cleaner than what she was wearing.

Mama gave Willa shoes, too. If there's one thing the family has—'cause of where Papa and Agnes work—it's shoes. Usually they have something wrong with 'em—cut or badly sewn—or they wouldn't get 'em. But they are shoes.

When Willa sees Maks, she says, "Do I look better?" She offers a small, shy smile. Maks hasn't seen one of them from her before.

He says, "Like Queen Louise."

"Who's that?"

Maks points to the picture on the wall. "The queen of Denmark."

Even Mama smiles.

Papa comes out of the back room. He's looking no better than Mama—maybe worse—his face pale, full of worry lines.

After a few moments Agnes follows, her blond hair looped in careful braids. She's coughing. The rims of her eyes are red.

Willa watches her intently.

Papa and Agnes are dressed for work—Papa in boots,

trousers, cotton shirt, canvas jacket—same as yesterday. He needs a shave, but he only does that on Sundays.

Agnes is also wearing what she wore the day before: a blue gingham shirtwaist, black boots that are too big for her.

Not much talking this morning.

Mama gives them breakfast: coffee in bowls and a roll each. Papa eats and drinks quickly. Agnes drinks too, but she puts her roll in a pocket for later.

Mama hands Papa his lunch pail. "Just bread," she says. "I'm sending the meat to Emma."

"That's good," says Papa. "Maks, understand? Come to the factory right after you see her."

"I know."

"And in case they don't know arresting her was a mistake," he adds, fussing with his mustache, "I'll ask about a lawyer. Make sure you tell Emma we're doing everything to help."

Maks is thinking they're not doing much, but he don't say it.

Papa bends over Mama and says something in Danish into her ear. Not something he often does. Mama hugs him back, eyes full of tears.

Agnes looks over at Maks. He knows what she's telling

him: that while he's with Emma, *she'll* be trying to find a lawyer.

Just as they're leaving, Monsieur Zulot comes from the front room. He's dressed for work in his suit, overcoat, and tie. The whole family thinks he times his coming to get a glimpse of Agnes.

As Papa and Agnes go out the door, he bows. Maks sees Agnes dart a forced smile at Zulot over her shoulder.

Mama gives Zulot his breakfast—also coffee and a roll. He bows to her, saying, as always, "*Merci*, Madam Geless. I wish you an excellent day." He goes off.

That's when Maks routs out his brothers and makes sure they're dressed right. Mama scrubs their faces with a cloth—regular baths are Saturday nights—and sends them to the privies. When they get back, she gives each of 'em milk with coffee and a roll. Offers the same to Willa and Maks.

"I'm supposed to take the boys to school," Maks tells Willa.

"I'll go with you, if you want," she says, not comfortable under Mama's gaze.

But all Mama says is, "Maks, when you see Emma, tell her what Papa said: We're doing everything to help. Give her lots of love. After seeing her, go right to Papa. Then come home so I know everything too."

She gives the young boys a kiss on their foreheads, tells them to be good, to mind their teachers, to learn a lot. They hug her.

To Mama, Willa says, "Thank you for letting me stay. And for the food, dress, and shoes."

Mama seems 'bout to speak, but all she says is, "You're most welcome."

"Maks," says his mother, "here's food for Emma. A sausage and roll wrapped in a piece of paper."

The three brothers head out the door with Willa, who has her stick in hand. Maks is wearing his jacket and cap. Just as he's leaving, Mama suddenly calls, "Maks!"

He looks to her.

She beckons for him to come back. Maks, not knowing what's the matter, does as she asks.

"Shut the door," Mama whispers. Hands pressed together, she says, "Should I go with you to the jail?"

Maks, not wanting to deal with his mother's upset, says, "Naw. Bet you anything they already let her out. You'll see. Be all a mistake."

Mama's face brightens. "Do you really think so?"

"Mama, she didn't steal nothing."

"No, no. Of course not. But—"

"I gotta go," says Maks.

"Maks!"

He stops.

Mama says, "I . . . I want you to bring that girl—Willa."

"Where?"

"Here. It's not right for a girl to live on the street alone. And winter's coming."

Surprised, Maks says, "You mean . . . live here?"

Mama nods.

Maks says, "Told me she likes living alone."

Mama shakes her head. "I won't feel right unless you ask."

"You want to tell her?"

"She's your friend."

"You sure?"

Mama nods.

"Okay."

Maks goes into the hall, where the others are waiting. Willa gives him one of her question looks, but Maks decides he's gotta get the boys to school 'fore telling her what Mama said. He does say, "Bruno's not there."

"Who's Bruno?" Jacob says.

"No one."

"How come you got your stick?" Eric asks Willa.

"I'm going to my home."

"You ever coming back?" Ryker says.

Willa, lips pressed tight, shakes her head.

Like most days, people—kids and adults—are swarming the streets, their eyes half shut with sleep. Mostly, they're going to jobs, though a few kids are heading to school.

As Maks, Willa, and the boys pass through the streets, stores, stalls, and pushcarts are opening for business. Calls are heard: "Hot corn! Here's your hot corn! . . . Mend your pots and pans! . . . Fresh fish!" The knife grinder sings: "Sharpen your scissors and knives. Make them sharp for your wives!"

Newsies are on every corner, crying the headlines: "Extra! Extra! 'Awful Railroad Wreck in Canada! Nineteen Persons Killed!' Read it in *The Times*."

Sandwich board men have begun to wander, though most can't even read what's written on their signs.

Bootblacks are lugging shoe boxes as they head up

or downtown, all the while yelling, "Shine! Shine! Bright boots gets the loot! Shine 'em up!"

Girl peddlers are out too, offering ribbons, bread, and handkerchiefs. "Look pretty! Eat nice!" they cry in high, piping voices.

Midst 'em all, beggars picking through the early garbage in search of food.

Maks herds his brothers—along with Willa—to school. When they arrive, crowds of kids are waiting by the fenced-in entrance for doors to open. Some parents are there, but mostly older girls—"little mothers" they call 'em, the girls taking care of younger sisters and brothers while mothers work.

Maks gathers his brothers, puts his arms round 'em, leans in. "Remember: No telling no one nothing 'bout Emma. *Nothing!*"

They promise they won't.

"She gonna be home when we get back?" asks Eric.

"Sure," says Maks, shoving them toward the school.

"Hey, Maks," says Ryker, "guess what happens Friday?"

"What?"

"Friday the thirteenth."

"Can't wait."

Eric turns back, grins, and calls, "Good-bye, Waddah!"

"Come on," Maks says to Willa.

They head for The Tombs.

For a while they don't talk. Then Maks says, "You ever go to school?"

Willa shakes her head.

"When I went," Maks says, "a hundred kids in my class. So noisy, half the time I couldn't hear what teacher's saying. Got so restless, she kept sending me out of the room. I'd just go play on the streets."

Willa says nothing.

They go on, not talking. Maks, not sure how he feels about it, is trying to decide when he should tell her what Mama told him. It's five minutes before he says, "Guess what Mama said when we left?"

Willa shakes her head.

"Said that when I come home, I should bring you. That you shouldn't be living alone."

Willa stops short. Looks at Maks with hard eyes, mouth clamped tight. To Maks's surprise, she seems angry.

"Honest," he says, trying to understand what she's thinking, why she's looking so mad. "What she said."

Willa starts walking again, fast, as if trying to get away.

Maks catches up to her. "What's the matter?"

Willa shakes her head.

After a couple of blocks Willa stops. Not looking at Maks, she says, "Did your mother really say that?"

"Honest," he says, wishing he knew what's bothering her.

"You mean," she says, "live with your family?"

"I guess."

Willa stares at Maks as if searching for something. Same time, she's smoothing down her dress. Then she shifts away, looking elsewhere. Maks don't know what's happening.

"Hey," he says, "don't worry. I told Mama you probably wouldn't."

She swings toward him. Tears are welling in her eyes. "Why did you say that?" she cries.

"Thought you told me you liked being alone."

Willa stands there, breathing fast. Without looking at Maks, she says, "I didn't tell you."

"Tell me what?"

Willa tries to find her breath, then says, "My mother died."

"Thought you said she was . . . gone."

"Can't be any more gone than dead, can you?" Willa says, her voice wobbly. She's still not looking at Maks. "And . . . and later on, my father . . ." She can't talk.

"Your father . . . what?"

"He died too, I think."

"Just think?"

"Sometimes," she says, "I think . . . I think he didn't die. That he just . . . went away."

"Why'd he do that?"

"I don't know," she says. "Maybe . . . because of something . . . I did."

"Like what?"

"I don't know," Willa says again, her voice a shambles. Tears run down her cheeks. She wipes them away furiously.

"Come on, Willa," says Maks, "this city, people always dying. Last year, in our building, seven people died. Kids, a mother, a father. Agnes's school told her it's bad water, bad milk, bad dirt, bad smoke. Ain't nothing you done bad."

He waits for her to say something, but she don't. Just stands there, smearing tears away. In her hands her stick is twitchy. As far as Maks is concerned, she may be standing right there, but she looks lost.

He's wishing he knew what to say but can only mumble, "Sorry."

When he realizes Willa ain't gonna say no more, he says, "Gotta get to the prison."

They start walking again, neither talking. As they

go, Maks keeps glancing at Willa, feeling sad for her, same time holding on to Emma's food while keeping a lookout, hoping, hoping they'll meet his sister coming home.

In his head he's thinking, *Papa's right. Times are hard.*

Now, this jail, what they call "The Tombs," it takes up a whole city block. Built of stones so huge and heavy, it's partly sunk into soft ground. Means you have to walk *down* a slope to get to the main entrance steps. Fact, people say going to The Tombs is like taking the first steps to Hell.

Lots of folks think they call it The Tombs 'cause it's a place for people getting buried. Sort of. But it actually got its moniker from looking like a temple in a country named Egypt.

Has these up-front gigantic windows, but you can't see through 'em. Too dark. So you never know what's going on in there. Creepy.

Okay. Now, when Maks and Willa get near the front doors, policemen are on guard, letting only a few people in.

These mugs are all swell stiffs, white-haired gents, dressed in black suits, shiny top hats, and gray gloves. Got turkey faces and big mustaches, muttonchop whiskers, trimmed beards. Some even have canes with silver handles. Looking at 'em, Maks thinks, *These guys wouldn't share spit.*

When these men arrive—brought by hansom cabs with fancy-dan horses, snooty drivers up and behind—the cops salute 'em.

Maks supposes some of these guys are judges. Or police chiefs. Maybe even the famous City Chief Detective Byrnes. Or they could be, he thinks, what people call "bosses," them political crooks who really run the city. People like Joe Gorker, whose picture is always plastered all over *The World.*

Maks wonders if any of 'em are lawyers. They look greased enough. He keeps spinning thoughts that detectives might cost less.

'Course, him and Willa ain't the only ones waiting for doors to open. Lots of women, men, and tons of kids. Maks wonders if he looks like these kids: pale and nervous and frightened.

Some of the people have paper bags or packages, with food and clothing for prisoners. Though he knows it ain't much, Maks is glad he's brought something for Emma.

He goes up to a kid. "Hey, pal, what time they open the doors?"

"Ten thirty."

"What time is it now?"

The boy points 'cross the way, to City Hall, which has a clock on its tower. It's almost nine thirty.

"Hey, you know if there are any lawyers here?"

"You off your trolley?"

"Maybe."

"Always vultures round here," says the boy, pointing to a man standing not far off.

Maks looks. What he's seeing is this short, squat, bald-headed guy, with more chins than three people could use, plus side-whiskers that look like weeds gone wild. He's wearing a dark, lumpy, patched coat that reaches the tops of his dirty boots.

Two large books—stuffed with papers—are tucked under each of his arms. Other papers stick out of bulging coat pockets. Little eyeglasses perch on his big, blue-veined nose. Around his neck something that, to Maks, looks like a dead snake. As Maks studies him, the guy suddenly turns and—as if he don't want anyone looking at him—glowers at Maks.

Maks turns away fast, thinking, *Whatever this mug is, he sure ain't rich.*

"We've got some time," he tells Willa. "Wanna talk to my friend Chimmie."

They head over to Chatham Street, the other side of City Hall. What's there is a row of large buildings, factories for writing and printing newspapers. People call it "Newspaper Row."

"See that building with a dome?" Maks brags to Willa. "Print *The World* there. Twenty-six stories. Biggest office building in the city. They say *The World* has a lot of power."

"What kind of power?"

Maks grins. "If my paper don't like you, you get it in your chops."

He leads the way behind *The World* building. There's an open space where the downtown newsies pick up their papers round two in the afternoon. *The World* don't mind if they hang round and wait.

Though it's hours 'fore the newsies can buy their bundles, a couple hundred boys—and a few girls—are milling round, not doing much. Some dressed pretty good, others raggedy, with no shoes. Some are playing toss-penny, dice, cards. Others sleeping on the ground.

"They always here?" asks Willa.

"Some lives in regular homes. Or, like you, don't have no parents. They stay here or on the streets. Some sleep in those newsboys' lodging houses. There are five of 'em. One for girls. Hey, I know a couple of mugs who use old sewer pipe for homes. Some even live in rope houses."

"What's that?"

"Rooms with ropes stretched 'cross. For two cents, you can hang your arms over the ropes, stand there, and sleep. Got a roof, don't it? In the mornings they just untie the ropes."

With Willa by his side, Maks stands by a group playing cards.

"Hey, Maks," a kid called Toby shouts. "Who's the lady?"

"Name's Willa."

"She your best girl?" says a kid Maks knows as Isaac. Heads turn, all grinning and smirking.

Maks says, "Don't laugh. She got me away from the Plug Uglies last night."

"Bruno's gang?" says a kid they call Blink, 'cause he's blind in one eye.

"Yeah."

"That true?"

"Said it, didn't I?"

The grinning fades. These guys know Bruno and the Plug Uglies. The gang has caught, beat up, and stolen money from many. Some, like Maks, got away. A lot not. For a moment the playing cards are put down as they look at Willa and Maks—but mostly at Willa.

"How'd she do that?" someone asks.

Maks grabs Willa's stick and holds it up. "This."

"What happened?" Toby says.

Maks tells the story. When he's done, they're all studying Willa. Maks can't tell if she likes it or not.

"Hey, Joan of Arc," Blink calls out, "anytime yous want to be my best girl, okay with me. Just bring that stick."

Some laugh, but nothing mean. Then the guys start swapping Bruno stories. No question: They hate the mug.

"Someday," a kid named Rufus says, "we gonna have to get Bruno. Bash him plenty."

The others agree, but they go back to playing cards.

"Anyone see Chimmie?" Maks asks. "Got to talk to him."

"Playing ball."

Maks looks. On the street some kids are playing some kind of game with a stick and a ball made of wrapped-up string.

Maks spots Chimmie. He's a big kid and fast runner who's always talking baseball. Roots for the Giants and his hero, Shorts Fuller, the Giants' shortstop.

"Hey, Chimmie!" Maks yells. "Got to talk to you! Right now!"

Chimmie comes over. "What's going?"

Maks says, "Hey, remember telling me 'bout some private detective you know?"

"Bartleby Donck? The mug who finds missing husbands?"

"That all he do?"

"Tracks crooks, gets stolen things back for people. Works with the cops too. Helps people find evidence, all that stuff that shows if a person did or didn't do no crookery."

"He expensive?"

Chimmie shrugs. "Lives near me."

"Where's that?"

"Delancey Street. Got an office next to our building. Number six twenty-four. Sign in the window. Yous need a detective?"

"Naw."

"I bet," says Chimmie. "Who's yer pretty gal?" he asks, nodding toward Willa.

"Friend of mine," says Maks. "Thanks. See you paper time."

When Willa and Maks get back to The Tombs, the doors are open.

Halfway up the steps, Willa stops.

"What's the matter?"

She says, "You need to see your sister without me."

"How come?"

"She's not going to be happy," Willa says. "And she doesn't know me. Don't worry. I won't disappear."

Maks, thinking Willa is probably right, says "Okay." Clutching Emma's food tightly, he goes on up to the entry. *Don't be there!* he's wishing for his sister. *Don't be there.*

So many people trying to get into The Tombs, Maks has to stand in line. The bags and bundles people have brought are unwrapped and inspected. Maks is standing behind a lady carrying a baby—they even check the baby.

When he finally gets through the big main doors, two policemen, one on either side, stop him. They're big coppers with large, turned-down mustaches, making them look fierce. Their dome helmets remind Maks of skyscrapers.

"State your business," one of them demands. He's holding a pack of papers.

Maks, heart thumping, says, "Please, sir, I want to find out if my sister is here."

"Name?"

"Emma."

"Emma *what*?"

When Maks don't answer right away, the policeman shouts, "You hear me, kid? Your sister's last name! Or don't she got no father?"

Maks winces. "Geless. Emma Geless."

As the cop flips through his papers, Maks holds his breath.

"Yeah. She's here. Arrested for larceny."

Maks's stomach churns. "What's . . . larceny?"

"She's a thief. How old?"

"Me?"

"Your sister!"

"Six—sixteen."

"In the women's prison. Not the kids'. Keep going."

Maks looks round to see if anyone has heard. If they did, they don't seem to care.

He follows the woman who's carrying her baby. A few steps along, the lady is told to go into a side room where women are being searched. Maks stays put, and another policeman—standing next to a barrel—pats him down, yanks the candle out of his pocket, studies it, frowns, flips it into the barrel. Maks grimaces: Candles cost two for a penny.

The cop opens Maks's newspaper-wrapped parcel, sniffs the food, makes an ugly face, gives it back, and hands Maks a ticket.

"What's this?"

"Admittance ticket. Gets you in. Gets you out. 'Less you want to stay here, kid, make sure you hold on to it. Keep going."

Clutching ticket and food tightly, Maks goes forward.

Most everything—floor, walls, ceiling—is made of stone. The echo-bouncing walls have gas jets stuck in them, the light dull yellow. The cold air smells of sewer.

"Keep moving!" a policeman shouts, and shoves Maks forward.

A few steps on he's stopped by another cop. "Ticket?" demands the cop.

Fumbling, Maks shows it.

"Who you seeing?"

"Emma Geless."

The policeman checks *his* list. "Women's prison," he says, pointing.

Along with other visitors, Maks walks down a long, narrow corridor lit by dreary light that seeps through high, dirty windows. No talk. The only sound is shuffling feet. It's clammy, colder than outside, giving Maks the shivers. His stomach hurts.

At the end of the corridor there's an open gate where men and women guards are standing around. Maks joins another line. When he reaches the gate, he's asked, "Where's your ticket, kid? Who you here for?"

"Emma Geless," says Maks, showing his crumpled slip.

A guard runs a stubby pointer finger down a list on the wall. "Emma Geless!" he shouts. "Top level! Cell four!" He spits into a spittoon.

Maks hates him.

Once through the gate, Maks is met by a fat woman guard in a long, dark skirt and jacket. She holds a billy club. "What's in your hand, kid?"

"Food."

She grins and gives him a poke. "This way."

Maks steps into a huge, high hall. One wall is dull red brick with large dirty windows set so high that no tall person could reach 'em. Or look out.

Two squat iron stoves sit on the stone-paved floor like fat, ugly toads oozing a bit of heat. In the middle of the hall, there's a long wooden bench and a set of washing basins.

Opposite the brick wall are four long rows of prisoner cells, one atop the other. Fifteen cells on each level. The highest row is eighty feet above the ground. On the side facing into the room, the cells have crisscrossing iron bars.

Maks thinks 'bout animal cages he once saw in a Ninth Avenue circus parade.

At the far end of the hall, steps lead up.

On the lower level, where Maks stands gawking, some cell doors are open, so prisoners are walking in and out. Plenty of people selling things: bread, apples, jars of water, cigars. Though it's the women's section, men are wandering up and down calling, "Anyone want out? . . . Get you out for bail money! . . . Lawyer! Who wants a lawyer?" Hester Street in jail.

In fact, the main floor is so crowded, Maks can't tell who are the prisoners, who aren't.

Maks is standing in place, not sure where to go, when another lady guard shouts, "Lower floor, lunatics and convicted. Second floor, murderers and arsonists. Third, burglars. Top, small-time thieves. Who you seeing, kid? Your mother? Grandma?"

"Sister."

"What she do?"

"Nothing."

"Then she wouldn't be here, would she?"

Maks feels as if the guards are hitting him again and again. He forces himself to say, "They say she stole something."

"What? Money? Drink? Food?"

"A watch."

"Forked a super, eh?" the grinning guard says. "Top row."

The guard leads Maks along the bottom cell row. Though each cell has a small, high window, they're all dark and murky. Eight or ten women prisoners in each cell. A few women dressed well. Most not. Some are sleeping on the floor. Others sit on skinny benches, heads bowed. Others pace. One lady, on her knees, is praying. Children in the cells too, not just babies. Everything smells and looks sour, sick, sad.

Following the guard, Maks climbs the steps to the top level. As they go up, he notices that the higher the cells, the smaller they are, and the more crowded. When they reach the top level, they walk along an iron balcony.

"How come no doors are open here?" Maks asks.

"Too many suicides."

Maks hears moaning and crying. Women press against

the bars, stretching out their hands. "Help me! . . . Would you run a message to home? . . . Have you come for me, boy? Hey, boy! Take me home!"

The guard stops in the front of a cell, bangs the bars with her billy club. "Emma Geless!" she shouts. "Emma Geless! Someone seeing Emma Geless!"

Maks peers into the dim room. At the far back someone lifts herself from the floor. Takes a few moments for him to realize it's Emma.

Emma's face is not only smeared with grime, her hair's a tangle, her eyes bloodshot, and the blue hotel uniform she's still wearing is dirty.

Emma is in such a rush to get to him, she stumbles over bodies. When she reaches the front of the cell, she shoves her hands through the bars and grabs him, pulling so hard, it hurts. Her questions tumble: "Maks, thank God you're here. Where's Mama? Is Papa here? What are they doing to help me? Are you gonna get me out?"

"We're trying to help," Maks says, squeezing her hands back. "How come they put you here? You gotta tell me what happened."

"At the hotel . . . a man said . . ." Emma struggles so hard to talk, she's gulping. "He said I stole a . . . gold watch."

"What man?"

"The hotel detective. But I didn't take no watch, Maks. I didn't. You know I wouldn't. I never would."

"Why'd they think you did?"

"First they told us girls that someone took a fancy watch from a guest's room. Then they searched our dormitory where we sleep." She pauses. "They found a watch chain under my pillow."

Maks's mouth opens, but he can't speak.

"But I don't know how it got there," Emma says quickly. "I swear to God, I don't." She's gasping and sobbing. "I didn't take it, Maks."

"I believe you."

"They took me to the manager's office, and that hotel detective tried to make me confess. Said he'd go easy on me if I gave the watch back. But I couldn't 'cause I didn't know nothing 'bout it."

Maks says, "You got any idea who put the chain there?

Someone mad at you? Something like that? Anything you can remember?"

Emma bites her lower lip. Rubs a reddish eye. Tries to smooth her hair. "I can't think of anything," she says. "When I got here, they took me to a judge. Some kind of court. All these awful people. That hotel detective was there, said he had proof I took the watch. A policeman swore he saw the proof, but I never seen him before. Not at the hotel."

"What kind of proof?"

"The chain under my pillow. Then the judge sent me here. Said I'd have to go to trial. Then be sent to that Blackwell's prison. On the island in the middle of the East River. For a year! Maybe more. I don't know where that watch is. You gotta help me, Maks. I just want to come home."

He keeps telling her he's trying. That the whole family knows she didn't do nothing wrong, that they're gonna make sure she gets free. "Agnes is finding a lawyer. Look, Mama sent you some food."

Emma rips the package open and gulps it all down right then.

"Ain't they feeding you nothing?"

"You have to buy food."

"Got any money?"

"A little from my last pay." She lowers her voice. "People try to steal it. Tell Mama I really need to see her."

"I'll bring her. I promise. And you won't be here long," Maks says without knowing it to be true.

Emma grips his hands again, pressing and kissing them. She wants to hear family news, everything, even 'bout Monsieur Zulot.

Maks tells her what he can: Ryker being given an American name, Ronald. She smiles at that. Tells her 'bout Willa. "Her parents died. She was living in some alley. She helped me, and Mama told me she should move in with us."

"Bless Mama!"

"But I don't know if Willa's gonna do it."

It's hard for Maks to leave, but he promises he'll come back soon. Emma can't let go of him. She keeps holding on to him, saying she loves him.

The guard leads him out. "Can't my sister get a better cell?" he asks.

"Kid, The Tombs got six decent cells. You want 'em, you grease palms. You're old enough to know that. What's in charge is money."

Maks goes back through the building. It's busier than when he first came, full of people looking either important or miserable. He wants to go up to one of the important ones and tell 'em Emma is innocent. But he knows no one's gonna listen to a kid.

At the entrance a policeman asks for his ticket. For a moment Maks forgets where he put it. Thinking it's lost, he panics, only to find it inside a pocket. When he finally gives it over, it's all creased and wrinkled.

When he's told he can go, he all but runs.

Except, when he gets outside The Tombs, Willa ain't there.

Okay. What happened to Willa?

She's on the steps of The Tombs when Maks heads up them toward the entryway. When she sees him go in, she stares at the big building, trying to make up her mind what to do. Then she turns round and starts walking.

She goes quickly, only to stop and then go on again, slower. Tense and uncomfortable, she speeds up. See, during the past few months, working by the East River on garbage barges, or under the docks picking out usable rags, people avoided her. She was alone most of the time. Became used to it. Didn't care what she looked like.

Now she's uneasy that Plug Uglies might be watching her, that she's in danger. She don't like having to walk crowded streets on guard, holding her stick so if that gang sees her, they'll know she'll hit back. That time in the alley with Maks wasn't the first time she'd used her stick, but it was the worst. That fight frightened her, made her feel unsafe—not that she was going to tell Maks.

And she knows she's dirty.

Willa reaches Birmingham Street, and when she gets to Maks's tenement, she stands on the stoop, scanning the street. No Plug Uglies. But two little girls on the street run up, and one of them calls, "Hey, lady, you live here now?"

"I . . . don't know."

"What's your name?"

"Willa."

"Mine's Miriam."

"Mine's Selena."

Giggling, they run off.

Willa goes slowly up the murky stairs, not sure what she's going to do. She pauses on the third floor, considers going down. But keeps going up. Then, just as she's 'bout to open the flat door, she halts. Realizing she'll be alone with Maks's mother.

And more . . .

Senses that by going in, she'll be staying with this family. That this will be her home. That these people will become her family. That she'll return here always.

Those thoughts bring memories.

Willa remembers her mother as warm and close, someone who liked to smile. She had a quiet voice with a German accent, which Willa noticed only when they went marketing and her mother talked to people.

Those times with her mother were calm and steady. Though her father wasn't around much, it didn't seem to matter. Then her mother got ill—coughing more and more, talking less and less. Ate less. Became very thin. Weak. As she grew sicker, her eyes seemed to get larger, darker. She hardly smiled. Spat blood. A lot. The day came when she took to bed and stayed there.

Willa took care of her, was her constant companion. She cooked for her. Cleaned the rooms where they lived. The only time Willa went out was to the market. She had no friends.

Their rooms were like those where Maks lived. But Willa's building wasn't as old, the kind of tenement called a "dumbbell," with an open central shaft that allows for light and air. Electricity and running water. Each floor, its own toilet. The house smelled cleaner too.

Willa's mother often asked her to sit by her side. Not that they talked much. Each day Willa combed her mother's hair. She thought it very beautiful.

For long hours Willa just held her mother's hand. As her mother's hands grew thinner, her wedding ring kept slipping off. One day she gave the ring to Willa and told her she must take good care of it. "Use it for your own family," she said with a sad smile.

There were moments when Willa thought she'd caused her mother's illness. No reason to think so, 'cept that being well, she felt guilty. Fact, sometimes she wished she'd get sick, so she could be the same as her mother.

Most days and nights her father was gone. As Willa understood it, he was working, but she didn't know what he did. She asked her mother, but her mother never said, not exactly. Something 'bout collecting money for an important person. Willa sensed that what her father did wasn't a good thing. That it worried her mother, made her ashamed. But Willa felt it'd be better not to ask.

When her father and mother spoke to each other, it was mostly in German, so Willa didn't understand what they were saying. But they usually sounded angry.

Sometimes, after her parents talked, her mother cried. When Willa asked her why, her mother only said, "Promise me that you'll never lie."

Willa promised.

Those times when her father came home, he would give Willa some money to buy food and pay the rent to Mrs. Barsis, the landlady who lived on the first floor.

He didn't give much attention to Willa. Mostly, he read a newspaper. Willa tried to please him by being quiet, not asking for anything.

Her mother grew weaker. Sicker.

The day Willa's mother died, Willa's father wasn't home. Terrified, not knowing what to do, Willa waited for him to return. When, after many hours, he still didn't come, she went to Mrs. Barsis and told her what had happened. Mrs. Barsis came right to the rooms. She covered the body with a sheet and told Willa to go find a policeman, tell him what had happened. Then the woman fled to her own rooms.

Frantic, sobbing, Willa ran through the streets looking for a policeman. It took an hour.

When the body was taken away, a city medical officer told Willa her mother died of wasting disease.

"Are you alone?" he asked Willa.

"My father will come," she said.

That night Willa stayed in the apartment alone, struggling to keep from crying. Next day, when her father did return, she told him what happened.

"Where did they take her?" he said.

"I don't know."

"Didn't you ask?"

Willa shook her head.

He said, "What kind of a daughter are you?"

Willa wept.

That evening her father sat in his chair. He was very cross. When Willa tried to talk to him, he said she needed to leave him alone. When she made supper for him, he wouldn't eat.

In the days that followed, Willa stayed home, tried to keep up the rooms for her father and herself. Never knowing when he might return home, she remained inside, 'fraid if she went out, she'd miss him. When he did come, he barely talked.

Two weeks later Willa waited three days for him to return. She sat in their rooms or on the front stoop by the sidewalk. He didn't show up.

On the fourth day she wandered though the city looking for him. She searched for a week, spending days on the streets, nights at home, looking and waiting. For food, she ate what was left in the pantry.

He did not return.

On the eighth day of her searching, she came home to find people living in their rooms. She didn't know who they were. They spoke a language she didn't understand. She got Mrs. Barsis to go with her into the apartment, where she took a doll and a tin box.

"Where are you going to live?" Mrs. Barsis asked.

"I have to find my father."

"He's not a good man," said the woman.

"Why do you say that?"

When the woman wouldn't answer, Willa didn't want to have anything more to do with her.

From then on, Willa lived on the streets.

Always clinging to her doll and box, she went and sat on the front stoop of the house where she used to live, hoping her father would return. Or maybe he'd leave word where he went.

He never did.

After a while Willa stopped going back to the house, but she stayed on the streets. One day a street peddler noticed her sitting on a curb, begging. He told her she might find work in the garbage dumps by the East River.

She worked there picking rags—sometimes finding food—earning ten cents a week. And—as another girl working there told her—if she stood on line after midnight at St. Peter's

Church near Fulton Street, she might get a loaf of old bread.

When Willa could, she searched for a safe place to sleep. It took weeks to find the walled-in place in the alley. She'd been living there for five months when Maks found her, too tired to climb back into her hole.

Now, as Willa stands outside the door of Maks's family's flat, she tells herself again that this is her new home. That it's a good thing. That she likes Maks. That he's a good friend. That his family is kind.

This is my new home, she tells herself, pushing down the sadness she keeps feeling. *It's good.*

Willa opens the door and steps inside.

Mama is sitting at the table. Startled, she looks up.

"Willa! Is something the matter?"

"Can . . . can I have a bath?"

Back to Maks.

When he comes out of The Tombs, all he can do is sit

on the steps. He's exhausted, upset, scared, his chest hurting as though he were breathing fire.

He keeps thinking how awful it is for Emma to be locked up like some animal. To be told she stole something when she didn't do nothing.

Find the watch, he's thinking. *Sure, might as well find a way to keep Agnes from coughing. Or keep the shoe factory open. Or find a million bucks on the street.*

He reminds himself he needs to buy the day's papers, start selling. They're gonna need every penny. Maks even thinks 'bout getting a job selling a morning paper—maybe *The Times.* He'd have to get up by four in the morning. Peddle *The World* in the afternoon. He could do it.

Though Maks knows he needs to get to Papa and then Mama to tell 'em what Emma said, he keeps sitting there.

He's worried what's gonna happen when he tells his parents how bad it is for Emma. He knows how scared they are. Even if they get a lawyer, how are they gonna pay him? What's a lawyer supposed to do, anyway? Talk 'bout sending Emma back to Denmark is terrible. And now she needs money for food. And they need a doc for Agnes. Nobody's saying it, but the money Emma made at the hotel was big. It's gone.

What are his parents gonna *do*?

———

And Willa. Where'd she go? Maks wonders if he'll ever see her again. The thought comes to him that maybe the Plug Uglies got her. *Naw, she knows how to fight back. Glad somebody does.*

But Willa never said she'd move in with the family. He thinks 'bout how mad she was when he told her what Mama said. Don't understand why.

He remembers Willa's alley. It's the only place he knows where she might have gone. Could look for her there. But he don't have the time. Has to get to Papa.

Forcing himself up, Maks walks the twenty blocks to Stanton Street, to the shoe factory where Papa and Agnes work. Dreading talking to Papa, he goes slowly, stopping to watch men dig in the streets, as they always seem to be doing.

As he looks on, he thinks 'bout that joke how in America it's easy to find gold in the streets. With all the digging they do round town, Maks sometimes thinks they're looking for it *under* the streets.

Well, good luck!

The factory where Papa works is a three-floor wooden building. On the first floor they make chairs and tables. The second floor, suits and coats. It's on the top floor that they make the shoes.

Maks goes up the wide steps, which are on the outside of the building. As he climbs, he hears hammers and saws on the first floor; steam and clacking scissors on the second.

The third floor is big, open, crowded, murky. Just a few skylights, mostly coated with soot and ash. Most light comes from dangling, flickering electric lamps. People work half in light, half in shadow, over large tables. It all stinks of leather, dye, horse glue, and people. Tobacco smoke floats through the air like layers of cake.

There's constant noise: the steady slicing of knives and scissors, the ripping of leather, the *tat-tat-tat* of shoe nail hammers. The *wizzy-wizzy* of stitching machines. Always gives Maks a headache.

The foremen—there are a few of 'em walking 'bout the floor—bark at workers, praising 'em or pointing out mistakes, urging everyone to work faster, reminding 'em that they make their money by the number of shoes they turn out each day.

In one corner there's a big, whining electric motor that runs the leather drive belts—belts that go up to the ceiling and then down, running the cutting and stitching machines on the floor. The wide belts and machines scare Maks. People have lost fingers. Someone lost a hand. Agnes once told him the factory joke: "What do you get if you lose a hand? A free, one-way carriage ride to the hospital."

Well, good luck, again!

It's always hot—even in winter—with maybe fifty guys working in sweaty undershirts, hairy chests open. Every time Maks visits, he's reminded of the goblin shoe-makers from the bedtime stories Mama used to tell.

What Papa does is cut thin leather for ladies' shoes. Works twelve hours a day with large scissors—thank goodness—not a machine. The pay? Dollar twenty cents each day, depending on how many leather pieces he cuts.

Naturally, if you get sick, you don't get paid.

As for Agnes, she puts laces into finished shoes. Her wage: twenty-five cents the day.

Papa once told Maks he got his job because his hands were big, but Agnes got her job because her fingers were small. "Best thing 'bout America," Papa once said, "she uses all kinds."

It takes Maks a while to spot Papa. He's at the far end of the floor bending over a large table cutting red leather from a pattern. Every time he cuts a piece, he sets it in a pile, then marks a little book. That way the foreman can't cheat on his wages, which Maks knows they sometimes do.

Papa is so hunched over his work that even when Maks is standing right next to him, he don't notice.

"Papa?" Maks shouts. "Papa!"

With a start, Papa looks round. Seeing Maks, he drops his scissors and leans toward him, big hands gripping Maks's shoulders, sweaty face close. "Did you see her?"

Maks nods.

"Is it . . . bad?"

"Yeah."

Papa groans.

Agnes appears from somewhere, listening, staring at Maks with her big eyes. She says, "What did she say?"

Quick as he can, Maks repeats his conversation with Emma. As he speaks, he keeps looking away from Papa 'cause his father's eyes are full of misery. It upsets Maks. Mostly, he talks to Agnes.

Agnes gazes at him, hardly blinking, listening intently, now and again clearing her throat or stifling a cough.

"And," says Maks, "she's going on trial."

"On trial!" cries Papa, stepping back, like a boxer getting hit by a really hard punch.

"She can't get free," says Maks, "till we find the watch."

"What watch?"

"The one they say she stole. And, Papa, she needs money for food."

"Don't they feed her?"

"Geless!" a voice booms over Maks's head. "Why ain't you working?"

Maks looks up. It's the foreman, a man he knows as Mr. Purnham. Tall, with curly black hair, Mr. Purnham always wears a straw hat cocked at an angle. "You're losing money, Gelesses. The both of you! Who's the kid?"

"He's my son," says Papa, fingering his mustache.

"You find a lawyer?" Maks whispers.

Papa says, "Agnes is trying. Expensive, probably."

With a worried look at Purnham, Papa steps away from Maks, picks up his scissors, and bends over his table, starting his clipping again.

Agnes heads back to her work, calling, "Maks! Go tell Mama!"

"Go to school, kid!" Purnham yells. "Learn to make money. Take care of your pa in his old age! Ha-ha!"

Papa darts a look at Maks. "Go tell your mother. We'll talk later."

In the dim light Maks sees Papa's eyes are brimming with tears. The sight fills Maks with pain.

"Bye," he mumbles, and walks away till he reaches the outside steps. He stops, looks back. Papa is making a mark in his book. Agnes is somewhere else. The thing is, the factory don't seem no different than when he got there: loud, with everyone slaving. All Maks can see is that all these bad things are happening, but people just keep working. Makes him angry. But the next moment—like a punctured balloon—he's telling himself, *What else people gonna do?*

When Maks gets out of the factory, it's lunch hour, so the streets are packed. People are alone, in twos, threes.

Some talking, some laughing. Staring straight ahead. Going, always going. He wonders where. Wonders if it even matters.

Maks, standing at the bottom of the factory steps, only sees crowds of people who don't care. He's full of heartache, but no one is seeing it. No one even looks at him.

For a moment he thinks of going to Willa's alley. No time.

Feeling bad, he starts for home, going slowly. His head is filled with images of Emma, Mama, Agnes, Willa, Bruno. Papa's word—"expensive"—keeps beating inside his head like a dull drum.

He's struggling with his thoughts, staring at his feet, not paying attention to where he's going, when someone suddenly slams him. The jolt sends him spinning so hard, he falls to the sidewalk. When he whips round to see who hit him, the guy who did it looks back and grins.

One of Bruno's gang.

Maks jumps up and searches the crowds to see if other Plug Uglies are close. He don't see none. All the same, it's scary thinking those mugs are watching and waiting to get him. Standing up just seems a way of being knocked down.

Rattled, Maks tries to tell himself that being hit by that guy was just bad luck. Trouble is, he can't be sure.

But the shock of being hit makes one thing clear: There ain't time to wait for Papa. Or Mama. If Emma's gonna get out of jail, he's the one who got to do something—fast.

Maks hurries home, watching all which ways so he don't get into no more trouble. By the time he hits Birmingham Street, he's running, half expecting to see Bruno, or one of his pals, waiting for him on his front stoop. By then he's ready to fight them all. Almost wants to.

Still, he's glad no one *is* waiting, least no one from the gang. Only a bunch of neighborhood kids and their sister-minders, all of whom he knows by name.

"Hey, Maks. Whatcha doin'? Wanna play?"

Looking at them, Maks has this sudden longing to be like them again—young, not knowing enough to worry. Same time, he feels sorry for 'em 'cause they don't know nothing 'bout anything, not like he does. *But they're gonna learn*, he thinks. *Oh, boy, they gonna learn how bad things are.*

"Gotta hurry!" he calls, just wanting to be home. Gasping for breath, he races up the steps—all five flights—flying into the flat.

Mama ain't there, but sitting at the table is Willa.

31

"Whatcha doing here?" Maks cries, not sure if he's glad or mad.

"I wanted to get clean," says an embarrassed Willa. "Your mama gave me a bath."

"She did?"

"Can't . . . you tell?"

Maks looks. Willa is a lot cleaner. Even her hair been washed.

Willa shrugs. "Didn't have one for a long time."

"Could have told me you were coming," Maks says. "I was worried."

Willa, wanting to change the subject, says, "Did you see your sister? She all right?"

"I saw her. And she ain't okay. It's an awful place. Where's Mama?"

"Went to the privies. Can you get Emma out?"

Maks slumps against the door frame. Gestures to

the picture on the wall. "Yeah. Me, Lincoln, and Queen Louise."

"Maks . . . did . . . did she steal anything?"

"I told you, no."

"What are you going to do?"

"Not sure." He glances at the clock. "I gotta get my papers."

He takes up his cigar box, dumps the coins on the table, and shovels them into his pocket. "Just now, when I was coming home," he says as he works, "one of them Plug Uglies knocked me on the street. Can't tell if they was waiting and watching or just happened to see me."

Willa glances away. Maks follows her look. Her stick is leaning against the wall.

"Maks . . ."

"What?"

"Sorry I didn't wait for you."

"Yeah. Okay."

Mama appears at the doorway. Soon as she sees Maks, she says, "Did you see Emma?"

"Yeah."

"Tell me."

Maks repeats what he told Papa and Agnes. When he's done, Mama sits down on one of the kitchen chairs. Stares

at her hands. No one speaks. She looks up. "Emma . . .
Emma didn't steal that watch . . . did she?"

Maks shakes his head.

"Is it awful there?"

"Yeah.

"She miserable?"

"Yeah."

"What's going to happen to her?"

"A trial."

"Dear God! When?"

"Soon. Not sure."

"What did Papa say?"

"Not much."

The grief on Mama's face is too much for Maks. He
wants to leave. Says, "Agnes is trying to find a lawyer.
Costs a lot, probably. And we need to bring Emma money,
for food. They don't feed her. And she really wants to see
you. Anyway, I gotta do my papers."

Mama nods.

Maks turns to Willa, says, "You coming?"

Willa gets up and grabs her stick.

"Be back," Maks calls to his mother.

Mama is still staring at her hands. "Maks!"

"What?"

Mama gives him a pleading look. "I'm sure Papa's trying as best he can."

"I know," Maks says, not believing. He shuts the apartment door behind them.

Soon as he does, Willa says, "I'm sorry about your sister."

All Maks can say is, "Come on. Can't be late."

They start down the steps, Maks first. Halfway down, he stops, lets out a big breath as if he's been holding it a long time. Turns to Willa and says, "You gonna stay?"

She gives a quick nod, then says, "Your mama is very kind. Do you know what she said about you?"

"No."

Willa says, "That you're the hope of the family."

All of a sudden, Maks feels like crying. "Wanna know why she says that?"

"Why?" Willa asks.

"'Cause she and Papa don't know how to help Emma."

Willa waits a second and then says, "Do you?"

"Have to."

"How?"

Maks shrugs. "Got an idea, but I need to sell my papers first. Come on."

By the time Willa and Maks get behind *The World* building, newsies are waiting for the papers to be dished, lined up in twelve restless, ragged, chattering, and fooling rows.

What you need to understand here is, the faster you get your newspaper bundle and reach your corner and start selling, the better the sales. Being quick makes a big difference 'cause there's tons of competition. City has something like *thirty* newspapers—and that's not even counting all them papers not in English. Still, *The World* has the bloodiest headlines, so it sells best.

Anyway, Maks and Willa get on what looks like the shortest line, behind a kid named Rory. Few minutes later a bell clangs. The back doors of the newspaper building swing open. Burly men start lugging out tied-up copies of *The World*, forty copies a bundle. Soon as they dump them on long tables, the lines of newsies surge forward.

BRUNO

"What's the headline?" Maks asks Rory as they edge closer.

"'Bodies Burned to Ashes.'"

"That'll work," says Maks.

Rory looks at him. "Somebody told me the Plug Uglies tried to get you."

"Got away okay."

Rory eyes Willa—and her stick. He says, "Last night some guys didn't. Lost their papers and their money. Got beat up, bad."

Maks says, "I hate Bruno."

"Rumor going round that he's doing all this stuff so the paper will stop headlining that Gorker guy."

"That true?"

Rory shrugs.

With the newsies in such a hurry, the line moves fast. When Maks and Willa reach the front, the newspapers are still piled high.

The way this works, a man is standing behind the spot Maks has come to. Next to the papers is a copper bowl hanging from a weight scale. Maks dumps his pennies into the empty bowl. The man bends over to look at the weight, rakes his fingers through the coins.

Maks says to Willa, "If he finds a slug, they kick you off the lines."

With Maks checking out okay, the man pours his pennies from the scale bowl into a big wooden bucket. "Take 'em!" he says.

Maks grabs a bundle, hefts it under his arm, turns to Willa, and says, "Let's go."

Going fast as they can—sometimes running—Maks leads the way to his spot, Hester Street and the Bowery.

Now, the rule among newsies is, you don't hustle your sheets till you reach your own corner. See, you're not supposed to go 'gainst your own guys, either, which in Maks's case are *World* newsies. Course, you don't care if it's some kid peddling another sheet, like *The Post*.

As Maks and Willa run, they don't talk much. Maks is too busy scanning the front pages, figuring his shout. Same time, both of 'em are watching for the Plug Uglies. They don't see none.

When they get to Maks's corner, Willa sits down on some steps just outside a small pickle shop, stick 'cross her knees. Maks goes to his selling spot, holds up a paper, and starts his cry: "Hey, read all 'bout it! Latest news! 'Bodies Burned to Ashes!' Terrible horror! Up in Canada. Blood! Bones! Awful news! Right here in *The World*. Just two cents! The world's greatest newspaper."

Whenever Maks sees someone looking his way, he runs

and shoves a paper at him. "Here, sir. Here, ma'am! All the hot news!"

Being near the El station, lots of people come by, 'specially during evening rush hour. Sometimes Maks makes his sale, sometimes not. Hard work making a sell, but it's great having Willa there 'cause Maks don't have to lug his whole bundle every which way.

He does have to be louder than the elevated train that's rumbling overhead. And the yelling teamsters. And the street sellers' cries. And the fire wagon, which goes racing by, bells clanging, horses charging, pumper pouring smoke, firemen in helmets and rubber jackets running alongside. If Maks wasn't selling papers, he would chase 'em. The city is full of fires, and he loves to watch.

After two hours Maks has only four newspapers left. That's fast. Hands Willa three of the papers and says, "Put these behind your back."

"Why?"

"You'll see."

When she does, he goes back to his corner.

"'Bodies Burned to Ashes!'" Maks yells. "Hey, lady. This is my last paper. Buy it and I can go home and take care of my sick mother! Honest. Come on, give a helpin' hand. Awful horror up in Canada! My very last paper! Only two cents. . . . Sir, I really need to get home 'cause of my sick ma. Yes, sir. My sick mama will bless you!"

Soon as he sells that paper, he runs back to Willa, grabs another. Does the same thing again with the same "sick mother" shout. In twenty minutes he hustles his last sheet.

"See," he says, "I just can't do it too much."

"Does it always work?"

"If it don't, I can go into a drum and sell to drunks. But they give you too little or too much. You get arguments either way. Anyway," he says, patting his pocket, "made my eight. You ready to go?"

"Where?"

"Gonna see that detective Chimmie told me 'bout."

"You serious?"

"Got a better idea?"

"Won't he be expensive?"

"Guess we'll find out, won't we?"

They run all the way to Delancey Street. By the time they get there, it's pretty dark. Even so, crowds are thick, the street swarming with carts, trolleys, wagons, the usual people selling and buying. Kids all over the place, dodging whatever moves, playing as if they might never play tomorrow.

As for house number 624, when Maks sees it's a tenement, he's disappointed. Then he reminds himself—he don't need rich.

On the building's lower level someone has put a hand-lettered sign inside the right side window. Knowing Willa can't read, Maks says it aloud:

LOST HUSBANDS FOUND!

Bartleby Donck, Lawyer—Private Detective

Helpful if Paid

145

"Are we looking for husbands?" asks Willa.

"All we need is the 'helpful' part. Come on." They go in. The building's entryway is like Maks's house: dim, narrow, smelly, little kids playing jacks on the steps. On the right side, a warped door, with a sign tacked to it: DETECTIVE—KNOCK LOUDLY!!!

Maks knocks but gets no answer. Knocks again, louder. No one comes. Presses his ear to the door. "Someone's there," he says.

Willa says, "Try the door."

Maks looks, but there's no doorknob—just a hole—so he puts his shoulder to the door and shoves. With a *pop*, the door opens.

They're looking into a murky kitchen laid out like Maks's house. Some light leaks in from the up-front room.

What they see is all junk and jumble with roaches scrambling away from a half-eaten loaf of bread on the floor. There's a small table but no chairs. On the table, moldy dishes, dirty glasses, a blackened pot. Tipped-over bottles and papers. No stove. Open books on the floor near a full spittoon. The place reeks of mold.

Wheezing noises come from the front room.

"Snoring," Maks whispers.

Trying not to step on anything, which ain't easy, they go up to the front room doorway. Look in.

The room's like most tenements, with two windows in front. Against one sidewall is a large rolltop desk, with square compartments—what people call "pigeonholes." The holes are stuffed with enough papers to look like wasted weeds.

'Gainst the opposite wall is a bookcase crammed with dried-out leather-bound books turned every which way, some of 'em tumbled to the floor.

In front of the desk there's a high-backed chair, with leaky stuffing. And in the chair, slumped over the desk and papers, there's a man.

The guy's bald head—like a moon that's fallen from the sky—is half buried in his arms. At his elbow an oil lamp is burning a small blue flame, a curl of black smoke spiraling up into the gloom. On the desk there's something that looks like a thick rope lying near a pot of ink, from which a pen is sticking out. Looks as if the guy was writing, 'cause in front of him sheets of paper are covered with scraggly script and inky blots.

Maks and Willa wait. The man snorts and snores.

"Mr. Donck!" Maks calls.

The man rumbles, making his whole body shake. All the same, he stays drooped over his desk, over his papers.

"Mr. Donck!" Maks shouts louder.

With a jerk, the man sits up and swivels round. He peers at Willa and Maks with bloodshot eyes through small, wire-framed eyeglasses perched like butterfly wings on the tip of his fat, vein-lined nose. Side-whiskers give him the look of a bristly chimney brush.

When the man breathes, there's a rattle deep in his throat. His chins go wobbly. Then he makes a couple of hacking coughs that cause his entire body to shudder.

Maks recognizes him. He's the guy that kid at The Tombs pointed out as a lawyer.

The man reaches out a dirty hand—fingers shaking— plucks up that thick rope. It's a rubber tube with wood bits at each end. One wood end is three inches wide, the other end narrower. The guy sticks the narrow end into one ear, holds the fat end toward Willa and Maks.

"What do *you* want?" he demands, his voice loud,

thick, and gravelly. "Talk to the tube. I'm mostly deaf."

"Please, sir," yells Maks. "Are you Mr. Donck, the detective?"

"What do you want?"

"Advice."

"About what?"

"My sister."

Donck glares at Maks. Clearing his throat, he bellows: "Have you any idea how many children come to my door, wanting me to find fathers, mothers, sisters, brothers, all of whom have abandoned them? Or who want my legal help when their relations are arrested, evicted, dead? Have you?"

"No, sir," says Maks.

"Hundreds! Thousands! I don't—can't—won't give advice to children." He yanks the tube from his ear, turns away, and lurches forward, his head sinking back into his arms.

"Sir," shouts Maks, "it's my sister! She's been arrested. She's in The Tombs."

Donck, not stirring, yells, "What did she do?"

"Nothing!"

The man jerks back up, coughs, snatches up a filthy, spotted handkerchief, wipes away bloody spittle that's bubbled to his lips. Adjusts his eyeglasses, turns and sticks the tube back into his ear.

"The hopefulness of children," he yells, "is equaled only by their naïveté! Do you have any idea what I just said?"

"No, sir."

"I said, children hope for the best and get the worst. Now get out!" He coughs and falls back into his arms.

But Maks steps forward and shouts, "She didn't steal nothing! And they say she'll go to prison."

"They spoke the truth!"

"Didn't!" says Maks angrily.

Donck groans, leans back in his chair, shoves his eyeglasses up to his smudged, bald forehead, rubs his red eyes with dirty thumbs. When he moves, lint leaps from his whiskers like from a dust mop.

"Our Constitution," proclaims Donck, wheezing between words, "proclaims that a person is innocent until proven guilty. But . . . in *this* city, innocence costs. Justice costs more. A bribe is what really works but costs the most." He puts the tube back in his ear. "Have you any money? Speak into my tube."

Maks leans forward. "No, sir."

"All statues of Justice show that sainted lady to be blindfolded. Do you know why?"

"Don't know what you're talking 'bout."

"So she can't see how our law actually works!" shouts Donck. "No money. No justice."

"Please, sir," Maks yells, "my sister needs help!"

"Everybody needs help!" Donck roars, only to cough so badly that he gags and has to struggle to clear his throat. "What the devil is your name?"

"Maks, sir."

"Maks what?"

"Maks Geless."

"You?" he says to Willa, shifting the tube toward her. "Willa."

"Willa, Maks," says Donck—and it sounds as if he's pleading—"I'm poor because I help people who can't help themselves. If I use my time helping your sister, I'll starve. Ergo, I *am* starving."

"Please, sir, I don't know what to do."

"Then you're no different from everybody else in this wretched city! My hands are not so much tied as they are empty. The poet said, 'Mercy has a human heart.' What he should have written is, '*Money* is the human heart.' Now get out! If I had any strength, I'd throw you out."

Donck yanks the tube from his ear and flings himself

back into his arms. The only sound in the room is his rattling breath.

After a moment Willa goes up to him, hesitates, and then pokes him with her stick.

Donck jerks up and shoves the tube back into his ear. Glares at Willa. "Did you just hit me?"

"You don't have to help us!" Willa shouts. "Just tell us what to do."

"What the devil does *that* mean?"

"We know all about detectives," says Willa.

"How could you?"

"Because," she says, "we read a story called *The Bradys and the Missing Diamonds*."

Donck's jaw drops. His face turns red, he coughs, struggles to speak, then manages, his mouth full of pink spittle, to shout, "Poppycock! Utter poppycock!"

"If you could just tell us how to start, we could do it," Willa says.

Breathing heavily, wiping his lips, Donck considers Willa balefully. "Why are you carrying that stick?"

"In case we're attacked."

"By whom?"

"A gang," says Maks. "The Plug Uglies."

"*Have* they attacked you?"

"Yes, sir."

"Why?"

"I'm a newsie, sir," says Maks. "They wanted my money. Willa saved me."

"Did she?" Donck stares at Willa again and takes a deep, clotted breath. "Lucky you," he mutters. Then, "Did you truly believe that . . . that story you read?"

"It was written by a detective," Maks says. "A *city* detective."

"It's nonsense!" cries Donck. "Garbage!"

His shouting exhausts him. Takes a few moments of heavy breathing before he says, "Why haven't your parents come?"

Maks says, "They . . . they don't know how."

"What does *that* mean?"

"They're new to America."

"Immigrants?"

Maks nods. "Don't understand the way things are done here."

"Do you?"

"I was born here," says Willa.

"And being birthed on this soil and having read that stupid story, you have—what? Wisdom?"

"Please, sir," says Maks, "I'm just trying to help my sister."

"The truth is," cries Donck, "nobody denies they are immigrants more often than the children of immigrants! And you immigrant children are all orphans *with* parents. Pha! It's a city of orphans!"

Donck flings his hearing tube down and, grabbing a rosewood cane, heaves himself up. Unsteady on his feet, he moves to the window. Using his ragged sleeve, he rubs the glass with shaky fingers, smearing grime away till he makes a lopsided circle. He peers into the dark street.

"I believe," he says—his back to Maks and Willa— "there are more wretched children on these streets than any other of the species. My Lord," he suddenly shouts, "the question before the heavenly court today is this: Do You wish *any* children to survive in this miserable city, this—this city of orphans?"

Maks and Willa stare at him.

Donck stays by the window, looking out, coughing, his body jolting.

"My sister coughs a lot too," says Maks.

Donck turns, lurches toward his desk, and snatches up his listening tube. "What did you say?"

"My sister coughs a lot."

"The sister in jail?"

"A different one."

"Consumption!" Donck yells. "Wasting disease! Tuberculosis! The cure, expensive, *if* it works. Each year," he shouts, "thousands in this filthy city die of it. Each month. Each week. Each day! Annually, this city has more than a million cases of illness. Smallpox! Diphtheria! Typhoid! Tuberculosis! I'm no exception. You are petitioning a doomed man!" He glares at Maks and Willa with bleary eyes, as if they were coming to bring him death.

Donck shuts his eyes, breathes deeply, raggedly. "If I were to teach you my skills," he says, "would you willingly become lawyer and detective for the thousands of children in this shameful city?"

"Yes, sir," says Willa.

"With your bludgeon," Donck sneers, "with which you so rudely struck me? So that when children come looking for relations who have abandoned or abused them, you could beat their oppressors?"

"What's an oppressor?" Maks asks.

"God protect the ignorant!" yells Donck. "Is your goal to starve along with me?"

"I don't eat much," says Willa.

"And I just want to help my sister," Maks pleads.

The kids wait.

"You!" Donck suddenly cries, pointing two fingers

right at Maks. "This morning. On the steps of The Tombs, you stared at me."

Taken by surprise, Maks can only nod.

"What," demands Dock, "was I carrying in my hands?"

"Your hands?"

"Are you, too, deaf?"

With Donck and Willa staring at him, Maks thinks furiously. "Nothing . . . in . . . your hands," he stammers, hoping he's right. "Two books tucked . . . under your arms. The books were stuffed with papers."

The only noise in the room is Donck's breathing.

"Good," Donck finally mutters. "Very good. You have eyes that see. Very well," he cries. "Why not? This is America. The New World. The noble experiment. Supposedly God's country. Pha! My Dutch ancestors began this city. It's time I was replaced. A new century comes soon to haul away my wretched carcass. When that moment arrives, you'll be of age. But I—I, Bartleby Donck—shall be dead. Dumped into a pauper's grave. The uncommon man sunk into the common city clay."

He drops into his chair.

"Sir," says Maks cautiously, "you saying you'll help us?"

"Do you wish to know why? Because you believed that pathetic story you read! I have an obligation to my profession to guide you from the pathetic influence of that junk. Besides, I admire loyal women," Donck says, looking at Willa. Looking at Maks, he says, "You seem able to use your eyes.

"Therefore!" cries Donck, pointing a dirty, fat finger at Maks, "you can be my farewell gift to this doomed city. A boy detective! Pha!"

Donck coughs a few more times. "All right," he says, aiming his listening tube at Maks. "Tell me what happened to your sister. All you know."

When Maks tells Donck what Emma told him, the detective listens, coughing now and then, wheezing, but saying nothing till Maks is done, which don't take long.

"Is that *all*?"

"What she told me."

"To summarize," says Donck, "your sister was accused of stealing a gold watch. This occurred at that new Waldorf Hotel, where she works. She denies she took it. But the watch was found beneath her pillow. Conclusive evidence, I should say. Not surprisingly, she's arrested, put in jail. Everything correct?"

"No, sir."

"Why?"

"Wasn't the watch they found. Just the chain."

For the first time Donck smiles. "Ah! Good. You can listen, too. Have you been to the Waldorf?"

"Walked my sister there."

"It's new. Cost four million Astor dollars to build. Not merely big, colossal. Thirteen stories with more than five hundred rooms. A thousand servants, of whom your sister was but one. She was—is—always will be replaceable. What else do you know about the Waldorf?"

"My sister told me rich people stay there."

"Rich? Pha! They claim only the *best* people patronize the establishment. The Waldorf is *the* most elegant hotel in New York. In America. The world, perhaps. Dear God, the rooms even have their own bathrooms. They wouldn't use people like you and me for doormats. What did your sister do there?"

"Cleaned rooms."

"How lucky for her. Her name?"

"Emma. Emma Geless."

"Emma Geless." After dipping his pen in his ink bottle, Donck writes the name on a scrap of paper. For a few moments he stares at it, coughing.

Maks says, "Can you help her, sir?"

Donck holds up a fat, flat, and dirty hand. "Advice only! You, the boy detective, will do the work. I've work to do. Return tomorrow. Same time. Now get out."

"Thank you, sir."

Willa and Maks step out to the street. Willa says, "I didn't understand half the things he said. Did you?"

Maks shakes his head. "Pretty strange. Sure ain't no money-spinner."

Willa says, "Think he'll really help?"

Maks shrugs. "Don't know what else to do. But it's hard shouting at him."

"He thought I was your sister."

"Don't mind."

"He's pretty sick," says Willa. "All that coughing and

spitting blood. My mother was like that. Before she died. I think it's what Agnes has."

"Agnes don't cough that much."

"She should go to a doctor."

Maks says, "My parents are saving for it. But . . . now . . ."

They stand for a while, gazing on the crowded street, until Maks says, "Come on. We better get home."

"Can we go to my alley first?"

"How come?"

"I need to get something."

"What?"

"You'll see."

Willa and Maks make their way through evening crowds of men and women, factory and office workers. Though people look tired, laughter can be heard as peddlers and pushcart dealers cry out last goods. When night falls, so do prices.

As they go along, Willa and Maks don't talk much. Willa is lost in her thoughts.

Maks is thinking 'bout Donck, how odd the mug was and wondering if he can teach him anything that'll free Emma. He's also worrying on the next day. He needs to bring Mama to Emma. Gotta tell his sister he's getting her help. Same time, he ain't so sure if he should tell his parents 'bout Donck. Not certain they'll like his going to a detective.

Don't take too long to reach Willa's alley. Some street-light seeps in, making it look like a hallway to nowhere. Save for the same old smelly garbage, it's deserted.

They step in, Maks holding Willa's stick while she climbs the fence. When she's gone, Maks can't help thinking of her living in the place. He's glad she's coming to Birmingham Street.

When Willa pops back up, he's surprised by what she brings: a small blue tin box, the kind in which candy comes. And an old doll.

The doll's head is chipped hard china, yellowish white, with only one glass eye and a floppy cloth body. Its dress is tattered.

"I got it when I was a little girl," Willa says. She's clutching the doll and box tightly, as if they're important. The box rattles.

"What's in there?" Maks asks.

"Show you later."

They start walking back down the alley, Maks still holding Willa's stick.

Next second, Bruno, derby cocked back on his head, lit cigar in hand, is standing at the entrance. He's blocking their way.

Willa and Maks are too scared to move.

As for Bruno, he don't do nothing but stand there, grinning, puffing his cigar. The cigar's ash glow makes his red hair shine, lights the tips of his ears. His squinty eye seems to glint with glee.

Maks thinks of the devil.

"Hey, Maks mug!" Bruno calls. "Still got that skinny girl protectin' yous?"

Maks moves Willa's stick so Bruno can see it.

"Just so yous understand," says Bruno, "I knows where yous live. Knows where yous sell your stupid papers. So me and my guys are watching. Pretty soon, we're gonna catch yous cold and plunk yous down dead. And when we do, we're gonna get your girlfriend, too. Soak the street with your blood. Both of yous."

Then he gives a fake horselaugh, steps out of the alley, and is gone.

Willa and Maks—she's clutching her doll and box, he's finding it hard to breathe, heart beating wildly—are afraid to move. They wait for something to happen, but nothing does, so it seems Bruno is really gone.

Maks gives a sigh. Says, "We ain't never gonna be rid of him."

Willa don't say nothing. Just stands there, looking down.

Maks takes a deep breath. "Come on," he says. "We need to get home. But you don't have to come with me if you don't want."

Willa spins on him, face full of fury. Starts to speak but can't. 'Stead, she turns and faces the wooden fence.

"Hey, what's the matter?" says Maks. "How come I'm always saying something wrong?"

Willa shakes her head.

"Is it Bruno? Come on. I was goosefleshy too."

Willa just looks at him.

"Hey, you gotta tell me what it is."

Not moving, Willa says, "Don't . . . don't you want me to go back to your house?"

"Hey, sure I do," says Maks. "We're pals, ain't we? Only saying you don't have to be part of this mess. It was me who put you in it. I mean, it's me Bruno's after."

"It's me, too!" she yells.

"Okay, sure."

"You want me to come or not?"

"Honest, my mother said you should."

Willa faces him. "What do *you* think? You never say."

"No? Really? Thought I did. Look, we're gonna do this together, ain't we? My sister . . . Bruno . . . all of it."

"But what . . . what if we can't?" Willa cries. "What if he does what he says? Or we can't help your sister? Or what if . . . if we can't do *anything*? I don't want to stay here anymore. I hate it! And . . . and I'm scared! I'm really scared." She stands there, sobbing.

Maks, full of his own misery, says, "Come on, Willa, don't know what else to do. We gotta try, right? Maybe that Donck guy will help. But if you and me don't do it together, it's gotta be worse. What I think. Honest. Come on."

Willa, her crying less, just looks at him.

Maks says, "We gonna be friends, right?"

Willa leans back against the fence. "Okay," she says, voice easier, stealing a look at Maks to be sure that he's still there. That she hasn't chased him away. Next moment, she jumps forward. "Did I get my dress dirty?" she says, showing him her back.

A few smudges, but Maks says, "Nothing really."

"Will your mama be mad? She likes everything clean."

"Willa, it's the city. Even the stinking air is dirty. Mama knows. Come on. Let's get home and eat. I'm starving." He takes a step toward the street.

Willa holds back. "You really sure you want me there?"

"How many times I have to say it?"

"There are so many people in your—"

"Hey, a few months ago, we had my uncle, aunt, and their five kids when they came over. All kinds of relatives come. People from our old town just show up."

"Where do they sleep?"

Maks shrugs. "Always find room. Come on."

Willa takes a deep breath. "I need to show you something first."

"What?"

"Not here."

"Fine," Maks says, glad she's coming, glad to get out of the alley.

The kids look up and down Chrystie Street. It's dark, but far as they can tell, Bruno ain't there.

Maks whispers, "Think we're okay."

"I need a place with light," says Willa. "Not the street."

They walk along, not talking, till Maks turns toward a small saloon. "This'll work."

The saloon—a sign names it THE BOTTOMS—sits at the base of a tenement. Like most city drums, it's a dingy room with a little stand-up bar and a few bottles. A gas jet in a blue glass globe hangs from the ceiling, its light somehow making the smoky gloom darker. On one wall there's a lopsided picture of the president, Grover Cleveland. On the wooden floor—sprinkled with dirty sawdust—sits a brass spittoon near a potted rubber plant with large, glossy, yellow-tinged leaves.

Only a few small tables with some people sitting and smoking. One guy drinking. Others just talking. A lady—her hat tipped down over her face—asleep in her chair.

The barkeep stands behind the bar. He's a big fat guy with a black beard and top hat. His name is Otis. Maks knows him 'cause he and his family live next to his tenement. Emma used to mind his kids.

"Hey there, Mr. Maks," Otis calls out in a deep voice when Maks and Willa walk in. "How you doing? How're the folks? How's Emma?"

"Fine," says Maks. "Okay if me and my friend sit and talk?"

"Make yourself at home. Who's the lady?"

"Willa. She's living with us now."

"Pleasure to meet you, Willa. Friend of Maks, friend of mine. Want something to drink?" He throws a wink.

Maks shakes his head, goes to a corner table, and sits. Willa takes the opposite chair, sets her blue box on the table. Checks to see if anyone is near. Satisfied no one is, she sets her china-face doll on her lap so the doll's eye is just above tabletop level.

Maks says, "Your doll is staring at me."

Willa, her voice small, gives a little smile. "She likes you."

"She got a name?" Maks says.

"Gretchen. My mother gave her to me."

"Pleased to meetcha, Gretchen."

Willa holds up her doll. Though the doll don't have no hands, just cloth stumps, Maks shakes one.

Putting the doll back on her lap, Willa draws the tin box closer to her, as if to hug it. Maks hears that slight rattle.

Willa, eyes fixed on box, strokes the tin top with her fingers. Slowly, she eases up the top on its hinge, swings it toward Maks so he can't see what's inside.

Reaching into the box, Willa picks up a photograph glued to a thick piece of cardboard. She holds the card carefully in two hands, stares at it. Then she sets it on the table in front of Maks, turning it round so he can see what it is.

It's a picture of a family.

There's a man standing behind a seated woman. On one side of the woman is a girl. Right off, Maks sees that it's Willa. She's leaning on the woman's knee, is dressed nice and clean, with long, smooth hair. She's in a white lacy dress. Hair in ribboned braids. The doll, Gretchen, is dangling from her hand.

As for the woman, she's wearing a long skirt with a high collar. She don't look particularly rich, but she ain't poor, either. Face is like Willa's—round, small mouth, nose somewhat sharp. Hair piled up with care.

But the woman ain't smiling. Even her eyes seem unhappy. She has one hand pushed forward so Maks can see the wedding ring on her finger, as if she's making sure everyone'll know she's married.

The man's wearing a dark suit, holding a derby in the crook of his arm. Hair combed back, parted in the middle. His face is long, smooth-shaven, eyes forward. One of his hands rests on the woman's shoulder. Got a smile, but it seems phony.

Willa's looking straight out, with a big, happy grin. A real one. As if she ain't noticing how the people behind are looking and feeling, which ain't so good.

Maks stares at the picture, then glances at Willa, not sure what to say.

"My family," Willa says softly, leaning forward to point them out. "My father. My mother. Me."

Maks says, "You all look nice."

Willa nods while gazing at the picture. It's a while before she looks up at Maks. "I just . . . I just didn't want you . . . to think I never had a family."

"I believed you. That's your mother, right? Who died?"

"They said it was that wasting disease. Like Mr. Donck. And Agnes."

Maks points. "Your father?"

Willa frowns but bobs her head.

Maks stares at the mug, fixing his face in his head, trying to get some idea what he was, guess what happened to him.

Willa don't speak. Or look at Maks. Just takes deep breaths, hunched over as if trying to hide. Maks feels waves of sadness coming from her.

Not knowing what more to say, he waits.

Willa looks up. "Is it really all right for me to come and live with your family?"

"Sure. Gretchen, too."

The fluttering gaslight seems to make Willa's face tremble. "She'd like that," she says.

"So will you," says Maks.

Willa stares at the family picture for a while before carefully placing it back into the tin box, closing the lid with a little *click* that sounds like *The End*.

Maks, glad the talk is over, says, "Come on. We need to get home."

"Home," Willa repeats with a shy smile. As if she's remembering a word.

40

Same time as Maks and Willa are going home, Bartleby Donck, over on Delancey Street, sits at his desk telling himself he was stupid to get caught up in those kids' problems. The girl, that Emma, means nothing to him. Her story is no different than ten thousand stories he's heard. They all seem the same.

Why did I get pulled in? he asks himself. But he knows the answer. *It was their telling me they read that stupid story! Believing it. Pha! Never mind law. I need to teach them what detection really is. And that girl, Willa. She spoke up. Didn't back away. Was strong. Wasn't scared of me.*

Donck scratches his side-whiskers, rubs his eyes, sighs deeply, wonders how long he'll stay alive. He looks at what he was writing, worries if he can finish it before he is finished. "Garbage!" he mutters, and shoves the papers angrily to one side 'fore picking up the scrap on which he'd written *Emma Geless*. He stares at it.

"I'm a fool," he says.

Coughing, Donck plucks up a stained cloth and spits blood into it. "I hate children," he says. "They believe in things. Like me."

Pressing down on the wooden arms of his chair, he rises precariously. Almost falling, he leans 'gainst his desk to catch himself. Then he snatches up his listening tube and hangs it round his neck. Grabs the cane that's leaning 'gainst the desk.

Walking slowly, leaning on the cane, almost shuffling, Donck passes out of his rooms. Don't even bother to shut the door behind him. Hey, there's nothing worth stealing.

When he reaches the street, he looks up and down. In the murkiness the only light comes from street-lamps. Donck glares at them. He hates electric light. As far as he's concerned, gaslight is better. Gives more light. Has life.

Standing there, he has a sudden memory of gaslight making a lady's diamond necklace glow so that when it hung round her neck it was like cold fire lighting up her face, her black hair, her dark eyes. The light made her even more beautiful than she already was.

He gave that lady the necklace.

With a rueful shake of his head, Donck moves slowly

along the sidewalk till he reaches a restaurant whose window has a sign in gold letters:

THE PROMISED LAND—*Cheap Eats!*
Telephone!
5¢

Over the window someone has stuck another sign:

Coffee and Roll
3¢

Donck enters. There are nine tables, two chairs at each. It all smells of stale grease and tobacco. A few people are sitting 'neath the feeble electric light, which hangs from the ceiling. A mournful waiter—pale, long-faced, big-nosed, thin-fingered, wearing a frayed black suit and a grease-stained apron tied high over his waist—steps forward like an undertaker.

"Mr. Donck, sir," he says, bobbing and squeezing his hands together. "How are you today? The usual table, sir? Complete dinner, sir? Beef and fried oysters. Twenty-five cents tonight, sir."

"I need the telephone," Donck growls.

"Very good, sir. Please step this way."

The waiter guides Mr. Donck to the back of the restaurant, where he opens a door. Beyond is a small room with one chair. Near the chair, attached to the wall, is a telephone.

The telephone—a new one—consists of two wooden boxes, one atop the other. The top box has a crank on one side, two bells on its face. From the bottom box, there's an electrical cord attached to a black tube. That's the listening end. To talk, you got to put your mouth near a hole in the same box.

When the waiter leaves, Donck leans toward the telephone till his mouth is near the talking hole. Takes down the listening tube with one hand, turns the crank a few times with his other hand.

"Hello, Central!" he shouts into the hole. "Hello, Central!" He shoves the listening end near his better ear.

"This is Central," comes a woman's voice, rough, crackly with static.

Donck shouts, "Connect me to the Waldorf Hotel!"

"Yes, sir. Just a moment, sir."

Donck coughs.

"Connection made," says the woman.

He can hear ringing sounds.

"Waldorf Hotel," says a voice as if from far away. There's static, too.

"I need to speak to Mr. Packwood, your detective," Donck all but shouts.

"I shall have to locate him, sir."

"I'll stay right here."

"May I tell him who's calling?"

"His almost brother-in-law."

"Sir?"

"Never mind! Just tell him it's his old pal from the Pinkerton Detective Agency, Bartleby Donck."

"Yes, sir, Mr. Donck. Please wait."

"Don't worry. I'm not going to disappear. Soon but not yet." A coughing fit shakes his whole body.

41

Maks and Willa get home. They haven't talked much. Just before they go up the stoop, Maks says, "I'm not gonna tell my parents 'bout Donck."

"How come?"

"What if they tells me not to work with him?"

Willa says nothing.

"Told you," Maks goes on, "they don't feel good doing new things. If I don't tell 'em, can't say not to, right?"

After a moment Willa says, "I don't know them."

"Come on," says Maks.

In the warm kitchen Papa is seated at the table, smoking his pipe. Mama is giving him dinner. Agnes ain't there. Maks hears his three brothers fooling in the front room.

Mama says, "You're home late tonight."

"Papers took a long time," says Maks. "But we sold everything." He dumps his coins on the table, makes the usual divide, putting most of the pennies in his cigar box over the stove. He slides eight cents 'cross the table to Papa. "All eight," he says.

"Good, Maks," says Papa. "We need every one."

"Where's Agnes?" Maks asks.

"At class," says Mama.

Papa turns to Willa. "Please, young lady, if you would be so good as to sit." He puts a hand on the back of the nearest chair. "I should be pleased to talk to you."

With a nervous glance at Maks, Willa sits with her doll and tin box on her lap. She looks down.

Papa pushes his soup bowl away and turns his chair

so he's facing Willa. "My wife," he says to her, "tells me you're going to live with us."

Mama, at the stove, listens. So does Maks.

Willa peeks up at Papa. "Yes, sir. If . . . if that's all right."

"Your parents are . . . no longer with you," Papa goes on. "Do I understand that properly?"

Willa swallows. "Yes . . . sir."

"I'm truly sorry to hear it. I'm sure they were fine people. But it's not right that a girl should be living alone on the streets. And now winter's coming. So the whole family has agreed that you must come and live with us. We don't have much, but we shall manage." He holds out a large hand. "I wanted to welcome you."

"Thank you, sir," says Willa, her voice so low, Maks can hardly hear it.

Willa looks up, sees Papa's hand, and puts out her own. She and Papa shake, Willa's small hand swallowed up in his large one.

"I have a job, sir," she says.

"Which is?"

"I pick rags at the dumps. Ten cents a week."

Papa frowns, shakes his head. "No. No more of that. We'll find something else for you to do. And I think it best you call me 'Papa.' And my wife, 'Mama.' It's what all our children do. You're family now. No need for 'sir.'"

Willa bobs her head. "Yes . . . Papa."

"As for sleeping," says Papa, "we'll find a spot."

Mama says, "Agnes says you can share her bed."

Willa looks at Papa. "You are very kind," she whispers.

Maks, across the room, feels proud of his parents.

"Have you any belongings?" Mama asks Willa.

"Just these," says Willa. She lifts the doll and the tin box.

"And the doll don't eat much," says Maks.

Everybody is glad to laugh.

Monsieur Zulot comes into the apartment. He makes his usual bow. *"Bon soir,"* he says, and looks round as if in search of something.

"Agnes is at class," says Maks, grinning.

"Ah, yes. To be sure," says Zulot, his cheeks turning red. "A smart young lady."

"Girl," says Mama fiercely.

"Monsieur Zulot," Papa says. "This is Willa. Maks's friend. She has become part of our family. She'll be living with us."

Willa looks up timidly.

"Good that you are, mademoiselle," says Monsieur Zulot. "You have found fine people. Now forgive me. I will step from the way but come when called." He goes into the front room, shutting the door behind him.

"Papa," Maks says, keeping his voice low, "did you find a lawyer?"

Papa shifts uncomfortably. "Agnes is looking."

"Maks, we'll find a way," says Mama.

Maks glances at Willa. When she looks back at him, he knows she's thinking the same thing that he is: *Donck*.

Maks says, "Mama, Emma really wants to see you. Tomorrow, after I bring the boys to school, I can take you. And, Papa, she needs money for food. I need to see her again too."

Mama and Papa exchange looks. Then Mama says, "Yes, I'll go."

"We got any money to bring her?" asks Maks.

"We'll find it," says Papa.

Mama says, "And, dear God, Maks said her trial will be soon."

"We'll find a way," Papa says.

Later, Monsieur Zulot reads the boys some more from that detective story. A chapter called "The Truth Unfolds!" Willa and Maks listen. In the story the boy detective is

Independence Public Library

looking—and finding—what he calls "clues," bits of information that'll help him find the stolen diamonds so he can help that pretty lady.

Maks decides he must ask Emma if there's anything she can tell him 'bout what happened *before* she was arrested, some clue. If there is one, he can tell Donck.

While Monsieur Zulot is reading, Maks steals a look out the window down to the street. Bruno ain't there. But someone else from the gang is.

Maks takes a deep breath and thinks, *They ain't never gonna stop chasing us.*

Agnes comes home only after Mama and Papa have gone into their room for the night.

"What class you been to?" Maks asks as she takes off her shawl.

"Typing. I'm up to forty-eight words a minute." Looking tired, she sits down.

Willa jumps up and takes soup from the pot on the

stove. She serves Agnes. "Thank you," says Agnes, and picks up her spoon only to pause. "Willa?" she says.

Willa looks at her.

"I'm glad you're moving in. There's room for you in my bed."

"Thank you."

Maks gets his sister some bread.

As Agnes starts to eat, she coughs, once, twice.

"I found the name of a lawyer," she says to Maks, keeping her voice hushed. "Someone at the Educational Alliance told me. A Mr. Sisler. On Rutgers Square."

"How much he gonna charge?

"'Going to,' not 'gonna.' Fifty dollars."

"Fifty!"

"The Alliance people said he's good."

"We don't have no money like that."

"They said he'll take a little at a time," says Agnes, bending over her soup.

After a moment Maks says, "We might have another way."

"What?

"A detective."

Agnes pauses in her eating and looks up. "I don't understand."

"Get, you know, clues and stuff to show Emma didn't steal nothing."

"'Anything.' How are you going to find a detective?"

"One of my friends—Chimmie—told me 'bout a Mr. Donck. Over to Delancey Street. And"—Maks leans forward, lowers his voice—"Willa and me, we went and saw him."

Agnes shakes her head disapprovingly. "You're listening to too many of Monsieur Zulot's stories."

"No," says Maks. "Really. He's gonna teach us."

"Did he ask for a lot of money?"

Maks says, "He's gonna teach us how to be detectives for nothing."

"What's he like?" Agnes asks.

"Strange," says Maks.

Agnes looks at Willa. "Do you think a detective is a good idea?"

"I hope so."

"Did you tell . . . ?" She moves her head toward the back room.

Maks shakes his head. "They won't like it."

Agnes sighs. "Maybe your detective will help." Then she says, "At the factory they announced we'll be closing in three weeks."

"Three?" cries Maks.

Agnes nods, then eats slowly.

Later that night while Agnes is reading at the table, she has a real coughing fit. Maks sees her wiping her mouth. Tries to hide it, but there's blood on the cloth.

"You okay?" Maks says.

"Fine."

Willa watches Agnes closely.

When everybody goes off to sleep in their regular beds, Willa tells Maks she won't sleep in Agnes's bed. "It won't be good for Agnes. And I don't mind sleeping on the floor."

"You're scared of her sickness, ain't you?" Maks says.

After a moment Willa nods.

Maks spreads a blanket out on the kitchen floor. "You can sleep here."

"Where should I put this?" Willa holds up her blue tin.

"Be safe in my cigar box." Maks puts it in there.

"Maks," Willa whispers, "did Agnes ever see a doctor?"

"There's one over to Mott Street," says Maks. "Supposed to be good. Only he costs. Mama has a friend, a midwife. She comes sometimes."

Willa says no more.

Maks goes into the front room and looks down on the street. The Plug Ugly is gone. He goes back to the kitchen. "No one out there," he calls softly to Willa.

———

After a moment Willa says, "Maks . . . do you ever feel as if you live in a hole?"

"You mean . . . like behind your fence?"

She nods. "At the bottom of everything."

He says, "Want to see something?"

"What?"

"Come on."

Maks leads Willa out of the apartment and up the narrow steps to the flat roof. There are crisscrossing ropes and cords that people have strung up for drying their washing. The hanging sheets look like flags from nowhere. In the sky just one or two stars are visible. There's a full moon, but only a lick of light pokes out from behind billowy clouds. On a couple of roofs, fire escapes stick up.

"That's Mr. Floy's pigeon coop," Maks says. The gray birds, in a large screened box, cluck and coo. "He comes up and lets 'em fly. Don't know why, but they always come back.

"Look here," Maks says. He goes to the roof wall and points. Lights—like strung beads—show miles of streets cutting 'tween buildings. To the east and west, the East and Hudson rivers glisten. City sounds roll up: horses' hooves, carriages rolling, bells jangling, and human voices, shouts, calls, and sometimes screams.

Turning, Maks says, "Over there you can see the end of the city, the Brooklyn Bridge, all them ships. See the funnels. Some of 'em smoking. And masts.

"You know what? I just like coming up here to see how big the city is. Someday—don't care how long it takes— gonna fly round the whole thing. You could come, if you'd like. Or maybe get on one of those ships and go someplace. Take you, if you want. Emma and I come up here too."

"Why?"

"Just to talk." Maks suddenly grins. "And guess what? She's teaching me to dance the two-step. But you know what I keep thinking?"

"What?"

"If Emma's gonna be in prison, it'll kill her. Kill the whole family."

Later, in his bed in the front room, Maks tries to think 'bout what it would be like to get on a ship. Where would he go? But his thoughts soon return to Emma, wondering if Mr. Donck can really help. Wondering what he was writing. Willa, asleep, clutches her doll.

43

Just about when Maks is falling asleep on Birmingham Street, Mr. Donck has a visitor in his office on Delancey.

"Good evening, Bartleby!"

With a start, Donck looks up from his writing. It's Mr. Packwood, the Waldorf detective who arrested Emma. He's dressed like a gentleman: fine frock coat, vest, and silk tie, boots polished to a bright shine.

Donck puts one end of his speaking tube into his ear. "Ah, Philip," he says. "Thank you for coming. Forgive me for not rising."

"Bartleby," says Packwood as he considers the room, "why do you insist upon dwelling in the most miserable of conditions?"

"We can't all live the way you do," Donck growls as he puts his rag to his mouth and coughs.

"Someday you must visit me at the hotel," says Packwood. "That is," he adds, "when you get some decent clothing, clean yourself up, and stop coughing. To be honest, I don't think Mr. Boldt would allow you to step through our doors. Not the way you are now. Did you know, he won't allow any of his employees to have beards, mustaches, or even side-whiskers?"

"Who's this unpleasant man?" Donck says.

"Boldt? The excellent German gentleman who runs the hotel. I assure you, Mr. Boldt will do anything to satisfy the needs of his guests. Just today a short gentleman found the chairs in his room too high. Mr. Boldt had them lowered."

"You mean he *cut* the furniture's legs?"

"Just so. And last week a guest wished her pillows overstuffed. Nora Foley, our chief housekeeper, took care of that. Mr. Boldt has even installed that Prussian invention—showers for the staff."

"What's a shower?"

"Like standing under a waterfall. But inside. Keeps the staff clean."

"Pha! Disgusting."

"It's good business, Bartleby," says Packwood. "Of course, for the staff—such as me—Mr. Boldt does no more than what he believes necessary. Bartleby, is there no place for me to sit?"

"If I had chairs, my clients would sit and talk my head off. Better to keep them standing. They leave sooner."

"I'm glad to learn you still have clients. And a head. How does your work progress? Still writing trash?"

Donck waves a hand over his writing. "Penny a word." Then, after a moment, he adds, "People seem to read it."

"I suppose it can't do any harm and it keeps you alive," says Packwood. "Now then, my old friend, cab and horse are waiting outside. They don't like your neighborhood. Neither do I."

"I would have thought you still carried a pistol."

Packwood mutters, "Only for my office. Not yours. Come now, Bartleby, I'm here because you asked me to come and we're old friends."

"Friends . . ."

"Quite so," says Packwood. "I even bring you greetings from my sister, who—"

"I don't want to hear!" roars Donck, his face turning red.

"As you wish," says Packwood. "Now, what's so urgent that you insisted I come immediately?"

Donck glances at a piece of paper and reads what he's written: "Emma Geless."

"How in the world do you know about her?"

"My rooms may be slovenly, Philip. I may be growing

deaf. Your sister once rejected my offer of marriage because I was too poor. I'm quite ill, but my mind remains keen. For a while, anyway. What do you know about this Emma Geless?"

"Age sixteen. Immigrant child. Don't know where from. Housemaid at the hotel. A gold watch and chain were taken from one of our guests. I found the chain under her dormitory pillow.

"Naturally, I had her arrested. She was arraigned and now sits in The Tombs awaiting trial. What else is there to say?"

"And the watch?"

"A Breguet."

"Indeed! Worth a fortune. Did you find it?"

"No."

"What happened to it?"

"The girl probably gave it to the boyfriend who put her up to the job. No doubt, that chain was her reward. Her real reward will be time in prison."

"And the boyfriend?"

"No idea."

"But you're convinced a boyfriend exists?"

"Usually the case."

"As certain that the girl is guilty?"

"The evidence was there."

"Beyond a reasonable doubt?"

"She claims she's innocent. But, Bartleby, you know as well as I do, they all claim that. The truth of the matter is, the watch chain was found—"

"Do you know her boyfriend's name?"

"Not the slightest idea."

"If you believe in his existence, don't you want to find him? Don't you want to recover the watch? Doesn't the man who lost it want it back? Breguet watches are unique. Very expensive. Pull that from your pocket and everyone knows you're a wealthy man. No wonder someone stole it. But . . . taken by a sixteen-year-old immigrant girl from nowhere? Pha!"

"She could pawn it."

"Such a watch would be easy to find. I promise you, whoever took it still has it. Didn't you give the victim reason to believe that you would try to find it? Don't you wish to protect the reputation of your new hotel?"

"Well, yes, all of that, of course, but—"

"Then what have you done, Philip," Donck shouts, "other than arrest that poor, ignorant girl?"

Packwood is quiet for a while, shifting uncomfortably on his feet. "Nothing," he says. "Not really."

"Exactly," shouts Donck. "You took the easy way! Pha!" His effort brings him a coughing fit. When he recovers, he says, "I intend to give you the means of recovering that watch *and* your reputation."

"My reputation is fine."

"Not with me," snaps Donck.

Packwood gives a mock groan. "Am I to hear about your illustrious Dutch ancestors again?"

"I intend to tell you what I know. Then you must tell me what you know. Finally, I shall inform you what you must do."

"Are you giving me orders, Bartleby?"

"Pha!" says Donck. "Once a Pinkerton, always a Pinkerton."

"'We never sleep,' do we?" says Packwood, smiling as he repeats the agency motto.

"It's as I prefer it. So let this be as it was," Donck says. "Listen to your old chief. This shall be my last case. Your orders, Philip: Find the watch and you will have the thief. The real thief."

"Find the watch," repeats Packwood with a mock salute. "Yes, sir."

"To that end, I'm going to send a boy for you to put on your staff."

"A boy? Why?"

"I need him to look about your hotel."

"Who is he? Your client? Your apprentice?"

"He's the brother of the girl you arrested. Name's Maks. We'll call him Brown. Maks Brown." Donck snorts. "He's . . . he's my boy detective."

44

Okay. It's next morning. Wednesday.

First thing, Willa and Maks take the boys to school, then return home to fetch Mama. By the time they get to her, she's made up a package of food for Emma: bread and sausage wrapped in a sheet of newspaper.

When they get to the prison, the doors are already open. Mama, holding Emma's food tight in both hands, is very nervous. "Is it terrible in here?" she asks Maks at the top of the steps. "Are you sure they'll let me see Emma? What if they won't?"

"It ain't nice," he warns her. "But she'll be glad to see you."

Willa announces she'll wait outside.

Maks looks at her. "You gonna wait?"

"Promise."

"Keep your eyes open," Maks warns. "You don't want 'em to see you alone."

Willa, understanding, holds up her stick.

Mama, who barely listens to what the kids are saying, whispers, "It's such a big building."

As she and Maks go forward, she clutches his arm while keeping her eyes looking down. Maks can feel her trembling.

When they get to the entry doors, the policemen ask the same questions they asked Maks the day before. When they answer, they're given tickets.

The first hard moment comes when Mama is told to go into the room where women are searched. It frightens her, but it's over soon.

"They even looked through the food," says an astonished Mama.

Maks, not talking, leads the way to the women's prison. It's cold and gloomy, the way it was yesterday. The same hollow cries, shrieks of misery, the stink of people, the swaggering guards, the crowded lower floor. Mama stares round with wide, frightened eyes.

———

"Who are all these people?" she whispers to Maks.

Maks, trying to act as if knows, says, "Lawyers. People selling food to prisoners."

He don't wait but leads Mama to the top cell level. She climbs the steps slowly—like a little kid—one step at a time, holding tightly to Maks and the side rail. He's hoping Emma's cell door will be open.

When they find it closed, Maks calls out Emma's name.

She's at the far back of the cell, as if hiding. Hearing Maks, she stands up, looking dirtier, more dismal than before.

When Mama sees Emma, she's so startled, she cries out. At first Emma brightens at the sight of Mama, but when they get close, she starts to cry. Mother and daughter hug each other through the bars and start talking Danish.

Maks sees Mama slip Emma a dollar. He don't know where she got it, but he supposes it's Monsieur Zulot's rent money.

Maks, sure they want to be alone, walks off a bit, leaning over the balcony and watching the people milling below. Don't take long before he spots Donck on the first level. The detective is talking to a man, tapping him on his chest as if scolding him, even as he's holding up his listening tube.

The other man, looking annoyed, turns and walks away. Donck shakes his head, walks down the hall, and leaves.

Mama tugs on Maks's sleeve. "Maks, she hasn't eaten all day. Can I go to some of those people down there and buy something?"

"Want me to?"

"I'll do it. She wants to talk to you."

Maks goes back to the cell. When Emma puts out her hands, he holds them.

"I found someone to help you," he says right away.

"Who?"

"A detective. Name is Donck. When I come back tomorrow, I'll tell you how he's gonna help. But I didn't tell Mama. So don't go telling her."

Emma says, "You asked me yesterday if I could remember anything unusual happening at the hotel before I was arrested."

"Did you?"

"Just something small."

"What?"

Emma tells Maks this story: "At the hotel my job is to clean rooms on the ninth floor. We start at nine in the morning. You're supposed to knock to make sure no one's in the room. See, when we clean, the guests can't be there. And we always keep the door open. The hotel has strict rules 'bout that. The chief matron, Miss Foley, is always checking to make sure we do things right.

"Sometimes when we're cleaning, a guest comes back. Because they forgot something or they need to change clothes. When that happens, we're supposed to leave. Wait outside till the guest goes.

"The day before I was arrested, I was cleaning one of the rooms and a gent came in. He must have been a guest in that room 'cause when he sees me, he apologizes for interrupting. Guests aren't always so polite. Says he forgot something.

"Right away, I says, 'I'll wait outside.' But he says, 'Pay no heed to me, young lady. Just go on with your fine work. I'll be but a moment.' Talked fancy like that. 'Thank you, sir,' I says, and kept working.

"As he was leaving—ain't more than a few minutes— he says, 'You're doing an excellent job here. If you tell me your name, I'll praise you to the management.'

"That's a good thing, so sure, I told him my name, and he left, and I went on with my work."

"But what happened?" Maks says, baffled.

Emma, disappointed by Maks's reaction, shrugs.

"We don't get praised by guests very often. It's the only unusual thing I remember."

Before Maks can say anything more, he sees Mama coming back along the balcony. She's got a jug of water, which she gives to Emma. The girl drinks greedily.

Mama and Emma make their good-byes with lots of hand-holding, hugs and kisses, as well as promises to return. Then Mama and Maks go back out the way they came in—Mama being quiet—and hand their tickets to a policeman. When they get outside, the first thing Maks does is look for Willa. She's sitting on the steps.

Since Mama wants to walk alone, Willa and Maks stay a few steps back.

"When you were inside," Willa says in a low voice, "I saw Donck come out."

"Yeah. I saw him too."

"I don't think he even saw me. He seemed to be thinking very hard. And . . . I also saw a couple of Plug Uglies."

Maks stops. "They do anything?"

"Soon as I saw them, I moved up by the doors. Where the policemen are. I had my stick, so maybe that's why they left me alone. But one of them shouted, 'Don't worry. We'll get you soon.'"

"They're following us," says an uneasy Maks. "Watching where we go."

He tries to put his mind back to Emma, going over that story she told him. Didn't make any sense.

As they head back to the tenement, Maks notices how dank the air is, how it smells of smoke. And it feels like rain is coming.

He's thinking, *Nothing's right.*

Soon as they get Mama home safe, Maks and Willa horse it over to Newspaper Row, back behind *The World* building. The usual knot of newsies is there but bunched up in one big crowd. No games. No fooling. Lots of fuming, fussing, and angry, nervous talk.

"What's the matter?" Maks asks Toby.

"Plug Uglies," says the kid. "They beat up four guys last night. Burned all their papers."

"Anyone get hurt?"

"Abe got his arm busted."

Everybody understands the newspaper ain't gonna help. And cops? Forget 'bout 'em.

Maks hears one kid say, "That Bruno, you know what? He ain't gonna back off till he bosses us."

And it don't help knowing rain is coming. Rain always makes newsies twitchy. No fun peddling papers when it's pelting.

The bell rings. Mugs line up while the papers are dished. Maks grabs his bundle. Then he and Willa head uptown, Maks reading the headlines as they go.

"Anything good?" Willa asks.

"Not bad. A town was wrecked."

"Where?"

"Says . . . Eng-Land."

"Where's that?"

"Don't know. Don't matter."

Soon as they get to Maks's corner, he starts hustling: "Extra! Extra! Read all 'bout it! 'Town of Sandgate Wrecked! Citizens Driven from Homes in Panic!' Read it in *The World*! The world's greatest newspaper. Town in panic! News like you love it! Just two cents! Only two cents!"

The rain starts. Ain't much at first, mostly spatter, but it gets colder, too. The rain and cold make people move faster, which ain't good for selling. Besides, people don't buy wet papers.

But Maks, being near the El station steps, got a good place. It's partly protected and people keep coming. Helps having Willa there too. She stays by the pickle shop—they have an awning over the door—and that keeps the papers dry.

More rain and then thunder thumps, making people jump. Sales are slow, but by sometime after seven, Maks dishes his last sheet. Soon as he does, he and Willa start running toward Donck's rooms.

By then it's dark, cold, the rain coming steadily. In the gray wet, the only bright spots are red lamps—like bloodshot eyes—set on the streetlight posts so people can find fire-alarm boxes.

Splashing through street puddles and mud, Maks clutches his pennies in his pocket. They hear one drop. They get on hands and knees and search till Willa calls, "Got it!"

Then they're up and running again.

When they get to Delancey Street, they go right to Donck's door. Maks knocks. He hears coughing and gasping 'fore he hears anything else. Then a voice yells, "What is it?"

"It's us. Maks and Willa."

"Come in!"

They enter into the same mess as before, the rooms cold, smelling of sour mold. Books in their cases looking like crumbling bricks. Rain drumming 'gainst the windows while water wiggles down an inside wall.

Donck is sitting behind his desk by his glowing lamp. Pen in hand, he's hunched over his papers, writing furiously, his bald head the only bright spot in the gloom.

Willa and Maks stand in the doorway, their hair dripping. At their feet puddles gather.

The detective shifts round and stares hollow-eyed at them. "Ah! The boy detective. You look as bad as the trash you read."

Maks says, "You told us to come back."

"So I did." The detective throws down his pen—spattering ink—picks up his listening tube, and holds it out. Immediately, he starts coughing, so much that he has to slap a hand over his mouth. Blood seeps through his dirty, stubby fingers.

Maks stares, horrified. He glances at Willa to see if she's seen it. Her eyes are big.

Donck wipes his hand down his chest. "Is it raining?" he says.

"Yes, sir," says Maks, hardly knowing how to react to this man.

Donck shoves his writing papers aside. "Pay no mind to my ill health," he says. "A rank case of rapid decline. Now then, your sister's case. What have you to report? I presume you spoke to her."

"Yes, sir."

"Did she tell you more? Admit she took that watch and chain?"

"I told you, she didn't take nothing."

"Of course," Donck sneers. "I forget. The whole world is innocent." He grinds an eye with the heel of his hand. "Then she told you nothing?"

"Just one thing."

"One is vastly more than none. What was it?"

Maks says, "Asked her if she remembered anything unusual at the hotel. Before she was arrested. A clue."

"Ha!"

"All she said was . . ." And Maks tells Donck how Emma was interrupted and praised by that guest. "That a clue?" Maks asks when he's done.

Donck, pondering Emma's story, sits still. Maks and Willa wait. The detective, scratching one side of his whiskers, says, "Does your sister have a boyfriend?"

"No."

"Would you even know? Sisters don't always tell brothers such things."

"She does me."

Donck holds up a dirty hand. "The first rule of detection: Nobody tells anyone everything. Now then, lessons. What a detective must do is look at the scene where the crime was committed. Study it. Search out people who might have noticed something. Determine if other people are involved—like a boyfriend. Your job is to notice as much as you can. The key: He who looks, sees. He who sees, knows."

Maks says, "How am I gonna do that?"

"When you learn one thing, connect it to another thing. Keep on connecting until you can go no further. Then go back and make more connections. Finally, connect the connections. There's your evidence."

Maks, with a glance at Willa, struggles to understand.

"Now then," Donck goes on, "at The Tombs today I inquired of a man I know as to what it would cost to release your sister on bail. Two hundred dollars. Twenty for deposit. Does your family have that?"

Maks shakes his head.

"I thought as much. Very well, I've arranged for you,

Maks, to work where your sister worked—at the Waldorf."

"*Me?* At the Waldorf?"

"You wish to be a detective, don't you?"

"Yes, sir."

"You can start there."

"Me too?" says Willa.

"Alas, no. Just your brother."

"When?" says Maks.

"Tomorrow morning."

"How I gonna do that?"

"I have arranged everything. Tomorrow morning, nine thirty, present yourself at the servants' entrance of the hotel. Ask for Mr. Philip Packwood."

"Ain't he the mug who arrested Emma?" says Maks.

"He is."

"Hate him," says Maks.

"Pha! Emotion clouds your eyes. I assure you, he's a good man. When you go, do not give your own last name."

"How come?"

"May I remind you, your sister was arrested there. People know the name. No. You'll tell people your name is Brown. Maks Brown."

Maks stares at him.

"Consider it a disguise. Packwood will treat you as an

employee. You won't be paid. Your task: Do what he tells you while you do your sleuthing."

"What's sleuthing?"

Donck sighs. "Detection. Still willing?"

"Yes, sir."

"Good! You need to discover three things. First, learn the room number from which—"

"What's a room number?" says Maks.

"Good God! You know *nothing*, do you?"

"No, sir."

"Who was the idiot who claimed that ignorance is opportunity? Ignorance is . . . is ignorance. Every hotel room has a number. You, Willa—a task for you: You will return to The Tombs to ask your sister where she was—the number of the room in which she received that promise of a compliment. You, Maks, at the Waldorf, will ask **Mr.** Packwood if your sister did, *in fact*, receive that compliment. Do you both follow me?"

"Think so."

"Now leave me in peace. Don't come back until you've learned something. If you do learn something, come immediately. Time—mine and your sister's—is short." Donck leans back in his chair, pulls his speaking tube out of his ear, and resumes his writing.

"Mr. Donck!" yells Willa.

He looks up.

"You never said the first thing to find."

Donck looks blankly at Willa and then, remembering, says, "Indeed. I did not. Very good. Excellent. Smart girl! It's the most important of all. Maks, ask Packwood in *which* hotel room the theft took place. That understood?"

Maks glances at Willa and says, "I . . . I think so."

"Now go," says Donck, and he turns his back on the kids and furiously resumes his work.

Maks and Willa—damp, cold, and uneasy—stand inside the tenement door, staring out onto the street. Rain is falling hard, bouncing off the glistening cobblestones like tiny iron balls. The flashing lightning throws gold onto the street while gutters float with garbage.

Only a few people are out. They're moving fast, as if they can outrun the rain. Some hold umbrellas. Others got newspapers over their heads. Most have nothing. A few wagons roll by, horses' heads bent, manes streaming. Drivers crouching beneath canvas capes as if they were the ones—for once—being whipped. An almost empty street-car rattles past, the squally weather turning its tinkling bell to taffy.

Maks is thinking 'bout what he's agreed to do: Go to the Waldorf. Just the thought of it makes him anxious. Hardly knows what he'll do once he gets there. *Find evidence. Sleuthing. Take on a different name.* Things he's never done.

Willa says, "You going to do what Donck says?"

"Wanna help Emma, don't I?" He shakes his head. "Those questions I'm supposed to ask that Packwood, you understand 'em?"

"Not really. Maks, if you go to the hotel, who's going to do your papers?"

"Forgot 'bout 'em. How 'bout after you go ask Emma Mr. Donck's question, you sell 'em."

"Will they let me?"

"Sure. The guys met you. Like you. And you seen what I do. I'll get Jacob to go with you—he done it before. You'll be all right."

"You still not telling your parents what you're doing?"

Not answering, Maks says, "Come on. Rain's not gonna let up. We should be home."

———

They take off, sometimes running, sometimes just walking fast.

Most shops are shut tight. The few streetlights still on have halos of mist. Peddlers' carts are covered with canvas, making 'em look like funeral wagons. Only small saloons, with their gaslights dreary in the thick, moist air, are doing business.

Maks leads them down Second Avenue, 'cause the overhead elevated train tracks block some rain. Cold and soaked, shoulders hunched, they try to keep out of the rain by hugging close to buildings. Their shoes splash in puddles. When Willa keeps pushing wet hair from her face, Maks gives her his cap.

Pausing to catch her breath, Willa says, "Is . . . is Mama going to be mad at me for getting my clothes wet?"

Maks notices: This is the first time he's heard Willa call his mother "Mama."

"Naw. She'll understand."

It's right near the Rivington Street station that Maks skids to a halt. "Over here!" he calls, and gives Willa a yank, scooting into a doorway.

"What is it?"

"Bruno and his gang are just down the street. Must be eight or nine of 'em."

Shivering with cold, Willa grips her stick and groans. "They see us?"

"Don't think so. Went into a saloon." Maks leans out of the doorway, peeks down the street. "The last one just went in."

"Can we get past?"

"Go 'cross the street. So wide and dark, they ain't gonna see us."

After taking another look to make sure none of the Plug Uglies are on the street, Maks jumps from where they are, races 'cross to the opposite curb. Willa's right at his heels.

As they start downtown again, Maks keeps an eye on the saloon in which the Plug Uglies went. The sign on its window names it THE SHIRT TAIL. There's another sign reading FREE LUNCH.

Maks stops, watches.

Inside the saloon, a gaslight hangs from the ceiling. They can see Plug Uglies standing 'bout, with Bruno in the middle. They're all drinking, talking, not that the kids can hear anything.

Willa tugs at him. "Let's go."

"Wanna see what they're doing."

"Why? We're not going in there, are we?"

"You heard what Donck said. If we're gonna be detectives, we're supposed to see things."

"Maks," Willa pleads, "we shouldn't be here."

But Maks wants to see what happens.

Within moments, the gang comes out from the saloon, Bruno in the lead.

Maks and Willa duck down behind the station steps. Maks peers out, watching as Bruno talks to his pals. Then the redhead goes up the El steps, the uptown side.

As for the rest of the gang, they walk just past the saloon and disappear between buildings, down what looks to be a narrow alley.

Willa pulls at Maks. "I'm really cold. We need to get home."

While the train rumbles into the station overhead, the two start downtown again. All the same, Maks keeps wondering where Bruno could be going that late. And the gang. Where were they headed?

Up at the American Theatre restaurant, the cold, rainy weather keeps the regular crowd down to half. On the stage the orchestra has stopped playing. Musicians are putting away their instruments.

But Bruno's boss sits at his usual corner table. His derby rests not far from the steak dinner he's all but finished eating. As a cigar propped on a plate burns slowly, he takes out his fancy watch and checks the time. Bruno is late again. But even as the guy puts the watch away, a waiter, white napkin over his arm, steps up to him.

"Excuse me, sir. There's a young fellow asking to see you."

"About time," the man mumbles. "Just show him along."

"Forgive me, sir," says the waiter. "He's rather wet and . . . what shall I say? . . . untidy. We'd rather not have him come onto the floor. I'm sure you can understand. Would you be willing to see him in the lobby?"

"You certain he wants to see me?"

"He asked for Mr. Brunswick."

The man frowns but stands up. "I'll see him."

"Thank you, Mr. Brunswick," says the waiter. "Much obliged."

When Brunswick reaches the restaurant's entryway, Bruno is waiting. He's quite a mess: wet hair, sopping jacket, muddy boots.

"Where have you been?" Brunswick demands. "I was just about to leave for home."

"Case yous haven't noticed," says Bruno, "it's stormy. Letting up, though."

"Good of you to come," says Brunswick, not speaking too nice.

"Nothing good 'bout it," Bruno throws back. "Yous tells me to come every day. Then they won't let me in."

"Never mind. I suppose you haven't managed much today."

"Not too bad." Bruno, grinning, holds up his bag of coins. "Usual haul. We shook some bones too."

"Fine," says the man. "But time is crucial. You need to work faster." He touches a hand to his breast pocket, where he keeps Bruno's photo—and his pistol.

Bruno, understanding the threat, frowns. "Hey," he

BRUNSWICK

says, "don't like yous pushing me all the time. Yous don't want to get me mad. Doing the best I can. I'm telling yous, them newsies are coming in. We'll bottle them soon. They're scared." He might as well be talking 'bout himself.

Brunswick smiles. "That's what I want to hear. Anything else?"

"Nothing. Just doing what yous told me."

"Good. I'll finish my dinner."

"Sure," says Bruno. "See yous tomorrow."

"Good night," Brunswick says, and goes back into the dining hall. When he sits down—thinking 'bout Bruno's threatening words—he pats his pocket, his revolver.

Down below, Bruno steps out onto the street and looks up. It's stopped raining. For once, the city air smells decent. Streamers of fog wrap round tall buildings.

Bruno glances at the line of horse-drawn hansom cabs at the curb. Be fun, he thinks, to ride one. He supposes Brunswick will take one home.

Just thinking 'bout the man reminds Bruno how much he hates the mug for forcing him to do his nasty work. If he could just get that pistol—and that picture—from him, he could be free. Nobody could touch him then.

Thinking 'bout Brunswick, Bruno wonders, as he often has, why the man don't want him to know where he lives.

Wants me to do his work, but don't want people seeing me with him.

Recalling that the man said he was almost done with his dinner and going home, Bruno decides to wait for him to come out. Maybe—if it ain't far—he can follow. Might help him to get that gun and picture.

Bruno stands in the shadows 'cross the street just opposite the restaurant. Turns out it's only a few minutes 'fore Brunswick appears. As Bruno guessed, the guy hails a hansom cab, speaks to the driver, climbs in.

When the horse and cab pull away, Bruno walks into the street. He watches the rear red night lamp swing from the back of the cab, then suddenly starts running after it.

The cab heads down Forty-second Street, then turns south onto Broadway. There's enough traffic to keep the cab from going fast. Bruno has no trouble keeping it in sight.

On Thirty-third Street the cab turns east to Fifth Avenue and stops. A run of only thirteen blocks. Bruno is hardly out of breath.

Keeping his distance, Bruno watches the man climb out of the cab and walk into an enormous building. Low clouds circle its top towers, making it seem something strange. But as Bruno stares at the building, he recognizes it as that new highfalutin hotel, the Waldorf.

Bruno grunts with satisfaction. *So that's where he lives.*

As he trudges toward home, Bruno tries to think of ways to make use of what he's learned. He tells himself once again that all he needs is to get his hands on Brunswick's pistol and the photo. Once he does, he'll be free of the mug. Forget the newsies. Lam it to Chicago. See that fair everyone's talking 'bout. Be anywhere but New York.

Just has to get that gun. And that picture.

When Willa and Maks get home, the kitchen is warm, smelling of the new bread Mama baked. The lone lamp casts a warm, yellow light.

The family has already finished supper. Since they know it takes Maks a long time to sell papers in bad weather, they don't even ask where he and Willa were.

Agnes, who's reading at the table, jumps up. "Come on," she says to a shivering Willa. "I'll get you something dry." Willa goes with her into the back room.

To Maks, Mama says, "Give me your jacket."

First Maks gives Papa his eight cents, then he dumps the rest of his pennies into the cigar box next to Willa's blue tin. Mama hangs his jacket on the back of a chair near the warm stove.

Papa, in a half whisper, says, "Maks, why does Willa always carry that stick?"

"Forget?" says Maks as he kicks off his wet boots. Sets them near the stove. "She beat off that Plug Ugly Gang with it. Makes her feel safer."

"But she feels safe here, doesn't she?"

"Oh, sure."

Mama places two bowls of hot soup on the table. Though she's always saying bread ain't done till it cools, Papa cuts it. Maks holds a warm piece in both hands, sticks his nose into it to smell its freshness. There's a family story 'bout how Maks once burned the tip of his nose smelling hot bread that way.

"Where the boys?" he asks.

"Monsieur Zulot is reading to them."

"That detective story?" Maks says, sorry he ain't hearing it. But he's so hungry and cold, he starts eating.

Willa comes out of the back room wearing one of Emma's dresses. Agnes, after giving the wet dress to Mama, who hangs it up, sits down near the lamp and picks up her book.

Maks says, "Papa, Emma's trial's gonna happen soon. Did you find a lawyer?"

"I'm trying," Papa answers.

The room is very silent. Papa unexpectedly stands up. "I'd best lie down." He starts for the back room only to pause. "Miss Willa," he says, "did Maks tell you? I have a little boat on the river. On Sunday—if the weather is good—we can go fishing."

"I'd like that," says Willa.

"Good night, Papa," Agnes says to him as he goes.

Mama says, "I'll come with you." Suddenly, she turns to Maks. "Shame on you!" she hisses. "What do you think? There's not a moment he's not worrying 'bout Emma. What are *you* doing to help?"

Maks bows his head. "Sorry," he mutters.

"The Tombs were awful," Mama goes on. "And Blackwell's Island will be worse." She shudders.

Agnes coughs, covering her mouth, but says nothing.

Mama takes a breath, sighs, bends over Agnes. "Don't tire your eyes."

To Willa, Mama says, "Stay warm."

To Maks, she grabs his hair, shakes it. "Papa's trying," she says, and leaves the room.

Neither Maks nor Willa says anything. It's Agnes

who says to Maks, "Can't you see how worried they are?"

"I know," mumbles Maks.

After a moment Willa eats.

Maks, leaning forward and keeping his voice down, says, "Agnes . . ."

Agnes don't look up.

Maks says, "Papa really looking for a lawyer?"

"We should use that Mr. Sisler I told you about."

"Okay with me," says Maks. "Listen. Didn't want to tell Mama, but Willa and me, we went and saw that detective—Donck—again. Guess what? In the morning I'm going to the Waldorf."

Agnes looks up. "Why?"

"Sleuthing. Looking for evidence. Clues. Gonna work there."

"How'd you fix that?"

"The detective did."

"What do you expect to find?"

"Stuff to prove Emma didn't steal."

"What about your newspapers?"

"Willa can sell 'em. The other newsies met her. Jacob can go too. They knows him."

Agnes says, "Why don't you tell Mama and Papa what you're doing? Show them you're doing something."

She turns to Willa. "Do you think it's a good idea?"

"I think he should tell them," says Willa.

Maks shakes his head. "What if they say no? Let's see what happens first."

"Will it be dangerous?" asks Agnes.

"At the Waldorf? Naw."

Later, Willa is under her blanket. Maks is sitting on a chair. They hear the storm outside rattling the front windows, beating on the roof overhead. From the back room comes the sound of Papa singing in his deep voice. They listen.

Vi drog fra Hjemmets Egne
Til ukjendte Strand,
Og snart vi os nu naerme
Til det fremmede Lans.
Hvad Tiden os vil Skikke
Der, Sorrig Eller Fred
Det Kjender vi jo ikke,
Det Gud alene ved.

"What's he singing?" Willa whispers.

"Danish song. It's the only song he ever sings. 'Bout coming to America."

"What's it mean?"

"I don't hardly speak Danish. But Emma once told me the words. Something like: 'We're traveling from our home to an unknown land. What will be there, sadness or peace, we don't know. Only God knows.'"

Thursday morning.

By the time Maks gets himself up and steps into the kitchen, Willa has already got water from the yard. Mama is making coffee.

Maks grabs the ash and milk cans and heads down the steps. At the front door he peeks out. No Plug Uglies.

It's a relief, but looking reminds him what the gang shouted at Willa when he was in The Tombs: "We'll get you soon." And what Bruno told them in the alley: "We're gonna soak the street with your blood."

He shivers, and it got nothing to do with the early-morning chill.

After dumping the ashes, Maks, wanting to look decent

at the hotel, gives himself a face wash in the backyard with cold water. As he does, he looks up and sees blue sky. Least he won't have to walk to the hotel in rain.

When he gets the milk, Mrs. Vograd reminds him 'bout the family account that's due.

Maks feels like the whole world is pounding on them.

Back in the kitchen Papa and Agnes are getting ready to go to work. As they leave, Agnes gives Maks a look. He's sure she's telling him to tell Mama what he's doing.

He still don't want to.

It's when he and Willa are walking the boys to school that he says to Jacob, "Willa's gonna do my papers today. I need you to go with her."

"What you doin'?"

"Something for Emma."

"What?" asks Eric.

Maks gives him a punch on his shoulder. "Just do what I'm saying, okay?"

"Did you tell Mama?"

"Hey, I'm telling you."

"How come Willa only needs Jacob?" Ryker wants to know.

"'Cause she does, that's all. So be outside school 'bout one thirty."

"Got class," Jacob says.

"Teacher won't care. Willa be waiting."

"You gonna bring Emma home?" Eric asks.

"I'm trying. Now shut up."

The boys know Maks well enough to know he ain't gonna answer no more questions.

Maks and Willa leave the boys at the school gate.

"Should I go with you to the hotel?" Willa says when they've gone a block. She hefts her stick.

"Be okay," says Maks. "Anyway, you gotta take Mama to The Tombs. And you need to see Emma. Remember? Donck's question."

"The room number?"

"Yeah. And you're living with us, right? So now on, Emma's your sister." He starts walking north.

"Maks," Willa calls, "if your mother asks me where you are, I don't want to lie."

Maks looks round. "Say what you want. Just don't forget: My paper money is in the cigar box. Make sure Jacob goes with you when you do the papers, okay? And take your stick."

Willa nods.

"Hope you find something!" she calls after him.

"Keep a look out!" he shouts back.

Maks heads uptown, moving at a steady pace, hands in pockets, his slightly damp cap on his head. It's something like three miles to the hotel.

Streets are crammed full of people going to work: women in long dark skirts, big hats. Men in rough clothing, carrying tools, lunch pails, derbies or caps on their heads. Kids everywhere, running, walking, scooting in between the adults. He sees one kid steal an apple from a stand, then eat it on the run, like he never ate before. A couple of kids are sleeping in a deep doorway.

Horses and mules hauling wagons. Hansom cabs crowding one another. Pushcarts on streets and sidewalks. It's early, but mugs are standing in front of stores calling people to come in, look round, and buy. Sidewalks spilling open baskets, barrels, crates, boxes full of food, shirts, dishes—you name it, it's there. To hear the calls, ain't nothing but bargains.

Maks makes his way through it all, walking so fast that it ain't too long 'fore he's moving the most direct way, which is under the Second Avenue El. As he's going, he's thinking mostly 'bout this Packwood mug he's supposed to meet, going over the questions Donck told him to ask. Keeps hoping he can find the clues Emma needs.

Maks is thinking so hard that when he looks up, he's surprised to find himself near the same place where he and Willa saw Bruno and the Plug Uglies the night before.

Since the last thing Maks wants is a tangle with them guys, he crosses over to the other side of the street. Same time, he can't help being curious 'bout the place where the gang went. So he keeps going under the El, up Second Avenue.

He reaches the Rivington Street station steps and stands behind a couple of pillars and looks over the buildings 'cross the way.

Being early, the Shirt Tail saloon ain't open yet. As for the house next door, downtown side, Maks sees now it's wooden, which means it's old. They don't build 'em that way anymore 'cause wood burns easy. And there are lots of fires in the city.

As Maks studies the old building, he realizes it's been abandoned. Which is to say, the windows as well as the front door are covered with boards. Peeling reddish paint on sagging walls. A buckled roof with just a few torn shingles left and a big hole that won't keep out much rain. A brick chimney—soot black at the top and without much chinking—seems 'bout to tumble.

The downtown side of this old building is set against a newer brick tenement. Right in front of it—on the sidewalk—there's a streetlamp with a fire-alarm box attached, its red light faded in the morning sun.

It's between the old house and the saloon that Maks notices a gap. The space ain't much bigger than two feet 'cross. Can't hardly even call it an alley. But Maks figures it must have been where the gang disappeared the night before.

Gazing at it, Maks wonders what's at the far end, where the gang was heading.

Sure, Maks knows he's got to get to the Waldorf, but he figures he's got some extra time. Least, that's his excuse for taking a closer look at that gap.

A bit nervous, he checks the street, uptown and downtown, but don't see nothing or nobody worth a nod.

Maks crosses the street, stands on the sidewalk, and peers into the little alley. Since the day is bright and sunny, the space dark, he don't see much.

Telling himself he'll be safe, he squeezes in. As his eyes adjust to the gloom, he's seeing a well-worn path. Gradually, he makes out a wall at the far end. Looks to be the back wall of another building. A tenement, he supposes. But he don't see no door or window. Nothing but wall. Makes him think there's another way out of this gap—which ain't the end.

The more he stares, the more Maks is sure that the gang probably didn't go *out* the far end of the narrow alley. Used the alley to go *into* the old house.

He can't resist checking.

Though it's dingy in there, he keeps telling himself to be careful, that this is the worst place for him, that he's doing something risky, dangerous, even stupid, that he needs to get uptown. But what's he do? He goes farther in.

Inching forward, he moves slowly, hands on opposite walls to steady himself, as if he's walking a tightrope. With every step he takes, he's telling himself, *Get ready to run.*

Then he spots what he thought he'd find—on the side of the old wooden house. Ain't a door or a window, but a large, jagged, door-size hole big enough to let someone pass through. What's more, Maks can see that it's covered—on the inside—by a curtain of splotchy yellow color. Just hanging there.

Though Maks's head is screaming at him that he's seen enough, that he needs to get out of there, his legs keep creeping forward till he's right outside that hole.

Carefully, he eases the curtain aside—it makes a squeaky sound—and peeks in.

It's dark inside the house, save for rods of light poking through chinks in the boarded-up windows. So it takes Maks a few moments to see that on the floor is an unlit oil lamp.

And right behind it, a body.

Maks gawks. But even as he looks, the person rolls over.

It's Bruno.

And Bruno's eyes are wide open.

"Hey!" he yells. "You!"

Maks whirls round and busts out of the alley. He don't stop, either, but keeps racing, looking back every few seconds to see if Bruno is coming.

Only when he's gone seven uptown blocks does he slow down. He's breathing hard, heart pounding, telling himself what a busted brain he's got. Creeping up that way, spying on Bruno, was no better than poking an angry dog in the eye. If he'd been caught, he'd have been chewed.

All the same, Maks keeps wondering, *Did Bruno see me? If he did, what'll he do about it?* Maybe waking up that way—suddenly—meant Bruno thought Maks was only a dream.

The notion calms Maks down.

Still, he keeps walking fast, getting farther away, always checking back over his shoulder.

No Bruno.

After a while Maks tells himself, *I'm safe. He didn't really see me. Naw, he won't do nothing.*

It's just before nine thirty when Maks gets to Thirty-third Street and Fifth Avenue: the Waldorf Hotel. He stands 'cross the street and stares at it.

With thirteen stories, it's a lot taller than most nearby buildings. Maybe not as big as *The World* building, but big enough—so tall that Maks wonders how long it'd take to walk steps to the top.

The first two levels are stone, the rest brick. As for windows, there are huge ones down low, smaller ones higher, far too many for Maks to count. Poking out here and there are large balconies. At the top, lots of small roofs with pointy tops and chimneys. One corner of the building is rounded off, like a fortress.

Along the Fifth Avenue side, there's a two-story entryway that sticks over the street. Has a metal awning complete with fancy, curly ironwork. Under it stands a doorman who looks like a guard.

This guy is wearing a long blue coat with double rows of bright brass buttons, glossy black top hat, white gloves on his hands, and spats on his boots. Maks wonders if this guard is there to help folks in or keep them out. Hardly seems big enough to do either.

As Maks stands there trying to get his courage up to go 'cross the street, good-looking horses hauling fancy carriages trot up to the entry. People spill out of the carriages: pale ladies with fine long skirts, furs over their shoulders, big hats with feathers on their heads, lace hiding their eyes. There are gents, too, with dark suits, shiny black hats, cigars in hand, side-whiskers and mustaches—what they call "muck-a-mucks." And servants buzzing 'bout 'em like flies round old meat.

Though Maks sometimes walked with Emma to her job here, knowing he's going inside this time makes it all different. He don't see one newsie, flower girl, or shoeblack. Nobody like himself. Truth is, Maks never felt so small in his life. Everything so far above him, he might as well be jumping the moon. How's he gonna find clues?

From those times he's been with Emma, he knows that people who work in the hotel ain't allowed to go in through the main doors. Got a servants' entrance over on Thirty-third, the one Donck told him to use.

Maks walks round the corner to a driveway. It leads to an open court and the service entrance. Men are unloading food wagons. Other wagons are waiting with piles of trunks.

Then there's the servants' entry and, next to it, a small, high table with another mug in green uniform with a shiny cap. He's checking goods and people going in.

To Maks, the folks here look a lot more regular than the ones going in on Fifth Avenue. Except he notices that none of the men have whiskers or mustaches.

There's a short line of people going in, so Maks tags on

the end. When he reaches the guard, the man looks down at him. "What you want, kid?"

"I need to see Mr. Packwood."

The man stares at Maks as if he don't believe him. "He expecting you?"

"Guess," Maks says.

"What's your name?"

"Maks. Maks . . . Brown."

The guard pulls out papers, flips through them. Maks thinks, *Like The Tombs.*

"All right, fine," the man says, and touches what looks to be a button on the wall behind him. He yanks the door open. "Go inside and sit down."

Maks does what he's told, stepping into a long hallway—so long, he can't see its end. It's wide, with fancy polished wood on the floor, as if no one is supposed to step on it. Walls painted dark red. Electric lights hanging from the ceiling.

There's a wooden bench over which is a sign: JOB SEEKERS SIT HERE. Maks figures that's him, so he sits, remembering to snatch off his hat. Hopes he's not making the bench dirty.

As he's sitting there, the outside door keeps opening. People passing in and out, but they don't pay no mind to Maks.

On the wall opposite where he's sitting there's a large painting with a wooden frame. It's nice to look at, with its hills, trees, flowers, and a river. If this is a picture of Heaven—and Maks thinks it just might be—he's thinking Willa's alley was the other place.

As he gazes at it, Maks can't help thinking 'bout where *he* lives, down on the East Side, their flat on Birmingham Street. The painting makes him think how dirty and run-down it is. Gives him a bad feeling.

Maks sits on that bench long enough to begin worrying that nothing will happen—that being here is a mistake—but then a man comes rushing up to him.

He's young, clean-shaven, neatly dressed, with a smooth jacket and blue tie. "Maks Brown?" he says.

Maks grabs his hat and jumps up. "Yes, sir."

"Here to see Mr. Packwood?"

"Yes, sir."

"This way."

The man walks down the hallway so fast that Maks skips to keep up.

The guy opens a door. Gesturing, he tells Maks to go on.

He steps into a big room with cubbyholes against the walls, low benches in the middle. What looks to be a closet in the back. Couple of men changing their clothes.

The guy who brought Maks into the room points to the back of the room, to that closet.

"Go take a shower."

"Take what?"

"A shower. To get clean. Don't you know what I'm talking about?"

Maks shakes his head.

"Go into that little room. Shut the door. Stand under what looks like a pail and pull the cord that's hanging there. Water will come down. Use soap to clean yourself. Rinse yourself off with more water."

Maks stands there, eyeing the mug. Donck didn't say nothing 'bout this.

"Please do as you're asked."

Maks goes into the little room. It's paneled in wood, with a hook on one wall over a little bench. On the hook a cloth hangs.

He pulls the door shut. Not sure what to do, he looks up and sees what that guy told him would be there: something hanging over his head that looks like a pail with holes in it. Near it a rope hangs down. Maks reaches up and pulls the rope. Cold water pours down.

Shocked, Maks jumps to one side. Now that his clothes are soaked, he peels 'em off, hangs 'em on the hook.

Using a chunk of yellow soap that's there, he scrubs himself. Mutters to himself, "It ain't even Saturday."

Then he reaches up and pulls the rope again. More cold water pours down, washing soap away. Shivering, not knowing what else to do, he gets back into his damp clothing. Steps out into the large room.

The mug who brought him eyes him. "Your clothing is wet," he says.

"Yeah."

The guy smirks and, as if measuring his size, leads Maks to one of the cubbyholes. A suit of dry clothes is hanging on a peg.

"Change into this uniform," the man says. "Leave your own clothing." He walks away but stands by the door, waiting.

Maks does what he's told fast as he can, getting into a uniform. It's dark red, the trousers having a blue streak down the legs and the jacket with shiny metal buttons up front. It's a little big for him, itches, and the collar is tight. But it's clean, smells nice, and is dry. Except for his boots.

He goes back to the man who's waiting for him. The guy looks him over—like he might examine a bug—adjusts one of Maks's buttons, smooths down his hair, then says, "Follow me."

Maks heads out of the room and goes along huge, wide halls. The place is nothing like he's ever seen before. Rugs with pictures hanging on walls. Paintings in fancy frames. Wood carvings everywhere. White stone statues, mostly— Maks don't know what to think—of naked people. There are fancy chairs, huge tables, clusters of electric lights hanging from ceilings, plants in pots. It's all smooth, thick, lush.

Maks always knew there were rich people. But this is more than rich. It's rich times ten—as Agnes might do the math—and even then, Maks ain't sure he's got it right. *This place*, he's thinking, *is a palace.*

And the people! He don't see *one* rich person; he's seeing a *parade* of rich people. Women in fancy long skirts, wide collars, puffy sleeves with jewels on necks and fingers. Big hats. Umbrellas in hand. Men in suits. Coats. Top hats. Derbies. Walking canes with gold grips. Neckties. Spats. Glossy whiskers and mustaches. People talking, talking, and smoking.

Plenty of servants, too, a lot in uniforms, like Maks, moving like lean dogs on long leashes.

An hour ago Maks was in an old, wrecked house, scared to death. Now he's in a world that's flashing money and he has no idea what's gonna happen and he's scared to death all over again—but in a whole new way.

The guy leads Maks up to a glossy wooden door and stops. Maks looks up to him.

"Mr. Packwood is in here," says the mug, and he raps hard on the door.

"Come in!" calls a voice.

Maks, more than a little panicky, feels a push from behind. He hates this Packwood. But if he wants to help Emma, he's got no choice. He opens the door. Steps in.

What's Willa doing?

She stands on the street watching as Maks heads uptown. *He's my friend,* she's thinking, liking the thought. Then she heads back to Birmingham Street. At the apartment she finds Mama on her knees scrubbing shirts in the big tin bucket.

Mama looks up and smiles. "Is everybody safe?" she asks.

"We brought the boys to school," Willa says. "Can . . . can I help you?"

Mama sits back on her legs, pushes hair away from her face with red hands. "That would be good." Looks at the water in her bucket. "I can use fresh water. And once I get these five shirts done, I'm going to visit Emma."

"If you'd like," says Willa, "I'll go with you."

Not waiting for a reply, Willa puts her stick in a corner, takes up two buckets, and carries them down to the backyard. A girl is there, using the pump. Willa waits.

"*Hola*," says the girl.

Willa nods. "My name's Willa. I live on the top floor. With the Geless family."

"*Me llamo Rosa. Vivo en el tercer piso. En la parte de atrás.*" With a quick smile, the girl goes her way, hauling a heavy bucket.

Willa dumps her dirty water on the ground, shoos the chickens away, pumps up water. With a bucket in each hand, pausing on each landing, she carries them back to the rooms.

"It's a long way, isn't it?" says Mama. "Do you know how to do laundry?"

Willa shakes her head.

"Work one shirt at a time, scrub it hard against the washing board. Use that yellow soap. Like this, see? I'll string the drying rope."

Willa balls up her skirt, gets on her knees, reaches into the cold water, and begins to rub a shirt against the washing board. Mama watches. "A little bit more this way," she says, taking a shirt and scrubbing it harder.

Mama ties a length of rope between two chairs. "It's such a filthy city," she says.

After a while she inspects the shirt Willa has been washing. "Good," she says, and hangs it over the line.

The two work silently. Suddenly, Mama says, "I keep thinking about Emma. Did you go into that prison with Maks?"

Willa shakes her head.

"Horrid. *Skraekkelig*, we say in Danish. And she's gonna be on trial. Ah, Willa, a child of mine . . . in prison. And . . . and none of us . . . we're not *doing* anything." She sighs deeply. Reaches up to smear some tears from her eyes.

Willa stares at her.

"When you have children," says Mama, "you'll see." She reaches out and touches Willa's cheek. "The good things that happen to them fill your heart with joy," she says. "The bad things . . . fill it with pain. I sometimes wonder why we give them life. It's hard to give them more."

Willa gazes at her.

"Where did Maks go?" Mama suddenly asks. "Did he tell you? That boy does what he likes."

Willa takes a breath. "He's gone . . . to that Waldorf Hotel. Where . . . Emma worked."

"Why would he go there?"

Willa is silent.

"Ah, Willa. My children often don't tell me things. They think I don't understand. That I'm stupid."

Willa, holding out the last wet shirt to Mama, stands up. "If we sit at the table," she says, "I'll tell you."

When the office door slaps shut behind him, Maks finds himself in a wood-paneled room as fancy as the other places he's already seen in the hotel. Three leather-covered chairs, books on shelves, a big table behind which a man is seated. Maks supposes it's Packwood. He's clean-shaven, wearing a fine frock coat, vest, silk tie.

Standing next to him is a woman. They look somewhat alike. As Maks sees it, the two must have been talking.

The woman is tall, wearing a big, flowered hat over black hair, dressed in clothes, Maks can tell, that must have cost a lot. Though he's sure he ain't never seen her before, she seems familiar. He don't know why.

Both man and woman turn and look at Maks standing there, shoes damp, cold, fidgeting nervously, not knowing what to do.

"Yes?" says the man. "Can I help you?"

"I'm Maks . . . Brown."

"Ah! Bartleby Donck's friend."

The woman starts and stares at Maks.

To Maks, the man says, "You are Emma Geless's brother?"

"Guess I am." Maks can't get himself to say "sir."

"Do you know my name?" asks the man.

"Packwood."

"Exactly. The hotel detective."

"I know," says Maks, pushing down the anger he feels. Balling his fists, he waits for Packwood to speak. Same time, he decides he don't care who the mug is. He ain't gonna let him bully him.

The man gestures to the woman. "This is my sister, Mrs. Winton." Then he says to her, "Maud, I think you'd best go."

The woman says nothing, just keeps staring at Maks. He wishes he knew why. All the same, she leaves the room, full skirts swishing. She smells like flowers.

Packwood studies Maks, takes a long time to say, "A few days ago I arrested *your* sister."

"She didn't steal nothing."

Packwood says, "Loyalty to one's sister is a fine thing. What makes you so sure?"

"She wouldn't."

"Not even for a boyfriend?"

"She don't have no boyfriend."

"How do you know?"

"She tells me everything."

"All?"

"Sure. Don't your sister tell you her secrets?"

Packwood is silent for a few moments. Then he says, "Tell me one of your sister's secrets."

"Wouldn't be a secret if I tells you, would it?"

Packwood smiles. "True enough. But by telling me you might help her."

Maks considers and decides to try. "Well," he says, "a couple of weeks ago she took the El home."

"Why should that be a secret?"

"Costs a nickel, don't it? Shouldn't have done it."

"The reason?"

"My family needs every penny we got. We walk."

"Ah! Anything else?"

Maks thinks. "A week ago she bought a ribbon. A blue one."

"Was *that* for a boyfriend?"

"I just told you, she don't have no particular gent. Just that she shouldn't have spent no money on that, neither."

"Same reason as before?"

"Yeah."

Packwood frowns. Presses his hands together, rests his chin on the tips.

Maks waits. He's wondering if he should tell this guy 'bout Emma being at a dance hall. Decides not to.

"If you know so much," says Packwood, "I assume you know that I found the watch and chain she stole beneath her pillow."

"No, you didn't."

"I beg your pardon."

"You only found the chain."

"How do you know that?"

"Emma told me."

"You've seen her, then?"

"Yeah. In The Tombs. In that cell they put her in."

"How is she faring?"

"You probably don't care, but it's awful. And she's going on trial."

"Indeed. In two days."

"Two?" cries Maks, his heart squeezing.

Packwood nods. "Saturday court."

"You gonna send her to Blackwell's Island?"

"Will the judge? Most likely."

"But she didn't do nothing wrong," Maks says, fighting back tears and struggling not to run off.

Packwood, eyeing Maks, stands and starts pacing behind his desk. "Do you go to school?"

"Used to," Maks scowls.

"No more?"

"Too old. I'm a newsie, ain't I? Need to sell my papers. People like you, you don't understand. My family needs all the money it can get."

"Perhaps that's why your sister took the watch."

"She didn't take nothing!" Maks yells.

Packwood stands still. "Very well. Why did Mr. Donck send you here?"

"Teaching me to be a detective."

Packwood suppresses a smile. "Going to replace me?"

"If I did, I wouldn't go round 'resting no innocent people."

"How well do you know Mr. Donck? Anything about his life? His career as a Pinkerton detective?"

Maks shakes his head.

"Never mind. What does he expect you to do here?"

"Supposed to find evidence that'll prove my sister didn't steal nothing."

"How do you intend to do that?"

"You're the detective, ain't you? You're supposed to tell me."

Packwood stands there, staring at Maks. Then he says, "I'm not doing this for you. Or for your sister. There's only one reason: Mr. Donck. I owe him much. But if, in any way, you do anything wrong, disobey me, cause problems, *anything*, I'll toss you out to the street. Is that perfectly clear?"

"You done it to my sister, so I guess you'd do it to me."

Packwood sighs. "You're wearing the uniform of a bellboy. Which means you'll sit in the main lobby. You'll be asked to do errands. All kinds. Anything a guest might ask. You will do so swiftly, silently, and politely."

"Supposing someone asks me to do something I don't know how to do," Maks says. "I ain't never been here 'fore."

"There's a bench for bellboys. Ask questions of the other boys. They can help. Nearby is the bell captain, Mr. Trevor. He'll instruct you. Is this all understood?"

"Mr. Donck says I'm supposed to find clues. Am I gonna be able to do that?"

"Keep your eyes open," says Packwood. "See if you can learn anything. If you do, inform me. Now come along."

Maks, not moving, says, "Donck says I'm to ask you something."

"Which is?"

"Couple of things. My sister, Emma, told me that some guy—some guest—said he was gonna say something nice 'cause she cleaned his room decent. Donck said I was to ask if he ever did. And if he did, who was the guy."

"Ah."

"Another thing: wants to know the number on that room, the place where that watch was stolen."

"Why?"

"Don't know."

Packwood remains still for a while before saying, "I'll see what I can learn. Now come with me."

Back in the apartment Mama hangs a wet shirt on the line, then sits on one of the chairs. "Is Maks doing something bad?" she asks Willa.

"He's trying to help Emma," says the girl. Then she tells Mama 'bout Mr. Donck, what Maks agreed to do.

Mama listens in silence. Then she says, "Willa, why didn't Maks tell me himself?"

"He's worried you'd say he shouldn't go, and he didn't want to disobey you."

Mama pushes a strand of hair from her face. "It's good we came to America," she says after a moment. "There was nothing back there for us. My husband—Papa—is a boat maker. Back in Denmark he couldn't find work. We thought it would be better in America. Me? I learned English as a laundry girl in an English merchant's house. In Copenhagen. It's not such a big city as here." She leans forward. "Willa, there's so much that's different here. And it's hard when your children know more than you do.

"Like Agnes. Do you know, she wants to marry Monsieur Zulot. I told her, 'You're too young! Just fourteen!' She says, 'But I may not live long.' Then she says, 'Look at Juliet.' I think that's some person she met in one of those classes she takes. But I don't know who this Juliet is. Why would her parents let her do such a thing? Fourteen!"

Mama holds Willa's arm. "Do you think it's right that Maks went to the hotel? Will it help Emma?"

"Hope so."

"When will he come home?"

"Not sure."

Mama is quiet for a while. "Willa, if he didn't want to tell me, why did you?"

"I don't want to lie."

Mama grows thoughtful. "That other day," she says, "did you really save him from a beating?"

Willa nods.

"You're a good person," says Mama, patting Willa's hand. "I like you. I'm glad he brought you home." She's quiet for a moment. "Do you know what I miss most? Here? In America?"

Willa shakes her head.

"*My* mama." After a moment Mama smiles and says, "Do you know what I like best about America?"

Willa waits.

"Coffee. At home it's a rich person's drink. Here everybody drinks it. Even my children."

"Mama," says Willa, "how sick is Agnes?"

"We're not sure. At that place where Agnes goes to night school, someone told her about a doctor who might help. On Mott Street."

"Did she go to him?"

"It costs a great deal. We've been saving. I tried to sell my hair." She smiles. "I couldn't. Too much gray. Imagine being told such a thing! But now, with Emma . . . Willa, if Emma has a trial, what will happen?"

"I don't know."

"Papa says if she's sent to prison, he'll break in, steal her away. Take her back to Denmark." She reaches out and grips Willa's hand. "He and I, we're very frightened."

She looks at the clock. "Ah! We should go to that prison and see Emma. I have more food to bring. I'll iron later. It will be good if she meets you."

It don't take long for the two to set out. Willa has her stick. They walk silently at first.

Then Mama says, "Why do you always take that stick?"

"It keeps me safe," says Willa.

Mama suddenly stops. "Willa, while Maks is at that hotel, who'll sell his papers?"

"I will. Jacob will come with me."

"Did Jacob say he would?"

"Maks told him to."

Mama shakes her head. "Those boys listen to him more than me. Ryker worships him."

They continue to walk. After a while Mama says, "Willa, I don't want you to tell me what you don't want to, but I'd like to know about your family. What happened to them?"

Willa is silent for a long time. Mama waits patiently. Then Willa tells Mama what she told Maks—the death of her mother, the disappearance of her father, adding, "I'm sure he died."

"I'm sorry," says Mama, taking the girl's arm and wrapping it around hers.

"I think . . . ," says Willa, "I think it would be better that way."

"Why?"

"I . . . I don't think he was a good man."

Mama squeezes Willa's arm. "So much is hard. But you have a home with us," she says. "You're welcome to take our name. Geless. It's a good Danish name. I don't even need to know your name."

But Willa says, "Brunswick." She says, "It used to be Brunswick."

Maks follows Packwood this way and that till he comes to what the man calls the "Lobby." Like everything else in the Waldorf, it's huge and fancy, dripping money like Niagara Falls.

Ceilings are wide and high—maybe thirty feet—held up by stone columns and arches. Floors made of colored bits of stone. Chairs with leather seats looking like thrones. Big paintings on walls. Potted ferns and flowers every-where, like an indoor forest.

Every few feet there are boys in the same uniform Maks is wearing. He guesses they're waiting to be asked to do something. They are too. Rich people stop them and

say things like, "Get my handkerchief from my room. . . .
Fetch my luggage. . . . Boy! Deliver this message." Ain't
things Maks knows how to do.

Packwood leads him to a small table with lots of carved
wood. Even has a telephone on it. Maks knows 'bout tele-
phones, what they do, but he has no idea how to use 'em.

"Mr. Trevor," says Packwood to the sour-looking man
at the table, "this is Mr. Brown, our new bellboy."

This Trevor mug sniffs his snooter. "And whom, may
I ask, hired him?"

"I did," says Mr. Packwood.

"Mr. Packwood, I have absolutely no—"

"Just do as I say," snaps Packwood, and walks away.

Mr. Trevor looks Maks over and don't seem pleased at
what he's seeing. "Have you been a bellboy anywhere?" he
asks.

"No, sir."

"Do you know anything about the Waldorf?"

"It's awful big."

Just as Maks is standing there, a gent comes up to the
desk, brushes Maks aside, and says to Trevor, "I'm looking for Mr. Yost. Is he in?" Trevor checks a big paper for
the name, reaches for the telephone. Cranks it. "Mr. Yost,
please."

Into the telephone, he says, "Mr. Yost, someone to see you, sir." To the gent, he says, "He'll be down shortly, sir." The guy goes off.

Trevor glares at Maks. "Go sit over there," he says, pointing to a bench where another bellboy is sitting. Maks is reminded how schoolteachers used to send him out of the room. But he does as he's been told.

"Hey," he whispers to the kid on the bench, "my name is Maks. I'm new here."

"Not supposed to talk," the kid says without even looking at him.

Nothing for it, Maks just sits there, gazing at everything. All he can think 'bout is Emma's trial in two days. Time ain't just tight, it's squeezing all the air out of him. He's tense. How's he gonna get clues just sitting there?

As Maks is sitting there, the kid he's next to is called to do an errand. That leaves Maks alone. Knowing he's gonna be called soon, he's more nervous than ever.

Sure enough, a few moments later he hears, "Boy!"

Maks jumps up and goes to the desk. Mr. Trevor is looking over a big book, running his finger down his list of names.

"Here it is," he says. "Mr. Coogan. Room six twelve." Trevor hands Maks a big key. Attached to it is a short length of chain, linked to an oval metal disk engraved with the number 612.

He says, "The gentleman left a pair of eyeglasses on his bed. Fetch them and bring them here."

"Excuse me, sir," says Maks. "Where is that?"

"Sixth floor."

"Where the steps?"

"Steps? Use the elevator."

Maks looks at him. "What's a . . . L-vator?"

"Good Lord," Mr. Trevor mutters, and stands up. "Come with me."

Maks trots after the bell captain through the lobby, round a corner, and into a hallway. On one side of this high hall are four—he don't know what they are, 'cept they look like cages, with crisscrossing bars on them. Reminds him of the cells in The Tombs.

Even as he's standing there, a tiny room drops in behind the bars. Maks has no idea where it came from.

Inside the little room are people, along with a young man in a hotel uniform. The young man slides the cage bars to one side. The people step out.

Maks, not sure what to do, just stands there.

"Take him to the sixth floor," Mr. Trevor tells the elevator operator, tapping Maks on the back.

Maks, baffled, doesn't move.

"Let's go, boy!" calls the man inside the little room.

Maks steps forward nervously. Soon as he gets into the little room—it's like a big box—the guy slides the gate closed, actually two gates, one outside the room, one inside the room. Grabs a bar sticking out of the wall, shoves it to the right.

With a sudden jerk that makes Maks almost fall, the little room jumps straight up, pushing at the bottom of his feet. The box *clicks* and *clacks*, wobbling slightly, as does the wall in front of him, which Maks can see through the cagelike door. It looks as if it's going down, but he feels like he's going up. *I'm flying!* he thinks.

Maks is so mixed up and shaky, his stomach so topsy-turvy, he's got to put his hand to the wall to keep himself steady.

The operator grins. "First time in an elevator?"

Maks nods. Maybe he shouldn't ever fly.

"The day they opened this place," he says, "back in March, a girl got killed by this elevator."

That don't help.

"You'll get used to it."

The operator shifts the handle, and the little room slows down till, with a sudden jerk, it stops. Reaching out, the young man pulls the inner gate open, then the outer one. Beyond is a hall. Maks can see it's different than the one where he was before.

"Hey, kid, thought you wanted the sixth floor."

"Yes, sir."

"This is it, pal," the man says, and makes a motion with his head that tells Maks he's to move.

Maks steps out of the box. Soon as he does, the L-vator gates shut. As Maks watches it drops away, he don't know where he is or where to go.

Only when Maks looks round does he realizes there's a sign that says FLOOR 6. Sitting under it is a guy wearing a uniform like the one he's got on. "What you looking for?" the guy calls.

Maks holds up the key.

"Six twelve? That way."

Maks starts down a long hallway, which has a whole row of doors. Next to each door is a number. He checks the key he has, and it's nothing to find the door with the same number. Unlocks the door and steps inside.

He can't hardly believe what's there: It's a room so big, Maks could take his family's *three* rooms on Birmingham Street and fit 'em all into this one.

A couple of big, squashy chairs. A telephone on the wall. A fireplace. A gigantic bed heaped with blankets and pillows. Maks figures his whole family could sleep in that bed. It even has a cloth roof over it, held up by four poles, one each corner.

The eyeglasses are right there.

Maks is so amazed, he can't help himself. He wanders, finds another room, smaller than the first. It's bigger than the one where his parents and Agnes sleep, only it has nothing but closets and drawers.

Then there's a bathroom with a window and a bathtub so big, Maks figures it must be for a horse. There's a sink, too, and a white toilet such as Maks has seen in a few places.

Maks knows there are rich people in the world, but what he's seeing astounds him. He's staring so, he's got to remind himself he shouldn't be taking all this time.

He goes back out into the hall, locking the door behind him.

"Find what you want?" the guy sitting by the elevator asks.

Maks holds up the eyeglasses. "Hey," he says, "I'm new here. Can I ask you something?"

"Sure."

"If a guest wants to give you a compliment—you know, to the boss—who'd he give it to?"

The bellboy grins. "You expecting one?"

"Maybe."

"They give it to Mr. Trevor. Or, if you're a chambermaid, to the lady in charge. Miss Foley."

"Thanks," says Maks. "How do I get that L-vator to come back?"

"Push that button."

Maks does, and from somewhere far off, he hears a bell.

Minutes later the caged room pops up, only it's different from the one he came up on. Maks has no idea where that other one went, but he goes down. The trip makes him queasier than going up did.

He brings the eyeglasses to Mr. Trevor. The guy says, "Take them to the Men's Club. Call out the guest's name, Mr. Coogan. He should be there."

By asking a couple of bellboys for directions, Maks finds the place quick enough. Turns out the Men's Club is a gigantic room, full of tables and chairs, three big fireplaces with logs burning in them. A bunch of chandeliers with fringes. A big, square bar where they're serving drinks.

Being morning, it ain't very crowded. Just a few customers are smoking cigars, reading papers. Waiters weaving among the tables serving food. Each table is topped with a placard reading:

Supper: Steak, Potatoes, Bread & Butter

83¢

Expensive.

In his best, loud newsie's voice, Maks shouts, "Mr. Coogan!"

A man lifts his hand. Maks gives him the eyeglasses.

"Thanks, boy." To Maks's surprise, the guy gives him a ten-cent tip. That's more than he makes selling papers most afternoons. He's thinking, *This ain't half bad.*

Feeling pretty good, he turns toward the door. That's when he sees Willa's father.

When Willa and Mama reach The Tombs, they get their entry tickets and make their way to Emma's cell. Soon as they get there, Emma hurries up to the bars. Her first words are, "Mama, they're gonna put me on trial in two days." She so upset, she's out of breath.

"*Two days?* God have mercy! Are you sure? Where?"

"Here. In The Tombs. Saturday. Is Papa finding a lawyer?"

"I don't know what Papa will do," says a flustered Mama. She pulls Willa close. "You need to meet Willa. She's Maks's friend. She's living with us now. She can tell you what Maks is doing."

Emma turns to Willa. Too upset to care 'bout the girl, all she says is, "Is Maks getting that detective to help?"

"Mr. Donck told Maks what to do. He's at the Waldorf right now."

"What's he doing there?"

"He's trying to find things to help you. And I'm supposed to ask you a question."

"What?" Emma says with frustration.

"You told Maks a man said nice things to you at the hotel."

Emma turns away. "Mama, what does it matter? This isn't gonna help me!"

Willa persists. "Mr. Donck wants to know what room you were cleaning—where the man spoke to you."

"Why?"

"I'm not sure," Willa admits.

"I don't know." Thinking hard, Emma says, "Maybe nine twelve. Yeah, that's it. Room nine twelve. Is that what he needs to know?"

"I think so," says Willa. Feeling dismissed, she steps back. "I'll tell him."

"Emma," says Mama, "I brought some food."

Emma begins to talk to Mama in Danish. Willa, not wanting to be in the way, goes and stares over the balcony at the people milling down below. "Nine twelve," she tells herself. "Nine twelve." She needs to tell Donck.

As Willa and Mama walk back to the tenement, neither of them talks much. It's Mama who says, "It's terrible. She didn't do anything. Going to prison. Willa . . . do you think your . . . detective can help?"

"I'll tell Donck what Emma said."

When they get back to the tenement rooms, Willa leans her stick in a corner while Mama cuts her a piece of bread. Seated at the table, Mama, all upset, begins to describe to Willa what her life was like in Denmark, the family who's still there, her own mother. "Sometimes I think we should go back. Lots do."

Willa tries to listen but keeps glancing up at the clock. Close to noon, she stands up.

"I think I better go to Mr. Donck," she says. "Then I'll get Jacob so we can do Maks's papers."

"Tell that Mr. Donck he must help Emma. Promise him money. I don't know how, but we'll find a way."

Willa goes to the cigar box and gets the newspaper pennies, puts them in her dress pocket.

Mama asks, "Are you going to bring Eric and Ryker home?"

Willa, glancing again at the clock, thinks for a moment. "If it's all right, it would be better if Jacob and I went right to the newspaper place."

"That's fine. I'll iron the shirts, then fetch the other boys," says Mama. "They always like that. You don't know when Maks will get home, do you?"

Willa shakes her head.

As she walks uptown, Willa keeps thinking of Maks and what he might be doing. It's only when she's gone seven blocks that she remembers: She's left her stick behind. Worried about time—seeing Donck, fetching Jacob, getting the papers, selling them—she looks up and down the street to see if there's any danger. Seeing none, she keeps walking.

I'll be all right.

Back to Maks.

The man who Maks is staring at, the one who looks like Willa's father, is sitting at a table with two other people. Maks knows one of them for sure: It's Joe Gorker, the big political boss whose face is peppered all over *The World*. The guy the paper is always thumping, 'specially now that he's been accused of stealing city money and is 'bout to go on trial. Even as Maks watches, the guy's reading the paper and frowning.

The other person at the table is a woman. She's dressed

in fancy clothing, complete with a big hat. A veil covers her eyes. It's hard for Max to know which man she's with.

But the mug Maks keeps looking at is the one who looks so much like the face on Willa's family photograph. Fact, it's such a shock, Maks can't believe it *is* him.

Hey, Willa told him she thought her father was dead. Maks has this creepy feeling he's looking at a ghost. Which is to say, he don't really believe what he's seeing. *Who is this guy? Why's he here? He a guest at the hotel? A visitor? Why's he with Joe Gorker? Who's the woman? Who's she with? What's going on?*

As the questions pop, Maks keeps gawking at the man, scared to think what he's thinking: *This ain't right. This don't work!*

Next moment, the man turns round, so Maks can't see his face no more.

Maks circles round the room to get another look. Same time, he's trying to remember the picture Willa showed him—trying to match it with this man's mug.

When Maks gets to the other side of the room, he stares at the guy. He sure looks the same. And Maks ain't got no doubt, whoever he is, he's cozy with Joe Gorker.

Same time, Maks keeps telling himself it *can't* be Willa's father. He's dead. Must be someone who just *looks* like that picture of Willa's father.

Flustered, Maks takes himself back to the hotel lobby, tells Mr. Trevor he delivered the eyeglasses. The bell captain gives him nothing but a nod, sends him back to the bench.

Maks is glad he's sitting there so he can try to figure out what seeing the guy who looks like Willa's father means. Keeps telling himself he's probably wrong, that he's making a mistake. Because if it is Willa's father—what she gonna do?

Then he starts asking himself if he should tell her what he seen or not? *It don't seem right to say, "Hey, Willa, guess what? I seen your dead pa today. Over at the Waldorf. He's with this crook, Joe Gorker. And a lady."*

See, Maks is also thinking, *what if it ain't him?* Be awful to tell her when it ain't.

So Maks decides 'fore he says something, he's got to be sure it's Willa's father. Thing is, the only way he can be sure is by looking at that picture of Willa's family again. Course, that picture is back home, in Willa's tin box. And Maks has to stay at the Waldorf.

Next moment, he reminds himself he's really here for Emma and her trial is in two days! *Gotta stay. Gotta find something to help her.*

He's being yanked two ways at once. Same time, he ain't moving anywhere.

On Delancey Street, Willa makes her way to Donck's rooms. Knocks on his door. As usual, no answer. After a few moments she pushes the door open. The rooms are as cluttered and dirty as ever.

She goes up to the dim, front room and looks in. Donck is bent over his desk, writing. Every once in a while he puts a cloth to his mouth. It's spotted with red.

Willa waits for him. Finally, she says, "Mr. Donck?"

He keeps writing.

"Mr. Donck?" she shouts.

The detective looks round. "Ah, you!" he says, throwing down his pen. Then he aims his listening tube at her. "Have you learned something?"

"You wanted me to ask Maks's sister a question."

"And?"

"It's the room number, at the Waldorf, the one where Maks's sister got a compliment."

Donck coughs and pats his mouth with a rag. Says, "I'm listening."

"It's number nine twelve."

Donck just stares at her.

"The other thing is," Willa continues, "she's going on trial in two days."

"Two days!" he cries.

"Yes, sir."

"Then we had better hope your brother finds something," says the detective, and he turns back over his papers and continues with his writing.

Willa watches him. "Mr. Donck?" she says. "Are you writing 'bout Emma?"

Donck shakes his head. "Your Emma is real. What I write is nonsense."

Willa waits for him to say something more. When he don't, she shouts, "Do you need me to do anything else?"

"Nothing. We must wait and see if Maks finds something."

Frustrated, Willa leaves the room.

She heads back downtown, head crowded with worries. She's thinking 'bout Emma and Donck, 'bout selling the papers. Keeps wondering, too, what Maks is doing, if he's found anything to help Emma.

By the time she gets to the school, Jacob is waiting for

DONCK

her outside. He gives Willa a big smile and asks, "Where'd Maks go?"

"He's at the Waldorf."

"What's he doing there?"

"Trying to help Emma."

"How?"

"Not sure."

As they walk toward Newspaper Row, Jacob looks up at Willa and says, "You really gonna live with us now?"

She nods.

"What happened to your mother and father?"

"They died."

"Sorry. But you know what?"

"What?'

"Glad you're living with us."

Willa takes his hand.

Willa and Jacob reach the area behind *The World* building. Right off, a few of the guys ask Jacob where Maks is.

Jacob lets Willa answer.

"He had to do something," she says.

When the bell rings and the newspapers are set out, Jacob and Willa stand in line with the other newsies.

Willa taps the shoulder of the boy in front of her. "What's the headline?"

"Pretty good," says the kid. "'Ship Fire on the Hudson. Boat Sinks. Three People Drown.'"

When Willa and Jacob get to the table where the papers are bundled, the man looks at Jacob and says, "Where's Maks?"

"Had to do something," Jacob says, looking to Willa. "We're gonna sell 'em."

"Got your money?"

Willa dumps the pennies into the scale bowl. The man checks the weight, rakes the coins with his fingers, slides the papers over. Willa wraps two arms round the heavy bundle, then she and Jacob head uptown.

"Can you read headlines?" Willa asks him.

"Not really. Can you?"

Willa shakes her head.

"Don't worry. That kid told us," Jacob says.

"Let's figure out the shout," says Willa.

They reach Maks's corner. This time it's Jacob who

sits down on the pickle store steps, half the newspapers by his side.

Willa stands on the corner, tries to remember just how Maks does it. She calls, "Extra! Extra! Read all 'bout it! 'Ship Fire on the Hudson. Boat Sinks. Three People Drown.' Read it in *The World*! The world's greatest newspaper. Just two cents!"

At first Willa finds it hard even to be loud. And she wishes she'd paid more attention to how Maks hustles his bundle. But as the afternoon goes on, she gets louder, stronger, better. One by one, the papers sell.

It's close to five o' clock when Willa suddenly sees Bruno. Not even sure where he came from. He's just there. With his gang. Instant she sees him, she remembers she don't have her stick.

"Jacob!" she cries. "Come here!"

The boy jumps up and runs to her side. "What is it? What's the matter?"

It's too late. The two of them are quickly surrounded by Bruno and Plug Uglies.

"Where's your boyfriend?" Bruno shouts.

"None of your business."

"Yes, it is," says Bruno. "Grab them papers," he says to one of the gang.

One of the mugs steps forward, snatches the remaining copies of *The World* from Willa, scatters 'em. Pages flutter like busted birds.

"Help!" screams Willa. "Help!"

But remember how we started with this story, how city kids' doings is for kids? Far as passing people know, that's what's here.

So no one helps.

Bruno grips Willa by the neck, squeezing tight. When she kicks at him, he hits her hard, stunning her. Then he shoves a hand into her dress pocket, ripping it, but scooping out most of the coins she's earned. Some pennies scatter. One of the other Plug Uglies has a bag. Bruno dumps in the coins.

Jacob throws himself at Bruno, only to be knocked to the pavement.

They start dragging Willa away.

Bruno looks back and yells at Jacob, "Tell Maks to come and get her! He knows where!"

A frantic Jacob jumps up, runs after the gang, only to be knocked down again. He's hit so hard, he's groggy. When he shakes his head clear and looks to see where they took Willa, she's gone.

Sobbing, Jacob goes back to Maks's corner, searches

for fallen pennies. Finds four. Clutching them in his hand, still crying, he races for home.

Up at the Waldorf Hotel, Maks ain't having much fun running errands for rich people. He's stunned by what these people can't do for themselves. "Boy! Get my shoes shined. . . . Boy! Bring these flowers to my room. . . . Boy! Help me find my suitcase."

At one point Mr. Trevor tells him to go to the girls' dormitory to give a message to Miss Foley concerning extra blankets for room seven seventeen. That's an errand Maks is happy to do, hoping he can speak directly to the lady 'bout Emma. He just might find a clue.

The girls' dormitory is a big, dull, gray room in a basement area. When Maks reaches it, seems as if no one is there. As he looks 'bout, he realizes this must be where the servant girls sleep. Emma, too, he supposes. Nothing fancy, maybe a hundred narrow beds, each of 'em with a thin mattress, a gray blanket, small pillow. Under the beds are wooden boxes in which Maks supposes the girls keep their belongings. The beds are all the same, 'cept each one has a tag attached to it with a girl's name.

Maks walks about, wondering if Emma's name is there. Finds it fast enough. When he looks at it, he's reminded of where she is now, which makes him feel bad.

Maks finds Miss Foley in her own little room, set off from the dormitory. A big, plump lady, she's working on some ledgers.

Standing in her open door, he says, "Miss Foley?"

She looks up. "Yes?" she says, not too smiley.

Maks gives her Mr. Trevor's message 'bout the blankets. Then he says, "Miss Foley, he also wants to know if a girl by the name of Emma Geless got a compliment from a guest."

Miss Foley's brow furrows. She says, "Be so good as to remind Mr. Trevor that that's the girl who was arrested."

Maks, trying not to react, keeps standing there.

"I suppose the police are asking," says the woman. "Mr. Packwood asked me the same thing. You can tell Mr. Trevor that, far as I know, the girl received nothing in the way of a compliment." She sniffs. "I'm not surprised. Not a bit."

Eyeing Emma's old bed as he leaves, Maks goes back to the bellboy bench in the lobby.

The rest of his day is spent running errands and sometimes thinking of Emma, sometimes thinking 'bout that man, Willa's father—if it is him. Maks hopes he'll catch sight of him again, but he don't.

Mostly, he's wishing he could find something for Emma, but all he has is what Miss Foley told him. Keeps puzzling why that guy would say he was gonna report something nice 'bout Emma then not do it.

He has no answers. Not to anything.

It's pretty near seven in the evening when that Trevor guy calls Maks to his desk, tells him he can go home. "Be here on time tomorrow," he warns.

Maks is glad to leave. And by now he knows his way back to Mr. Packwood's room, where he knocks on the door.

"Ah, Mr. Geless. How did you get along?"

"Fine."

"Learn anything to help your sister?"

"Don't think so. You get any answers to Mr. Donck's questions?"

"You mean, someone extending a compliment to your sister?"

Maks nods.

"I asked the ninth-floor supervisor—that's where your sister worked. No compliment was given to her. Nor to Miss Foley, or, for that matter, to Mr. Trevor. Tell Mr. Donck if you wish. As for the room number where the theft took place: nine twelve."

"Nine twelve," Maks repeats. "Think Donck can do anything with that?"

"I have no idea. He's a clever man."

Maks keeps standing there.

After a moment Packwood says, "I'm sorry to disappoint you."

"Me too," says Maks, and he backs out of the room.

Outside the office, he tries to decide if Packwood's answers are good or bad. Has no idea. All the same, he knows that he needs to tell Donck the answers. And that Emma's trial is in less than two days. It's getting to be no time left.

Maks makes his way back to the men's changing room, pulls off his hotel uniform, and gets back into his own clothes, which are still damp. When he's in that room, he counts his tip money. Ninety-five cents! That's a whole lot of money for Maks. Can't wait to give it to Papa. Fact, he starts thinking, *Maybe I should keep this job. Let Jacob sell papers.*

When Maks leaves the hotel, it's dark. Streetlamps are on. But he gotta get to Donck's place before he can look at that picture of Willa's family. Knowing the walk downtown is gonna take an hour, and being chilly, he starts off fast.

After a few steps Maks stops. *Maybe that guy asked Emma her name so he could learn it. But why would he do that?*

Then Maks decides that since he has all that tip money in his pocket—money he don't usually have—he could take the El. Get there a lot faster.

Turning east, he finds a train station on Second Avenue and Thirty-fourth Street.

Trouble is, he's never been on the El before. So what Maks does is watch what people do. Then he buys a ticket from a man in a booth, and making sure he's waiting near the steps that'll take him to the downtown side, he stands where other people are waiting by a gatekeeper.

Ain't long 'fore a train pulls in, wheels and driving rods churning, smoke pouring from its stack, engine leaking steam.

"Downtown train!" shouts the gateman, flipping up the gate.

Like everyone else, Maks drops his ticket into the gateman's glass box and rushes onto one of the three crowded cars. No empty seats, so he holds the pole set from ceiling to floor.

With a whistle blast, the train jerks forward. Maks never moved so fast in his life. Fifteen miles an hour! It's like that elevator he was on—only instead of going up and down, it's going flat. City lights whiz by as fast as shooting stars. Makes Maks feel giddy, but he loves the feeling.

The train goes along at a third-floor level, so even if Maks didn't want to, he's looking into lit-up tenement rooms. In a few places, people have even put their names in the windows so he knows who's living there.

Names.

That guy asked Emma for her name. If you wanted to put that watch chain under her pillow, you could find it easy: Emma's name is on her bed.

A train guard calls out the station stops: "Twenty-third Street! . . . Eighteenth! . . . Fourteenth! . . . Eighth!" Every time the train stops, doors crank open. People get on or off.

When Maks reaches the station nearest Donck's place, he jumps off, goes down to the street, and walks to the detective's rooms. As he goes, he has new thoughts: *Miss Foley's room is off to one side. When I walked through the dormitory, no one even noticed me. Maybe it was the same for the real thief.*

Maks gets to the detective's door. It's open, with a little light coming from the front. Even so, it takes a minute for him to see Donck. The guy is leaning back in his chair, mouth open, a thread of blood slipping down his chin.

Maks gasps: *He's dead.*

"Mr. Donck?" he shouts. "Mr. Donck?"

With a start, Donck lurches up, putting eyeglasses on with shaky hands, then fumbling with his listening tube, which he sets into his ear. "Who's that?"

"It's me. Maks. The kid you're teaching to be a detective."

Donck looks at Maks for a long minute. "Ah, yes," he says, rubbing his face as though to wake himself up. "Your sister was here."

"Willa?"

"She told me your sister Emma is going on trial on Saturday."

"I know. You gonna be able to help her?"

"Have you learned anything?"

"Did what you told me: went to the Waldorf."

"And?"

"It's rich."

"Pha! I know that."

"But the cleaning girls' dormitory is ordinary."

"I don't care. Just tell me if you've learned anything to help your sister."

"I asked Packwood those questions you told me."

Donck leans back in his chair. Shuts his eyes. "Go on."

"My sister—Emma—she never got that compliment from that guy who said he'd give her one. And the room where the watch was taken—"

Donck holds out his hearing tube. "Loudly."

"It was nine twelve."

Donck sits up, eyes wide open. "*Nine twelve?* You're quite certain?"

"Yes, sir. What Packwood said. Nine twelve. That help any?"

"Nine twelve," Donck says again, dropping back in his chair.

"And . . . and I thought of something else."

"Thinking is always useful."

"That dormitory I was trying to tell you 'bout—where the cleaning girls sleep—they got name tags on all the beds. And guess what? They left Emma's name tag on the bed she was sleeping in."

"Why should that matter?"

"See, that guy told Emma he was gonna say something nice for her."

"So?"

"Well, if he knows her name, he could have found her bed in the girls' dormitory. Easy."

"How?"

"Just said: Every bed has a name tag on it."

Donck is now sitting straight up, staring at Maks. "But surely," he says, "people were there. A stranger coming into the girls' dormitory—if it was a stranger—would be noticed."

"What I'm trying to say. When I went in, nobody was there. I mean, the woman in charge—Miss Foley—her office is off some. So when I went in, I was alone."

"But how would the thief know your sister's name?"

"Told you! Emma said that guy asked her for it."

"Did he?"

"Yeah. And see, her bed had that tag. That help?"

Donck closes his eyes. Rubs his chin. "Perhaps. Yes. You're smart. Very smart."

"I am?"

Maks waits for Donck to explain why he thinks he's smart. But when Donck don't, Maks says, "Want me to go back to the Waldorf tomorrow?"

"Yes."

"You got more questions for Packwood?"

"Not questions. The watch. Tell him to keep looking for the watch. I believe it's in the hotel. Somewhere."

"How come you think that?"

Maks waits. But all Donck does is pull out his ear tube, bend over his desk, pick up a pen, and begin writing fast.

Maks says, "Want me to stay or go?"

Donck keeps writing.

Maks, thinking this is the oddest mug he's ever met, can't do anything but leave.

Maks walks toward home. He's discouraged, frustrated. Emma's trial is in two days! But maybe he did something to help. Tries to think why Donck said he was smart. Can't figure it out. *Just making fun,* he supposes.

Least, he tells himself, he didn't do too bad at the Waldorf. Actually had some nice things happen, like riding the elevators, the El. And something stupid—that shower. Still, he got all that tip money, only spent a nickel. Almost feels like a swell. Ninety cents gonna help.

As usual, the Lower East Side is dark, cluttered, smelly. Not so crowded as daytime, maybe, but still lots of people on the streets. But somehow things don't seem right to Maks. He's noticing how poorly people are dressed. How tired they look. Not so happy, neither.

As Maks walks on, he becomes aware of the rip under one arm of his jacket. Notices that he's tired too. And the rows of drab tenement houses make him think of tombstones with windows. Even the plodding horses, heading for their stables, look exhausted.

That's me, thinks Maks. *Like them horses. Ready to go into a tombstone.*

Never had such feelings before.

Next moment, he scolds himself for thinking that way.

Hey, this is my neighborhood. Up there, the Waldorf, that ain't home. This is where I'm supposed to be. I'm down here. Live here. Work there.

Maks struggles to put his thoughts to Willa and the man who looked like her father. Sitting with that Joe Gorker and the lady, he appeared rich too.

What's going on?

Once again Maks tells himself he better be sure before telling Willa anything. And he's gotta tell his parents that Emma's trial is in two days. The thought makes him ache. Everyone's gonna go crazy.

Hands in his pockets, feeling his coins, Maks turns onto Birmingham Street and looks up. Sees someone leaning against the streetlamp.

A Plug Ugly.

Maks scoots back round the corner, then steals a look. Between the light coming from the lamp and the light seeping from the saloon at the bottom of his own building, he sees that there are two of 'em.

Maks has no doubt they're wanting to grab him.

He tries to think what to do. Other nights when he saw 'em—looking down from his front room—they left after a while. So Maks tells himself he could wait. That'd be the best, safest thing to do. But he really wants to get home. The later he is, the more worried everybody's gonna be. He needs to tell everybody 'bout Emma's trial. And he wants to look at Willa's picture. It's all burning him.

Maks stands in a dark spot at the end of the street, watching. As he sees it, the Plug Uglies are talking to each other more than they're keeping guard.

Maks figures if he can get close, make a fast run, really fast, he should be able to shoot right by 'em and get into the house 'fore they even know it's him.

Thing is, he needs to be a lot closer.

Staying on his side of the street, keeping to dark patches and shadows, Maks goes forward in little bits.

The Plug Uglies don't seem to notice.

Maks keeps edging on, creeping closer to the stoop.

Then one of the guys turns and seems to be staring right at him. Maks, heart pounding, hardly breathing, freezes like a hunk of ice. When the Plug Ugly turns away, Maks starts sneaking forward again.

Maks don't have no plan when to make a move. Just all of a sudden, he *knows* it's right. Shoots like a Fourth of July rocket, tearing toward his house. Hits the stoop just as the Plug Uglies realize it's him.

"Hey!" one of them yells. "You! We got—"

Maks yanks the front door open, leaps inside, races up the steps. In moments he's standing in front of his apartment door, breathing hard but safe.

Soon as he catches his breath, he opens the door and walks in.

The whole family—Mama, Papa, Agnes, the boys, even Monsieur Zulot—is in the kitchen. They all look right at him, wide-eyed. Jacob is crying. And it's Jacob who, soon as he sees Maks, calls out, "Maks! Willa got kidnapped."

"Kidnapped?" Maks cries. "What are you saying?"

"When she and Jacob were selling your papers," says Papa.

Agnes says, "Jacob said it was some redheaded guy."

Maks stares at Jacob. "Bruno?"

"And some big boys," adds Ryker. "They grabbed Willa."

Mama says, "We've been out trying to find her."

"Only we don't understand where to look," says Monsieur Zulot.

Maks, trying to grasp what's happened, drops to his knees, holds Jacob's shoulders with both hands, looks into his face. "Tell me everything!"

Jacob takes a deep, weepy breath, says, "We were just there . . . selling papers . . . sold most of them . . . when this guy . . . he had red hair—"

Maks nods. "Bruno."

Jacob brushes tears away. "He and a bunch of other

guys surrounded us . . . threw down the papers that were left . . . took Willa's money . . . and though she was screaming at them, fighting, kicking . . . I tried to help her, Maks, I really did . . . but they knocked me down . . . then they took her away."

"Where?"

"I don't know. I really tried—"

"Which direction they going?"

"Uptown."

"Why would they do such a thing?" says Mama.

Maks can't begin to answer. Besides, he's trying to decide what to do. That's when he notices Willa's stick standing in a corner.

Jacob reaches over and tugs on Maks's jacket. "Maks," he says, "that redheaded guy shouted at me, said—"

"What?"

"Said, 'Tell Maks to come and get her. He knows where.' That's all he said. I'm sorry."

"What will they do with her?" Agnes asks.

"Should we go to the police?" says Mama.

But from what Jacob just said, Maks knows exactly where they took Willa: to the house, that old house, where the Plug Uglies live. Where he saw Bruno that morning. Where Bruno saw him. Where he should never have gone.

'Cause Maks knows, sure as anything, that's why Bruno done what he did.

Maks stands up. Everybody's looking at him, waiting for him to say something. But Maks—furious, upset, scared for Willa—is trying to think what to do. It don't take him long.

He snatches up Willa's stick. Even as he does, he hears the jingling of coins in his pocket—the tips from the Waldorf. Knowing there's too much to lose, he runs over, grabs his cigar box.

Opening the box, he flips in the coins. When he does, he sees Willa's blue tin. Don't matter what's happening. He has to know 'bout that man he saw.

He snaps the tin open. There are two things inside: a gold ring and that picture. Maks snatches up the picture and stares at it.

The guy he saw at the Waldorf: It's Willa's father.

Maks flips the picture back, puts the cigar box back on the shelf.

"I'm gonna get her," he says, and he's out the door 'fore anyone can say anything.

But clattering down the steps, he hears Papa calling, "Maks! Wait! Where you going? Don't go alone."

Maks don't stop.

He gets to the front door and almost opens it, when he suddenly remembers: Plug Uglies are out there. Now he understands what they're doing: want to drag him off to where Willa's at. Only that ain't the way he's going.

He spins 'bout, races back up the stairs to the top floor. Goes farther, tearing up the extra steps to the roof. In seconds he's there, popping out of the small shed that covers the roof steps. Rushes over to the low, front wall of his building, leans out, and peers down. Plug Uglies still there.

Backing away, Maks stuffs his cap into a pocket, grips Willa's stick tight, then scrambles from rooftop to rooftop, the buildings being pretty much at the same level, with no gaps 'tween them. The last one has a fire escape.

After twelve, thirteen buildings, Maks reaches the last roof, the corner house. He looks for the fire escape, finds it, climbs over the low wall. He's on the topmost part of an escape.

Feet planted on the rusty iron ladder rungs, he starts

climbing down, going floor level to floor level, fast as he can. When he reaches the final, bottom ladder, he's eight feet off the ground.

Maks peers down, trying to see where he'll land, not wanting to be seen or heard.

Checks the street. Plug Uglies ain't looking in his direction.

Maks lets himself drop.

The second he hits the ground, he slaps on his cap, grips Willa's stick, starts running. And he knows exactly where he's going.

It's close to ten thirty when Maks reaches Newspaper Row, the back of *The World* building. When he gets there, he finds—what?—sixty, seventy newsies under the feeble yard night-light. Some are sleeping. Others sitting round talking. A few playing cards, dice. Someone is tooting a tin whistle. All dull drowsy till he roars in.

"Hey, mugs!" he shouts. "You gotta listen! My friend

Willa—you met her, right? Who beat off the Plug Uglies. She was doing my papers this afternoon. With my brother, Jacob. Bruno and his gang grabbed her, stole her money, dumped her papers. Kidnapped her!"

The newsies, his buddies, his pals, they wake up, pop up, sit up, stand up. And if they're not up on their own, Maks pulls 'em up.

"That you, Maks? What you say? They got who? What's happened?"

Maks jumps on the table where they dump the newspaper bundles.

"Listen!" he cries. "I'm pretty sure they got Willa in a house up under the Second Avenue El. Near the Rivington station. It's where Bruno's gang lives. If we get there fast, we can fix 'em good. Won't be able to bully us no more. Only we gotta move right now!"

Maybe the newsies were bored. Maybe they got nothing better to do. Maybe they just needed someone to flash their fire. But the newsies get excited. "Yeah! Show us where! Let's go! We can get 'em."

Maks barely finishes hawking when he's heading uptown. Only this time he's leading an army of newsies. Moving fast, a parade on the run. As they go, guys find sticks, rocks, cobblestones. Anything they can lug.

On the street, people stop to watch 'em pass. Some even follow. Maks don't care. Only thing he don't want is the police showing up making 'em halt. Mostly, though, what he's thinking is, *Bruno better not hurt Willa.*

Not that he exactly knows what they're gonna do when they get there. Just knows they're going to do it. And by now they're racing under the Second Avenue El, going faster than before.

And pretty soon there they are. Bruno's place.

It's dark under the El. The single streetlamp throws out as much light as a fading firefly. Overhead, a train clatters by, dropping spits of sparks. The Shirt Tail is still open, but just a couple of people are at the bar. Some window light comes from that newer tenement building.

'Tween the saloon and the tenement is the old boarded-up house, the place where Maks is sure the gang's staying. Where they have Willa.

Maks remembers: In the morning when he saw Bruno

in the old house, there was an oil lamp. Since he's seeing a little fluffing light coming through chinks in the building's old walls, he figures the gang must be inside.

Maks is glad for the light. Not just 'cause it's telling him the Plug Uglies are probably in there, but it's hard fighting in the dark. Anyway, he has to find Willa.

"This is it!" he yells. "Here!"

The newsies, like riled rats, are milling round the front of the old building, sticks and stones in hand. The bricks weigh nine pounds. Cobblestones—which are granite—heavier.

Soon as Maks tells 'em this is the place, the guys don't wait. "Get 'em! Smash 'em! Collar 'em!" they're yelling, shouting, screaming.

The ones with sticks start beating on the old house like it's a drum. The ones with stones and bricks start hurling 'em 'gainst the building. The booming sounds like General Grant's cannons: *Thump! Slam! Crack!*

"Watch that little alley!" Maks shouts. "They may try getting out." Maks don't know if they will, but he's hoping some of his guys squeeze that way.

Meanwhile, a bunch of the newsies—and that includes Maks—are attacking the boarded-up front door. Others go after the first level of blocked windows.

The flying cobblestones and bricks crush and splinter the old wood. With the stones' weight, it don't take long 'fore holes are punched right through the building. One of the window boardings splinters. The front door caves. Soon as it does, the newsies pour inside, Maks right up front, Willa's stick in hand.

Inside, as Maks figured, there's that oil lamp burning, so he can see a bit. What's he see? That first floor, which once must have had two, maybe three rooms, is now one big space. Walls busted out. Floorboards bulging. The ceiling bowed, looking like it's ready to drop. There's a staircase going up, but steps are missing.

Maks don't see Willa. But the Plug Uglies are there. They're backed up—Bruno in the middle—into a corner, as far from the invasion as they can get. They're looking scared, shocked, and muddled, with eyes like slices of cold potatoes.

The newsies are screaming and swearing, cursing and calling, wanting revenge for what the gang done to them. In they go, slamming and smashing with fists, sticks, stones.

The Plug Uglies fight back. There's pushing, punching, kicking, tumbling, everyone yelling and screaming, with enough cursing to peel off whatever paint is left on the walls. It's a bursting bedlam in there.

———

The fight ain't one-sided neither. Some of the good guys get smacked, hard. Mostly, though, the Plug Uglies— that includes Bruno—are just trying to get out and away. It's the alley fight all over again. Only bigger.

And with everyone running all over the place, the burning oil lamp crashes over. Flaming oil splashes the floor. The old, dry wood bursts into flame as if it's been waiting to burn for ten million years. Within seconds, flames are roaring and crackling, filling the space with billowing smoke.

People start shouting. "Fire! Fire! Get out! Get out!"

That kills the brawl. Everybody—newsies and Plug Uglies both—frantic to reach safety, are bolting through doors, windows, any way they can get out.

Maks still hasn't seen Willa. But with the flames spreading, only one place to go. He races for the steps, heads up, watching where he's going 'cause not all the steps are there. All he's thinking is, *Where's Willa?*

Bruno, seeing right away it's a losing fight, knows he has to run. Course, he's got to knock down three newsies just to get out the hole in the side of the house and into the gap. Once there, he dashes toward the street. Reaching the entryway, he sticks out his head only to see a tangle of pushing, shoving guys.

The second he takes a step out, someone spots him.

"Bruno!" comes a shout. "There he is! Get him!"

Ducking a brick, Bruno charges back down the alley. Avoiding the house, he races to the far end of the alley. There, separating that tenement building from the saloon building, is a very narrow opening. Desperate, Bruno squeezes into the space.

Shouts of "Fire! Fire!" come from behind him.

Startled, he steps out and peers around. Sees flame and smoke pouring out of the wood building. Frightened, he jumps back into the gap. Moving sideways—barely room for even that—he squeezes himself 'tween the rough walls, scraping elbows and face, till he comes out the other side of the tenement.

He gives a quick look back to be sure he's not being chased. Then he races 'long the side of the building till he reaches the Bowery. Heading uptown fast as he can, he's moving farther and farther away from fight and fire.

Maks gets to the second floor. Soon as he does, he sees Willa. They lashed her hands together, tied her to the remains of a busted bed.

"Maks!" she cries, laughing and crying at the same time.

Maks runs over to her. Using teeth and fingers, he works to get the rope knots undone.

"How did you know I was here?" Willa's saying. "What's happening? Is the whole building on fire?"

By now the smoke is creeping up through the stairwell, up through the cracks in the floor. It's hot, getting hotter. Becoming hard to breathe.

Maks frees one of Willa's hands so she can work the other knot. He darts back to the steps to see if they can get down that way. The lower steps are burning. Nothing but flames.

Willa pulls the last knot loose.

Maks races to one of the front windows, tries to yank out the boards that cover it. When he can't do it that way, he starts whacking at them with Willa's stick, then kicking at them, till he finally knocks the boards out.

But when he does that, he causes a fierce, chimneylike wind. Flames roar up the steps. The floor starts to burn.

"Come on!" Maks yells to Willa.

Willa runs to the window. She and Maks look out and down to the street. His newsie pals are there, plus lots of gawkers. Maks is trying to decide if they can safely jump to the ground. Seems awful far.

Even as he's trying to decide what to do, firemen come down the street. First to arrive is a hook and ladder wagon, hauled by three galloping horses. Then a pump steamer comes—steel and nickel-plated iron, loaded with rubber hose—smoke chuffing from the steam engine that works the pumps, bells clanging. Firemen—in leather hats, rubber coats and boots—running right alongside.

Willa and Maks are yelling and calling from the window. "Hey! Help! We're up here! Here!"

Flames are moving 'cross the floor toward them. The air is all but burning. People below are pointing up at them, yelling, "Jump! Jump! Get out! The building's 'bout to go!"

Though Maks is scared, it seems too far to go.

Then he sees five firemen running toward the house. They get right below and spread a net, leaning back so it shapes itself into a big circle.

"Jump!" people are screaming. "Jump!"

Willa grabs Maks's hand, looks at him, and he looks at her, and then . . . they jump.

Bruno crosses Houston Street. Wanting to get as far from the burning house as he can, he keeps heading uptown and don't slow till he reaches Fourth Street. Once he gets there, certain he's not being followed, he sits on the curb to catch his breath, calm down. His favorite hat, the brown derby, is gone. His squinty eye stings. His heart is thumping. He's finding it hard to think.

He never thought anybody but Maks—brought by

his Plug Uglies—would show up to get the girl. Hadn't even planned what he'd do when the kid appeared, 'cept beat him. If he broke some of his bones, well, fine. Serve him and that girl right, trying to show him up, spying on him. . . .

Bruno does wonder what happened to his gang. If they got away. If they were hurt. Arrested. That alley fight was bad enough. This was worse. He's sure of one thing: The gang won't follow him no more.

But most of all, he's trying to figure what's gonna happen to him. The attack on the house didn't just take him by surprise, it shocked him.

Sitting there, rubbing his bruises, wiping blood from scratches, Bruno tells himself he should have known better. Should have posted guards on the street as lookouts to give warning.

He hardly can sort out what he's feeling. It's all anger, humiliation, fury. Some of it's directed at himself. Some at Maks. Some of it at the whole stupid city of New York.

Realizing he was dumb disgusts him, makes him feel desperate. That makes him feel weak. He hates the feeling. In moments he's full of rage. Nothing works for him. It's their fault. He has to live, don't he?

But I'm not weak, he tells himself. *Haven't I spent*

my whole life on the streets? Haven't I survived? With a few
friends.

He don't even have a memory of his parents, who
they were, where they came from, where they went. All
he is, is Bruno. Him, alone. Bruno can't remember when
he wasn't by himself, finding ways to live on his own. Now,
like always, he'll have to take care of himself.

As Bruno sits there, thinking how he came to be
where he is, he curses the time he ever tried to mug that
Brunswick. That guy, he's the real cause of all this.

The mug looked like easy prey. How was he to know
the guy carried a gun? That he was a part of some gang?
That he worked for some big-city boss?

How could he let Brunswick force him to take that
picture? Steal his face? But then, people are always forcing
him to do things.

Bruno tells himself he needs to get out of New York.
Away from everything. But first he's gotta get hold of
Brunswick's gun. And that picture that the mug keeps
holding over him.

"Hey, you!" Bruno feels a sharp smack on his shoulder.

Bruno jumps up. A policeman is standing over him,
billy stick in his hand.

"Can't sit there, buster. Get moving."

Bruno glares at the copper but decides this ain't his fight. Muttering to himself, he heads uptown.

Maks and Willa hit the firemen's net at the same time. Maks bounces up, gets caught by one of the firemen, who sets him on the ground.

Just as that happens, he hears a great *whoosh*, then *crunch*. A chorus of voices saying, *"Ahhh!"*

Willa, dazed, lies in the net, catching her breath, till a fireman helps her set her feet on the ground.

Maks goes right over. "You all right?"

She nods but holds on to his arm to steady herself.

"Hey, kid," one of the firemen says to Maks, "anyone else in there?"

"Don't know."

"Got out nick-time. Lucky yous weren't roasted."

Maks looks round and can barely believe what he's seeing. Or don't see. The building is gone. Those sounds he heard—it was the old house collapsing into a pile of black-gray, smoldering wood, the heap spiked by small cat-tongues of flames, the ground covered with muddy puddles crusted with ash. The air stinking of wet smoke.

The street is crowded with fire wagons, firemen, horses, snaking hoses. There's even an ambulance wagon. Police are holding back a gawking crowd.

Once Willa and Maks are safe on their feet, the firemen no longer care 'bout them. Maks grabs Willa's hand—she's still unsteady—and when he spots a bunch of newsie pals, they go over to them.

"Everybody get out?" Maks asks.

"Think so."

"What 'bout the gang?"

"Don't know."

"Bruno?"

"Somebody says they saw him trying to duck out of that little alley. But he ran back in."

"Into the house?"

"Nowhere else he could have gone." The kid looks at Maks. They hate Bruno, but even so. . . .

Maks feels sick. "Was he trapped? Killed?"

"Probably."

Maks turns to look at the smoking ruins. No one could have survived in that. In his head he hears that fireman's word—"Roasted." He feels like throwing up.

"Guess we got 'em," says one of the newsies.

"Yeah."

There ain't much joy. It's too big. People may have been killed. So everyone just stares at the smoldering ruins, scared by what happened. The thought that Plug Uglies— maybe Bruno—are in there makes it hard to think 'bout it. The fire was an accident, but still. . . .

A bunch of the newsies come up to Willa and ask if she's okay.

"Fine," she tells them. "Thanks. Thanks for coming."

"Sure. Glad we saved you. Don't worry."

The firemen begin to roll their hoses. The ambulance goes. The people who came to watch drift. Newsies share stories 'bout what happened, telling one another what they did and saw. Keep their voices low. No laughter.

They start heading downtown. Not celebrating. Just glad they did something to the Plug Uglies. Feel good, too, 'bout saving Willa.

Maks says to her, "Let's go home."

"Okay."

Side by side, they walk down Second Avenue, but not with the other newsies. Without saying it, they want to be alone.

At first, worn out from thinking 'bout all that happened, they don't talk. But Maks can't keep Bruno out of his head, wondering if he was killed.

He stops. "Hey, I lost my cap. And your stick."

Willa shrugs. "Maybe I don't need it anymore. Maks, I keep thinking about Bruno. You think he was killed?"

"Don't know."

Willa looks down. "My dress is a mess."

"Mama will understand. She was really worried 'bout you. Everybody was. 'Specially Jacob."

She says, "When Jacob and I were on the street and the gang showed up, they were pretty awful. Jacob tried to help me. Is he okay?"

"Fine." Maks asks, "They hurt you any 'fore I got there?"

"Nothing much. How did you know I was there?"

"They told Jacob I was supposed to come get you." Then Maks tells her how, that morning, he saw Bruno in the building. "I shouldn't have looked," he admits. "I had to run like nothing. Betcha anything that's why he came after you."

"Did you go to the hotel?"

To Maks, that seems like a long time ago. But glad to get away from Bruno talk, he tells Willa what he did there.

Tells her, that is, till he suddenly remembers 'bout seeing the man—her father.

He wants to tell her. He don't want to. In the end he decides he has to hold it till they get home. Even so, he can't help wondering what's she gonna do when she finds out.

All he knows, it's gonna be awful.

Bruno wishes he knew the time. He supposes he has missed his regular meeting at the restaurant with Brunswick. But maybe it ain't too late. He really wants to slam the mug when he sees him 'cause he's the cause of all this mess. Gonna give him a sucker punch. Grab that pistol and picture. Take his money, too. People will treat him decent then.

When Bruno reaches the entrance to the American Theatre, he finds the doors locked. He's too late.

His anger seething, frustration building, he leans 'gainst a wall. Nothing is right. It's so hard to breathe, he feels he's drowning. Then he remembers. He knows where Brunswick lives. That huge hotel. He can catch him there.

Bruno heads back downtown, walking along Broadway. At Thirty-third Street he turns east and takes himself to the Waldorf. Once there, he stands 'cross the way from the hotel's main entrance. As people go in and out of the building, Bruno watches.

Hate 'em all, he tells himself.

"Hey, buddy, yous can't stay here." Another policeman.

Bruno says, "It's a free country. Stand where I want."

The policeman raises his stick. "Not for mugs like you, it ain't. Now move!"

Bruno, muttering curses under his breath, shuffles away. He'll come back tomorrow.

He's exhausted. Needs a place to sleep. As he walks, he searches his pockets. All he's got from the money he ripped from Willa is seven cents. Barely enough to get a flophouse bed. If he spends that, won't have enough for breakfast. And he's hungry.

Then he remembers a place where he can sleep on the floor for three cents. That'll work.

With one last angry backward glance at the Waldorf, he heads downtown. "Tomorrow," he mutters again, "I'm gonna kill that mug. Get myself out of here. *Do* something. Be free."

Keeps walking till he comes to a place where digging

has been going in the street, where cobblestones have been stacked to one side. In the hole old wooden pipes are exposed, a shovel left behind.

Bruno looks into the hole, sees the shovel. He snatches it up, puts it over his shoulder and keeps heading downtown.

"I'll bury him," he whispers to himself. "That's what I'll do. Get my picture back and bury him deep. Be done with him for good and all. Be free. "

As Willa and Maks walk home, he tells her 'bout things at the Waldorf, how rich it is, the bathrooms, the elevator.

Willa hardly listens. The first moment Maks pauses, she says. "But did you find anything to help Emma?"

"Don't know," he says, and repeats what the hotel detective told him—that Packwood said Emma didn't get a compliment, how he went to Donck's place and told him.

Willa says, "This morning, at the prison, I asked Emma what Donck told me to, then I went over and told him."

"Yeah, he said."

"Is he going to do anything?"

"He might. Guess what?" says Maks. "He said I said something smart."

"What?"

Maks shrugs. "Not sure."

Willa looks at him. "Her trial is Saturday."

"Know."

"What's going to happen?"

Maks shakes his head.

They keep walking but don't say much more. That's all right with Maks, 'cause he keeps trying to decide how he's gonna tell Willa the news that all this time she been thinking her father is dead, he's alive.

They get home long past midnight. Soon as they step into the flat, Agnes, in her sleeping dress, rushes from the back room. "Willa!" she cries, and gives the girl a huge hug.

Papa and Mama come out in their sleep shirts too. So

EMMA

do the boys and Monsieur Zulot. Everybody makes a big fuss over Willa being back and safe.

Maks thinks she likes it.

Of course, they want to hear what happened. Maks does most of the talking.

Everybody is shocked. The boys, nothing but big eyes, keep staring at Willa and Maks. Agnes, too. Papa shakes his head.

"God have mercy," Mama murmurs.

"That mean the gang is gone?" Jacob asks.

"Hope so," Maks says, putting his hand on his brother's neck and giving him a squeeze. "And if you hadn't told me, I wouldn't have known where they took Willa."

Jacob, proud 'bout his part, grins at his brothers.

Mama gives Willa and Maks soup and bread.

Papa shakes Willa's hand. "You're a brave girl," he says to her. To Maks, he says, "And you are a brave boy. These are hard times," he announces, "but good things can still happen."

Maks feels good.

But then it's Mama who says, "Maks, did you ever go to Emma's hotel?"

"Yeah," he says, surprised she knew.

"Did you find something to help her?"

"Don't know."

The room gets very quiet.

Mama whispers, "Her trial is so soon."

Nobody says nothing. The joy is gone. Everybody drifts back to their rooms to sleep. But not before both Mama and Agnes give Willa more hugs. So do the boys. Even Monsieur Zulot. But it's not the same as before.

Everyone's thinking 'bout Emma.

Except Maks.

He helps set up sleeping for Willa. All the while, he's glancing at the cigar box—with Willa's family picture—trying to find the right moment to tell her 'bout her father.

By the time they lay out her blankets and Willa settles down on the floor, it's almost two o'clock. She sits there, hugging her knees, holding her doll. Then she takes a deep breath, as if to suggest it's finally all done.

"Maks," she says, "I was really scared. Thanks for coming after me."

Maks is sitting on a table chair. "Hey, you saved me. I saved you. Guess we're even."

"Guess." She smiles.

For a moment they don't speak.

Willa lies down. Maks, knowing he's got to tell her,

takes his own deep breath and, with a pounding heart, says, "Something I need say."

"What?"

"It's big."

Willa, hearing caution in Maks's voice, sits up. "What?" she says.

Maks pulls the cigar box down, takes out her blue tin, and hands it to her.

Looking a question at him, Willa holds it.

Maks says, "Take out your family picture."

She stares at him but does what he says. "What is it?" she says again, almost as if she don't want to know.

"That picture—with your father," says Maks. "That's him, right?"

Willa nods. "What 'bout him?"

"Today at the Waldorf . . . I saw him."

Willa stares at Maks for a long time. To Maks, it seems like forever.

Then—her voice small—she says, "My *father*? You . . . saw him? Are you . . . sure?"

He nods.

"But—" She don't finish.

Maks waits.

Willa says, "I thought . . . he died." Her voice is broken, jagged. It's as if her heart is right there, but it's full of nothing but sadness and hurt. Her mouth is open, but it speaks no words. Her chest heaves, but there's no breathing. Her eyes well up, so all the while she's looking at Maks, she's not really seeing him, only her own tears. Or someplace else. Or nowhere. Maybe she's seeing only what she can see, but not wanting to see what's there.

She whispers, "What . . . what was he doing?"

"He was in this room—for eating. Sitting there, reading the paper. *The World*."

"The paper?" Willa asks, as if that's the most impossible thing of all.

Maks nods.

"But . . . why?"

"Why what?"

"Was he . . . there?"

Maks shrugs. "Don't know."

"Was he alone?"

"Uh-uh."

"Who was he with?"

"Joe Gorker."

"Who's he?"

"Big-city crook. And . . ."

"What?"

"A lady."

"Who was she?"

"Don't know."

Willa is still holding the photo in her hands. She bends over it, stares at it, and for a long time she stays that way, as if the picture can explain everything. Or nothing. As if the way the picture is trembling in her hands is its way of talking.

Maks waits.

Willa looks up. "But why . . . why would he leave me?"

It's the saddest thing Maks has ever heard.

"Don't know," he says, wishing there were something else he could say.

"Does . . . does he live there? At the hotel?"

"Could be. Maybe." Maks shrugs helplessly.

Willa leans over the photo again. Looks up. "Are you going back there?"

"Supposed to."

"Will you take me?"

"If you want."

"Maks . . ."

"What?"

"If I do see him . . . and if it is him . . . I won't know what to do."

"I know."

Willa puts the photograph on the floor, lies facedown, head in her arms, doll forgotten. "Maks?"

"What?"

"I hope it isn't him."

Maks takes a deep breath. After a while he hears her quiet weeping.

He goes over to her. Sits by her side. Says, "Willa . . . you can stay here. Be part of this family. We all like you. You can be another sister."

When Willa don't say no more, Maks goes back to his chair, just sits there in case she needs him.

As he sits, he's wondering: *Which family is Willa gonna be part of?*

Then his mind goes back to Donck. *What did I say that was smart? Is it gonna help Emma? All the things that happened today . . . it all seems worse. Emma's gonna go to prison.*

Maks feels ready to explode.

For the Geless family, getting up Friday morning is pretty regular. Except it ain't. It was a short night of long fears.

There's Maks, as always, making a privy stop, dumping ashes, pumping water, getting milk. He can think 'bout only two things: Willa and Emma. What's gonna happen?

A quiet, sad-faced Willa helps Mama make breakfast. Everybody supposes she's just tired.

Papa and Agnes go to work. Talk of visiting Emma. Mama says she'll go to The Tombs after doing her laundry. Monsieur Zulot leaves for his work.

The three boys stumble sleepily out of the front room. They get ready for school.

Everything is slow. Everything 'cept time.

Maks keeps stealing glances at Willa, asking himself, *What's she gonna do?*

For her part, Willa is wondering if it really is her father.

And if it is him, what should she do? And again and again, why did he leave her? She's having trouble just being.

Maks is also nervous 'bout what's gonna happen when they reach the Waldorf. He can get in. He's supposed to be working there. But how's Willa gonna get by the guard?

Then Maks gets an idea. All he says to Willa, though, is, "Make sure Mama gives you a nice dress. Fixes your hair."

"Why?"

"You'll see."

Willa and Maks bring the boys to school. They're still jabbering excitedly 'bout what happened during the night.

"Can we tell our friends?" asks Ryker.

Maks looks to Willa. She shrugs. He says, "Tell 'em what you want."

Ryker grins. "Guess what day it is?" he says to Willa.

It's Jacob who says, "What?"

"Friday the thirteenth."

"Shut up," says Maks.

The boys off to school, Willa and Maks start uptown.

Willa says, "At the hotel are you still going to try to find evidence stuff for Emma?"

"Don't know what to look for anymore," Maks says. "Besides, when we get there, we don't know what'll happen, do we?"

After a moment Willa says, "No."

"Anyway, I don't think it's good for you to be selling papers on your own. Not today. I mean, those Plug Uglies might come back."

"Bruno?"

"I'm thinking he's dead. Or gone. But maybe he ain't. Like I once told you—and I was right, wasn't I—he's all 'bout getting revenge."

Willa don't reply.

They keep walking uptown, only Maks decides it ain't smart taking Second Avenue. Not past that burnt-up house. So they go up Third, then over to Fifth.

Willa is sad, quiet, tense.

"I've been thinking," Maks finally says. "We both need to get inside the hotel, right? I'm okay. But I'm pretty sure they ain't gonna let you in the front."

"Why?"

"The way we look. But there's a door off to the side for people working there. Maybe I can get you in that way. And inside, there's this bench. For people asking for work. We'll tell them you're looking. Maybe that'll work."

"Then what?"

"Getting tired of saying, 'don't know,' but . . . don't know."

81

Standing on Fifth Avenue, the kids look at the Waldorf from across the street.

Willa shakes her head. "It's so big."

Maks shrugs. "Bigger inside."

"Is it all rich people?"

"'Cept the help."

Willa keeps staring. "My father can't be there," she says.

Maks don't reply.

She says, "Maks . . ."

"Yeah?"

"I don't know what I want."

"Understand."

After a while Willa says, "Okay."

They head for the side entry.

Just like the day before, the guard in his green uniform is on duty, checking in workers. Maks and Willa get on the line, and when they reach the desk, the guard looks down at Maks and says, "You started yesterday."

"Right. For Mr. Packwood."

"Go on." He waves him on, but then he sees Willa right behind Maks. "What do *you* want?"

Maks is ready. He steps back, holds Willa's arm. "She's my sister. She wants to get work here too. Maybe take the place of that girl they arrested."

The guy looks Willa over. "You and the rest of New York. Okay, go in. Sit on the first bench. Make sure you stay there till you're called. Just don't think you'll get the job. They want good-looking girls." He pushes the button on the wall.

They go through the door. Willa has her eyes cast down, as if afraid to see anything.

Maks points out the bench. "Sit there. I'll be as fast as I can."

"Where you going?" she asks nervously.

"Have to get my uniform."

Willa sits, hands in lap. Maks runs off but knows his way well enough now so that he quickly gets to where he can change into his bellboy suit. Which he does fast. Races back to Willa's bench. To his relief, she's still there.

Maks says, "Anyone ask you anything?"

Willa shakes her head.

"Good. Come on."

They get up, and Maks starts leading her though the hotel halls, Willa gawking at everything. Maks, meanwhile, keeping his own look about.

Now and again people glance at Willa—she's dressed odd for the place—but she's with Maks and he's in his bell-boy uniform, so it don't look as if they ain't supposed to be there. At least, that's what Maks is hoping.

They get to the main lobby. Lots of people going all which ways doing what they do. Maks keeps searching 'bout but sees no sign of the man.

"Come on," he says to Willa. He's heading for the Men's Club. When they reach it, he says, "Wait here."

Willa stands tensely at the entry while Maks goes in. Takes a quick look. Ain't many people there. Maks don't see the guy.

He comes out. "Not there."

Willa is so nervous, she has to work hard to keep from bursting into tears. Feels so lost, she needs Maks to tell her what to do. Trouble is, Maks ain't so sure he knows what to do either. Then he gets his idea.

"Follow me." They head back to the lobby. "I'm gonna take you to this table," he whispers. "There's this guy sitting there, Mr. Trevor, captain of the bellboys. He'll ask you what you want. You say, 'I'm looking for a guest. Mr.—' What's your father's name?"

"Gustav."

"No, last name."

"Brunswick."

"Okay. Brunswick. Say to the guy, 'I'm looking for Mr. Brunswick. Is he in?'"

Willa gives him an I-don't-know-what-you're-talking-'bout look.

"Just do what I say." Maks is trying to sound as if he knows what he is doing. Fact, he's making everything up as they go along.

He leads Willa up to the desk. Trevor is sitting there.

Maks says. "Sir, this lady is looking for someone."

Trevor gives Willa a funny stare, as if she don't belong, but he don't connect her with Maks. "And whom do you wish to see?" he asks.

Willa, her voice tiny, says, "Mr. Brunswick."

Trevor opens up his book, looks up and down the list of names, nods to himself. Picks up the telephone. Gives it some cranks.

"Mr. Trevor, here. Ring room nine thirty-two."

Willa, trembling, stares at Trevor.

Maks, watching her, feels like the world is gonna crash.

"Mr. Brunswick, sir!" says Trevor. "Good morning!"

Willa's mouth drops open. She slaps a hand over her mouth, as if to keep her insides in, then makes a half turn, trying to find Maks, or maybe looking for a way out.

Trevor, into the phone, says, "A young lady to see you in the lobby."

He looks at Willa. "Name, please?"

Willa can't speak. Not for her soul. Shakes her head.

Maks thinks, *Her father may not be a ghost, but she looks like one.*

Into the phone, Trevor says, "She doesn't wish to give her name, sir. . . . Very well, sir." He puts the phone down. To Willa, he says, "Please have a seat. Mr. Brunswick will be down in a few moments."

Willa, finding she can't breathe, throws a loopy look to Maks that ain't nothing but desperation. Maks had moved a few paces away, trying to act as if they're not connected, but, of course, they are. He tells himself, *This uniform I'm wearing, it don't matter no more. Just pretend. It's Willa who's real.*

He jumps forward, whispering, "Come on." Grabs her arm, tries to guide her from Trevor, to a place where she— and he—can see where the elevators let people off.

He figures that's the way this Brunswick guy—Willa's maybe father—will have to come down. At least, Maks is hoping so. Or maybe, he reminds himself, he's got it wrong. Maybe the guy ain't Willa's father after all.

Willa is barely moving on her own. She hardly seems alive. But Maks leads her near a big plant that's in a huge pot. It keeps them somewhat hidden. From behind it, they can move one way or another, be seen or not be seen.

Willa is clinging to Maks's arm with tight hands, her breathing coming in short gasps. She's blinking. Tears on her face.

At the same time the hotel is doing what it's supposed to be doing, which is people going 'bout their business, walking, sitting and watching, meeting, talking, going out the front entry, coming in. Only to Maks and Willa, it feels as if they're the real center, as if the whole world is spinning frantic fast, like that famous new Ferris wheel out at the Chicago World's Fair. Except nobody knows the world is spinning out of control but them.

Then, out of nowhere, Maks sees Packwood. The hotel detective is walking into the lobby. Coming easy. Nothing special. Maks don't think he's looking for him. But same time, Maks don't want the detective to see him. He might pull him away. So Maks reminds himself that he's not really a hotel employee. That Willa's what's real. She's what's important. He won't budge.

Maks eases the numb Willa farther back behind the potted plant, hoping Packwood don't see them.

As Maks does that, he all of a sudden hears, "Stop!"

Someone is yelling.

People look round. So does Maks.

"You can't go in there!" comes a shout.

Maks ain't certain what's going on. It's a commotion. But where? What? Then Maks realizes the shouting, which continues, is coming from the front of the lobby, near the main entrance.

"Stop that kid! Stop him!"

People—the rich people, the hotel people, everybody—back away, retreat, as if something awful is coming at them. Something they don't like. Something bad.

Maks leans out from where they are hiding, wanting

to see what's happening, why there is all the yelling. And what does he see?

He sees Bruno.

Maks don't believe it. Can't believe it. Don't want to believe it.

But sure as certain, it *is* Bruno.

The clothing he's wearing is ragged, dirty, full of rips, as if he just crawled from some hole. His good eye is glazed with fury, his squinty one twitching; his grin is nasty; and his red hair is flopping over his face like a veil of blood. Seems ready to fight anybody who's willing enough to come near 'cause he has a shovel in his hands, holding it like a weapon, swinging it wildly so that it *is* a weapon. Which is all to say, Bruno is crazy.

Men and women are shrieking, screaming. "Look out! Get away! He's mad!"

A couple of hotel mugs take steps toward him. But Bruno swings his shovel round so wickedly, they have to jump. You can cut a guy's head off with a shovel that's swinging. Which is just what Bruno's trying to do.

Then he starts yelling, "Where's Brunswick? I know he's here. I need to see Brunswick!"

Maks can't believe what he's hearing—that Bruno is after the same guy Willa is.

Maks turns and catches sight of Packwood. But Packwood is running in the *opposite* direction, going fast, away from Bruno. Maks don't understand why. Scared, maybe. The way he is.

Even as Maks is looking after him, he suddenly sees the person he thinks is Willa's father stepping out of an elevator, coming right into the lobby.

Where Bruno is.

People are screaming and yelling: "Stop him! Look out!"

Brunswick—not seeming to understand what's happening—stops and stands to look, Maks supposes, for the "young lady" he's to meet in the lobby.

When Maks turns back toward Bruno, the redhead is coming down the lobby—swinging that shovel wildly, trying to keep everyone away. Which is working, 'cause people are scattering everywhere, frightened like anything.

Maks turns to Willa.

Everything is happening so fast, he almost forgot her. He don't know if she saw Bruno—how could she not?—but maybe she hasn't. What he does know is that she's facing that man, Brunswick. She's looking right at him. Staring at him. And on her face is a look Maks never seen before. Maybe it's joy. Maybe it's pain. Maybe it's something Willa just invented, which is both things, and she can't tell the difference and don't know how to. Don't want to.

"Brunswick!" Bruno shouts. "I want that pistol. Give it to me!"

Maks is now sure that Willa—who's staring so hard at Brunswick—hasn't seen Bruno, don't know he's even there, don't understand what's happening. She can only see the man, her father. In fact, the next thing Willa does is yank away from Maks. He's so dazed, he don't stop her. She steps into the open lobby, going right toward the man, this man who's her father. The one who left her.

Maks don't know what to do. He stands there, tight with horror, but what he's seeing is two people moving toward this same Brunswick. One of them, Bruno, is acting as if he's wanting to kill the man. The other, Willa, is wanting to love him.

Maks can tell by the way Brunswick starts and stares

that he now sees Bruno. Even so, Brunswick just stands there, gawking, maybe amazed, maybe scared, maybe both, doing nothing. It's as if he can't believe that this crazy kid, this Bruno, is really in the Waldorf lobby coming at him. The point is, Brunswick ain't moving.

But Bruno *is* moving. He's coming closer, shovel swinging.

Suddenly, Brunswick reaches into his pocket. Now he has a pistol in his hand.

Which is just when Willa calls out, "Father!"

Brunswick must have known her voice, must have kept it in his head all this time, pushed it away but not completely, 'cause some voices you can't lose no matter how you push 'em away, not in a million years. And so he turns sharp toward Willa. Stares at her with this look on his face. Maks can't tell what it is. Shock. Anger. Disgust. None of it, maybe, but it sure ain't love.

The thing is, that moment, he's no longer looking at Bruno. Not paying attention.

Bruno, seeing this, drops his shovel and dives at Brunswick.

At that last moment Brunswick turns from Willa. Sees Bruno, but it's too late. Before he can shoot, Bruno is on him, grabbing hold of the pistol.

Now the two of them are wrestling, falling to the floor, rolling, fighting frantically for that gun.

Willa stops moving. Just stands there, watching, both hands over her face—but not her eyes.

People are still screaming and yelling: "Help! Help! Police! Police!"

There's an explosion. The sound is as huge as the whole gigantic lobby. Punches people's ears like boxing gloves. Makes ears hurt bad. Makes 'em ring like the final bell.

Brunswick jerks away from Bruno, flops down. The minute Maks sees him do that, he knows the guy has been shot down dead.

Same time, Bruno staggers back. In one of his hands is that pistol he took from Brunswick. Next moment, he dives forward, drops to his knees. He's reaching for the dead man, reaching into his jacket. Yanks out stuff. Out pops a picture, a wallet. And a gold watch.

Bruno grabs them all.

That's when there's another pistol shot, even louder than the first.

Bruno is hurled back and collapses in an instant. Dead. The things he took from Brunswick's body drop, scatter.

Maks spins around. Mr. Packwood is standing there, a pistol in his hand. He's just shot Bruno.

In the Waldorf it's quieter than Eden before creatures came. The only one in that whole gigantic space who's moving is Willa. She's rushing to the dead Brunswick. She's kneeling by his side. She's holding his hand. She's crying, crying, crying.

Maks runs to her, and he's on his knees in the spreading blood, and he is trying, trying to hold her.

People start edging closer, looking, looking.

Packwood is there too now, kneeling on the other side of Willa's father. He looks up and he sees Maks. "Do you know who these men are?"

Maks can only nod, yes.

Mr. Packwood bends over Brunswick's body, sees the watch on the ground, starts, picks it up, and stares at it.

It becomes wild in the lobby. More than wild. All kinds of people are swarming, yelling, screaming. That includes the police. The ambulance wagon has arrived, bringing docs. The bodies are taken away. Lots of hotel people gather and are working frantically to clean up the blood, trying to make sure there's not a spot left. The way the Waldorf is supposed to be. A place with no blood.

Packwood leads Willa and Maks into his office.

Willa is so stunned, she's not truly there. Maks don't know where she is. It is no place he ever visited. No place he ever *wants* to visit.

Sometimes she's crying. Sometimes she's not. The only thing she's really doing is keeping Maks close, clinging to him, gripping his hand hard, grabbing him if he moves an inch away. And sometimes he's holding on to her, keeping *her* from bolting away. If none of that makes sense, it's because there ain't much sense to this scene I'm telling.

As for Packwood, he keeps asking Maks who these dead people are. Maks tries to tell him. Only it's pretty confusing and hard to answer with the questions coming so fast, like someone threw a pack of cards at him, each card a question. Then the police get there and ask their own questions. More policemen come. More questions. They write down Willa's answers. Maks's, too.

"Are you saying that this Mr. Brunswick was this girl's father?" someone wants to know.

"Yes, sir," Maks says. "But he left her. She hasn't seen him for months."

"And the other one?" asks another.

"Named Bruno," says Maks. "Head of the Plug Ugly Gang."

"Bruno who?"

"Don't know."

"How are the two men connected?" asks Packwood. "Why did this Bruno kill your father?" he asks Willa.

She shakes her head.

Maks says, "We don't know."

Fact, the more questions there are, the fewer answers there are.

Then Packwood tells Maks and Willa they can go, and he's decent enough to get them a cab, guiding them in, even giving the cabbie some cash to get them home to Birmingham Street.

But as he puts Maks into the cab, he dangles the watch, the watch that Brunswick had, and he says, "Tell Donck I found the watch."

"What watch?" Maks asks.

"The stolen one. Mr. Brunswick had it."

"The one you said Emma stole?" cries Maks.

Packwood nods.

Maks can't speak no more.

As the kids go downtown, it's mostly quiet, save for the horse's hooves on the street stones, going *clop-clippity*, the carriage wheels jolting, Willa's crying. It's not hard crying. More like whimpering. Her face is gray as city sky, and all tight with pain.

She says, "Why did he leave me?"

Maks shakes his thoughts away from Emma, but he ain't sure if it's him Willa's asking or herself. Don't matter, 'cause he has no answer. No more than he thinks Willa does.

But then Willa says to him, "Where am I supposed to go now?"

That time Maks can speak. "Home," he says.

And Willa gives Maks the most grateful look that ever was grateful.

They get to the flat. Mama takes one look at Willa and cries, "What's happened?"

Maks says, "She needs to be in bed."

Mama puts Willa into her own and Papa's bed, covers her with all the old country blankets. Even then, Willa can't stop shivering. Mama sits with her, holding her hand, stroking it. Maks brings her doll.

Briefly, Mama comes out and says to Maks, "Tell me."

Maks starts at the end. "She found her father. He got killed."

"How?"

"Too complicated. Tell you later."

All that day Mama sits with Willa, and she does so into the night.

That afternoon Maks sells his papers. No Bruno. No Plug Uglies. Only newsies talking 'bout what happened in the night. Maks don't tell 'em 'bout the morning.

———

That night, back at the flat, when everybody is there, Maks tells the family all that happened. All he knows. Willa ain't there. She's still in bed and don't want to or can't talk.

When Maks finishes, no one speaks.

Papa shakes his head.

It's Agnes who says, "It's Emma's trial tomorrow."

Maks says, "But didn't you hear what I said? They found the watch they said Emma stole. That guy, that Brunswick, Willa's father, *he* had it."

Mama wrings her hands.

"Does that mean," asks Papa, suddenly breathless, "that Emma will go free?"

Maks, as he keeps doing, says, "I don't know."

But then sometimes "I don't know" is the most honest thing anyone can say 'bout anything.

Early next morning, Saturday, they all—the whole family— troop to The Tombs. Willa insists that she go along. Papa and Agnes are skipping work.

They enter The Tombs, and when Maks asks, they're told where the trial is being held. Finding it, they discover Packwood outside the doors of the courtroom.

He greets Maks, and Maks introduces him to his family.

"Where's Donck?" Maks wants to know.

"I spoke to him late last night," says Packwood. "I'm afraid he's very ill. But he had enough strength to tell me what to say. It will be me who goes before the court."

"Did Donck figure it out?"

"He says you did."

"*Me?*"

"We believe you are exactly right as to what happened."

"That mean Emma goes free?"

"That remains to be seen. It'll be up to the judge."

Agnes puts her arm round Mama as they all go into the court. It's a big room, full of wood and chairs. High windows and a tall desk, with an old mug of a judge in a black robe and white beard sitting up high.

Maks's heart sinks. It's another swell stiff.

Lots of people in the court. You can't tell who is who or what is what. You might say they all look innocent, 'cept they all look guilty, too. Only in one section there are these others—poor people mostly but not all—where Maks can see Emma in the middle of a crowd. The prisoners.

The cases are quickly heard. Most of the people are sentenced to time in jail on Blackwell's Island, some to Sing Sing. It all goes fast, as if what's important is the sentencing, not the people whose lives are being locked away.

When they finally call "Emma Geless!" she stands up, hands clasped, looking pale, fearful, tears wetting her cheeks. Packwood goes and stands by her side. What he says to the judge is this:

That Emma was working at the Waldorf Hotel cleaning room number nine twelve when a man, a hotel guest, a Mr. Brunswick, went into that room pretending it was his own. Then he stole a fine watch and chain, having probably observed the owner with it. He then proceeded to ask Emma Geless her name—under pretense of commending her to her superior—so Emma gave it. The man then slipped into the girls' dormitory, found Emma's bed, which he easily located, because of her name tag on it, and placed the watch chain under her pillow, knowing she would be blamed for the theft.

Packwood holds up the chain and watch. In the gloomy court the golden watch shines like a string of stars. The watch is its own sun.

"And did you detect all this yourself, Mr. Packwood?" asks the judge.

"Your Honor, it was my friend Bartleby Donck."

"And where is our Mr. Donck?"

"Gravely ill, Your Honor."

The judge sighs, says to Packwood, "Then you withdraw the charge against the defendant Emma Geless?"

"We do, Your Honor."

"And the real thief?" asks the judge.

"No longer alive."

"Good!" The judge bangs his desk with a hammer and says, "Case dismissed. Let the prisoner go free. Next!"

Quick as that, Emma is nothing but smiles and more smiles. There are hugs and kisses and more hugs and kisses, 'cause she's innocent—which she always was—the way Maks always said. But hey, being innocent and being free—two different things.

Maks gives her a huge hug. Then he turns and faces Willa. She's trying to smile. But she can't, not really. In fact, tears come again. Maks hugs her anyway. He whispers, "You're part of our family now."

And that reminds him of what Mama always says: "People are freer in America. But there are more tears."

Back in the tenement it's like a party. Everybody's happy. Willa's doll is on her lap, and Maks could swear the doll is smiling too.

Willa herself still tries to smile, still can't. But Mama sits next to her, holding her hand, 'cept sometimes it's Papa who holds her hand, or Ryker, or Agnes, or even Maks.

Then Emma announces that **Mr. Packwood** told her she could have her old job back. "And," she says, laughing at Maks, "he said to tell you if you wanted to keep on being a bellboy at the hotel, he will arrange it."

"There," says a beaming Papa, "when the whole family works together, we can manage anything."

Maks looks at Willa. She finds a little smile from somewhere and offers it to everyone.

Then, in the middle of this celebration, Agnes starts coughing. All of a sudden, nobody is happy.

That's when Willa says, "Papa, you must get Agnes to a doctor."

"My dear girl . . . ," Papa starts to say.

That's when Willa stands up and goes to Maks's cigar box, pulls out her blue tin box. Everyone watches as she opens it. What she takes out is her mother's golden ring. She puts it into Papa's large hand.

"It was my mother's," says Willa. "Sell it. She said I should use it for my new family. For Agnes."

Maks notices that Willa's family picture ain't in the box anymore. He don't know where it went, and he never sees it again.

I suppose you need to know that over on Delancey Street, in Donck's rooms, the old detective is stretched out in his filthy bed, his eyes closed.

There's a woman sitting by his side.

Before Willa and Maks sell the Saturday papers that afternoon—Maks wants to do it one last time—he and Willa decide to go see Donck to thank him for all he did.

When they get there—Delancey Street—they knock on the door.

"Come in," says a voice.

When they enter, they don't see Donck. 'Stead, there's a lady in his room. She's standing near his desk, looking sad. Around her neck is a glittering diamond necklace. The minute Maks sees her, he knows who she is.

"May I help you?" she says.

"Looking for Mr. Donck."

"He died this morning," says the sad lady.

"You his friend?" asks Maks.

"I was. And you were too, I believe," she says to Maks, recognizing him from the Waldorf.

"Yes, ma'am. Guess we all was."

Maks and Willa don't know what else to say. They just stand there. Then Maks glances over to Donck's desk and sees some writing. Across the top page it says:

The Bradys and the Missing Diamonds
Or
The Boy Detective
Written by a New York Detective

Out on the street Maks tells Willa, "I know that lady."

"Who is she?" says Willa.

"Packwood's sister. Remember that lady in the story, the one the boy detective helps? That was her. And guess what? Donck was writing it."

"Was that a diamond necklace around her neck?"

"Think so."

That afternoon, when Willa and Maks go out to sell the Saturday papers, he calls the headline as usual: "Extra! Extra! Read all 'bout it! 'Murder at the Waldorf. Terrible Struggle with a Crazy Man! Two Men Killed!' Read it in *The World*! The world's greatest newspaper. Just two cents! Only two cents! Here 'tis!"

For once, he is the news. And that night he makes his

whole eight cents. As I said when I first started to tell you this story, for them days, eight cents ain't bad.

And, oh yeah, that night, it being Saturday, everybody gets their weekly bath. Mama likes a clean family.

So there's the story. Too many coincidences? Or just miracles? You decide. Thing is, it's all true.

But you probably want to know what else happened, right?

Papa pawned Willa's ring and got enough money for Agnes to go see that doctor over on Mott Street and get some medicine. She got mostly better. She went on to become a typist at a bank earning ten dollars a week! Three years later she married Monsieur Zulot.

The shoe factory closed and never reopened. But Emma and Maks kept working at the Waldorf.

While Jacob started selling *The Times*, Willa became a newsie and sold *The World*. But she also went to night school and learned to read.

The three boys? Too many stories to tell!

Mama kept doing laundry.

The truth is, for a long time it was mostly the kids who took care of the family.

Fact, it was thirteen months before Papa got a job at the Fulton Fish Market, repairing barrels.

What I'm saying is, the family survived.

But these days, hey, that whole world is gone. Nothing left but those tenement buildings, which you can go see for yourself down on the city's Lower East Side. Call 'em tombs with windows, if you'd like, but millions of people were alive in 'em.

And when I do look at 'em, I'm reminded of that song Papa liked to sing:

We're traveling from our home
to an unknown land.
What will be there,
sadness or peace,
we don't know.
Only God knows.

Author's Note

From its earliest days as a Dutch settlement, New Amsterdam, which became New York City, has been home to all kinds of people, languages, and cultures, more than any other American city. Its history lives in the past *and* the present. "Wall Street"—the name we use to refer to the core of our twenty-first-century economy—takes its name from a wall built by the Dutch in the seventeenth century.

The United States experienced enormous changes at the end of the nineteenth century, nowhere more than in our large cities. It was a time of great wealth, great poverty, widespread crime, great charity, and major political reform. Many good things happened, particularly in the realm of science and technology. Nevertheless, many awful things happened too, such as the spread of urban diseases and cruel social discrimination.

This, too, was the time of a gigantic influx of immigrants who poured into the country through Ellis Island. The place where newcomers came and stayed in the greatest numbers was

New York. The histories and personal accounts of the time all mention how many children there were in city tenements, on the streets, at work, at play, and in jails.

City of Orphans is my attempt to catch a small bit of how New York City kids lived at the end of the nineteenth century. When thinking about the past, we often bring to it fanciful notions from books, movies, TV shows, and, not least, family stories. But as a wise man once said, "You are entitled to your own opinions, but not your own facts." Doing research for a historical novel is the process of discovering facts, then working to make real what has become lost, forgotten, invisible, and sometimes denied. The discovery of what was can be exciting, puzzling, funny, and sometimes even frightening.

My lead characters, Maks and Willa, are, I hope, unique individuals, but they're not so unlike thousands of other city kids of their day. Over the passage of time, we often forget kids in history, how they struggled to live and make livings—in short, how they survived. My hope is that in *City of Orphans* you will see them for what they were: amazing heroes.

Two final notes: The Plug Ugly Gang is not my invention. There really were gangs by that name. And "wasting disease" is what people used to call tuberculosis. That, alas, is still with us.

AVI

For Further Reading and Viewing

Alexander, June Granatir. *Daily Life in Immigrant America, 1870–1920.* Chicago: Ivan R. Dee, 2009.

Bial, Raymond. *Tenement: Immigrant Life on the Lower East Side.* Boston: Houghton Mifflin, 2002.

Byron, Joseph. *New York Life at the Turn of the Century in Photographs.* New York: Dover Publications, 1985.

Freedman, Russell. *Immigrant Kids.* New York: Dutton, 1980.

Granfield, Linda, and Arlene Alda. *97 Orchard Street, New York: Stories of Immigrant Life.* New York: Lower East Side Tenement Museum, 2001.

Hopkinson, Deborah. *Shutting Out the Sky: Life in the Tenements of New York, 1880–1924.* New York: Orchard Books, 2003.

Nasaw, David. *Children of the City.* New York: Anchor, 1985.

New York, episode 3, "Sunshine and Shadow." PBS Home Video, 1999.

Wheeler, Thomas C., ed. *The Immigrant Experience: The Anguish of Becoming American.* New York: Dial Press, 1971.

Independence Public Library

JF
Avi

9-11N